OLD SCORES, NEW GOALS

Other Quarry Press Books by Joan Finnigan

Finnigan's Guide to the Ottawa Valley:
A Cultural and Historical Companion

Legacies, Legends & Lies

Some of the Stories I Told You Were True

Tell Me Another Story

The Watershed Collection

Wintering Over

Old Scores, New Goals

THE STORY OF
THE OTTAWA SENATORS

BY Joan Finnigan

Quarry Press

The publisher gratefully acknowledges the financial assistance of The Canada Council, the Ontario Arts Council, the Department of Communications, and the Ontario Publishing Centre.

Canadian Cataloguing in Publication Data

Finnigan, Joan, 1925-
        Old scores, new goals

ISBN 1-55082-054-0 (bound)
ISBN 1-55082-041-9 (pbk.)

    1. Ottawa Senators (Hockey team)—History.
2. Hockey—Ottawa River Valley (Quebec and Ont.)—
History. I. Title

BV848.066F46 1992   796.962'6   C92-090054-2

Design by Keith Abraham.
Typeset by Susan Hannah.
Printed and bound in Canada by Tri-Graphic Printing, Ottawa, Ontario.

Published by **Quarry Press, Inc.**, P.O. Box 1061, Kingston, Ontario K7L 4Y5.

CONTENTS

For my mother,
Maye Horner Finnigan (1901 – 1992),
and my father,
Francis Albert Clarence Finnigan (1901 – 1991).

1

THE LEGEND OF "THE SHAWVILLE EXPRESS"

"If I were building a new team and were given my choice of all the players I have seen in action, I would select Finnigan as one of the wings. He was a perfect coach's player; he could score, patrol his own wing defensively and, as a penalty killer, he had few equals."

— **Frank Selke,** *Behind the Cheering*

I was born in Ottawa in 1925, the eldest child of Maye Horner and Frank Finnigan, both then aged twenty-four. The year before, my father, known then throughout the Ottawa Valley hockey circuit and later throughout the hockey world as "The Shawville Express," had signed his first National Hockey League contract for $1,800 per season with the Ottawa Senators. Bonuses from Frank Ahearn, owner of the Senators, brought my father's salary for that first year up to $3,400.

Prior to turning pro, my father had worked as a lineman for Bell Telephone in Pontiac County in Quebec and, according to Valley legend, was up a telephone pole when the long distance call came up from Ottawa proclaiming to the whole countryside "instamatically" that Frank Ahearn of Ottawa was calling Frank Finnigan of Shawville. Someone ran from the Chinese restaurant on Main Street to tell my father.

For years afterwards one of my mother's constant refrains was, "Oh, if only he had stayed with the Bell! He wouldn't have gotten a swelled head, and he wouldn't have taken to drink, and he wouldn't have got in with all those dreadful people . . . and we wouldn't have . . . '' The meteoric and chaotic life of the professional hockey star would have been bypassed for the more orthodox predictable life of the Big Company employee with what seemed to her, I am sure, all its enviable advantages: the punctuality of nine-to-five hours, the holidays with pay, the certain pension at retirement age, the "safe" life away from the constant threats and emotional dangers of living in the limelight.

Frank Finnigan, "The Shawville Express," sports the uniform of the Ottawa Senators with the distinctive "O" crest and black, red, and white stripes. Finnigan played for The Senators for over a decade, winning The Stanley Cup in 1923–1924 and 1926–27.

When The Senators disbanded in the early 1930s, Finnigan was sold to the Toronto Maple Leafs, where he starred on the 1932–33 Stanley Cup team with fellow former Senator Frank "King" Clancy.

Even though my father was a national idol in an era when the country seemed to have very few, he chose to live in Centretown Ottawa on McLeod Street, first block west of Bank Street, in an unpretentious one-bathroom house. Our middle-class neighborhood was home to such future celebrities as Lorne Green, Fred Davis, and Paul Anka. I suppose my father could have chosen a more prestigious area of the city in which to raise his family. But he had wanted Centretown, he told us later, because "It

Frank Finnigan rode the Push, Pull, and Jerk Express from Shawville to Ottawa where he became a hockey legend and gained his nickname "The Shawville Express."

Many other local hockey heroes would travel down the Ottawa Valley to become Hockey Hall of Fame legends playing for The Senators. The Pontiac train made twenty-six stops at stations like this between Ottawa and Waltham.

was close enough that I was able to walk to work." Yet he was never known to walk to work — or anywhere else, for that matter! He always drove one of his annual succession of new cars three blocks over to Argyle Avenue where the old Auditorium stood in those days on the site of the present-day YMCA. There, the only professional hockey club in the history of the Capital City, the Ottawa Senators, had their home base, practiced and trained, hosted the National Hockey League teams in an international

Pedlars with horse and cart sold their wares along the streets of Centretown Ottawa. Pictured here is Ben Polowin and his horse Jenny.

Frank Finnigan's youngest son Ross rides his tricycle in front of the family home on McLeod Street. Both Ross and his brother Frankie retained considerable memorabilia of their father's hockey career. But it was John who kept the scrapbooks — source of data and photos for this book.

circuit which included the Toronto St. Pats, the Montreal Canadiens, the Montreal Maroons, the Chicago Black Hawks, the Boston Bruins, the New York Americans, the New York Rangers, and the Detroit Red Wings. Two years after I was born, the Ottawa Senators won The Stanley Cup; my father, a wet-behind-the-ears rookie brought down the telephone pole to inject new blood into the playoffs, had scored the winning goal.

It is often said in Canada that children of hockey players are fitted for skates before they are fitted for shoes. In retrospect I recognize that, figuratively speaking, we almost grew up on our skates. Frigid, Siberian Ottawa was a good place for a professional hockey player to raise a family, some of whom he certainly intended to follow in his footsteps. Ottawa was then, as I remember it, nine months of ice and snow. The second fully recognizable season was two months of summer, usually spent at Sand Bay on the Quebec side of the Ottawa River. Spring was merely an undelineated period in between winter and summer, a few weeks of taking off your winter coat, and being told to put it back on again (I once skied on the 24th of May on the north slopes of Camp Fortune). Like spring, autumn was just a brief sigh of sadness for summer's end, the click of the furnace going on the first of September, the after-school aromas of mother's jams, pickles, and grape juice in the kitchen, the barrels of apples and bags of potatoes put into the cold storage in the basement, winter hems let down, snow shovels standing in position. Our profound Canadian yearning for winter would almost equate with the passionate longing of the English poet who wrote, "Oh, to be in England now that April's here!" Annually, we danced an ecstatic welcome to the First Snow.

We grew up in a glassy sea of skating rinks — one on Gladstone Avenue near us (now the site of MacNab Park); one at Glashan Street School (although they locked it on weekends and you had to climb with your skates on up the eight-foot-high chain-link fence to get in); and one on Second Avenue to which one sometimes aspired if one had a "crush" on a young man of the moment who lived in the Glebe. There was the Rideau Canal — until someone drowned and it was banned as a skating rink. Given certain quick-freeze ice conditions before too much snow had fallen, sometimes all the streets of Centretown became skating rinks. On Saturday afternoons for ten cents there was skating at The Auditorium, affectionately called "The Rink," to the "Skater's Waltz" and the "Blue Danube." And then there were all the backyard rinks.

We always had a backyard rink. Our days and nights were filled with the slashing of sticks and the crashing of pucks. Centretown was populated then by people raising families and, with five of us at home, it was easy to pick up a team anytime along the street. We played after school and on the weekends and even in the cold winter nights when we turned on the back porch lights and lit the ice. In time, flying pucks actually wore holes right through the wood in our back porch. Girls were not really welcome on the backyard rinks, unless there was a shortage of neighborhood boys, and my brothers tell now how sometimes they were told on the sly to take their younger sister off the rink for "ragging" (hanging onto) the puck.

On below zero nights when there was not the cutting of ice by sharp skates or the crashing of the puck on the boards, there was the steady sound of the necessary hosing. Indeed, one painting that has not yet been done by a Canadian artist, to my knowledge, is of that solitary figure, the rink-maker or the icer, standing out in the crispness of a twenty below January night, alone under the lights, moving the hose carefully over the ice surface. There should be an historic plaque somewhere to commemorate the passing of this unsung national hero. Along with the frozen ponds, lakes, and rivers of this country, the backyard rinks generated our national game and spawned some of our greatest teams and players.

During the day in the house on McLeod Street we lived the relatively ordinary life of all the children growing up in Centretown in that era. But, from an early age, on singular nights we had a heady and perhaps enviable experience when we went to watch our father's games at The Rink (and later when he was with Toronto Maple Leafs at Maple Leaf Gardens). My brothers and sister and I took turns going with mother, dressed in our Sunday Best, and sitting in the Special Box then reserved for families of players. As a little girl I was secretly mortified by the boorish manner in which the players, including my own father, cleared their noses by using their hands and then wiping the phlegm on their pants. I had already started to grow up in the world of beautifully-embroidered handkerchiefs for ladies, boxed in sets for Christmas-giving, and clearly the only proper vehicle known then to man for the business of nose-blowing. My sister later confessed that as a young child she was so bored that she could never sit still or even keep awake through an entire N.H.L. game, and remembers well going to sleep inside my mother's big black seal coat.

My brothers were much more aware of the course of my father's hockey career. They lived and breathed hockey. Not only did they practice to be great hockey players like their father before them, but they followed the games in amateur leagues throughout the "hockey city" which Ottawa was in those days.

From the very first time the cry "He shoots! He scores!" went out over Canadian airwaves, they listened to Foster Hewitt announce

Star's Daughter Reported Better

Finnigan Unable to go to Pittsburgh — Connell Reported Better.

Frank Finnigan, star right wing player of the Ottawa hockey team, was unable to accompany the Senators to Pittsburgh for their game there tonight against the Pirates on account of the serious illness of his little daughter, Joan. Little Miss Finnigan is at the Isolation Hospital recovering from scarlet fever and from an operation for mastoid trouble.

"She is getting along better today, I am glad to say," said her father this afternoon.

Word was received from Dave Gill at Pittsburgh, this morning, that Alex Connell, the Ottawa goalkeeper, is better from a heavy cold, but is still very weak. The team were glad to receive a report that Frank Finnigan's daughter was slightly better.

the games on radio. They collected gum cards with an avidity that verged on mania and forced the rest of us to swallow two-by-three squares of stale bubble gum, or let it go to waste. My brother John made scrapbooks of all the newspaper clippings and magazine writings in which my father appeared. While my brother Frankie began playing in earnest in leagues that led to the N.H.L., John sold programs at The Auditorium, both to earn himself some money and to keep himself within the inner sanctum of hockey.

But I don't ever remember listening to a game on the radio or reading a newspaper headline. Nor did I ever collect gum cards. I do vaguely remember going to the N.H.L. games with my mother when it was my turn to go and sit with her in the Family Seats. But I remember more what my mother wore on her head than any play or score or player, for that matter. In truth, I have only one or two memories of my father's career in big-time hockey.

I very vaguely recall my father winning The Stanley Cup with the Toronto Maple Leafs in 1932 (I would be seven then), and the memory takes on the hue of a nightmare. After the game my mother and I had made our way out of our Box Seats into the lobby of the arena where patrols of policemen were trying to keep the crowds under control. But the crowds went wild as the victorious heroes came out of their dressing-room. We caught sight of my father off in the distance and began to try to swim against the current towards him, my mother holding my hand. But my father was swept away from us in a sea of arms. "They are going to kill him now," I thought. The policemen fought valiantly to maintain crowd discipline but the mobs picked the players

Hockey heroes like Frank Finnigan endorsed every product imaginable, from Aylmer tomato juice to Dunlop tires, from Beehive corn syrup to R.J. Devlin and Biltmore hats. Their image appeared not only on the sports pages but in consumer magazines and on public billboards in every hockey town.

up and carried them away. My father disappeared from sight. The crowds surged around us like an ocean, almost tearing me from my mother's grasp. I was torn between tears and anger. Why were they bearing my father away like a piece of flotsam? He was ours. Not theirs. Or so I thought.

As a young girl growing up in Ottawa's Centretown in the 1920s and 1930s I soon discovered that going along Bank Street with my father was often an unforgettable experience. All kinds of unknown, unidentified people came up and slapped him on the back, crying out, "Great game, Frankie!" or pushed through shopping crowds to shake his hand, or pressed upon him for autographs for their kids. Ottawa then had a population of 120,000 but the fact that my father was a great right-winger in Canada's national game made the city a tiny village.

As a child, it seemed to me very puzzling that he knew everyone and everyone knew him. It required a number of years and a certain amount of learning before I realized that, as a hockey hero, he belonged to everyone — even strangers. I don't think, my mother ever accepted that. She was suspicious of every fan, every admirer who came near him. "Who was that? Who was

Frank Finnigan is shown here beside one of his annual sucession of new cars given to him by the automobile dealer as payment for his endorsement.

that?" she would demand. "How dare they call you 'Frankie' when they don't even know you!" To which my father would patiently reply, "I don't know who it was. They know me, but I don't know them. Everybody calls me 'Frankie'. They call Howie Morenz 'Howie'. They call Joe Primeau 'Joe'."

I soon became aware of my father's legend, sensing some of its negative implications as well as all of its more positive ones. "No bones about it," as my mother was wont to declare, it was exciting to go down the streets of Centretown in the shadow of my father, strangers greeting him with, "You're the greatest, Frankie boy!" Fair-weather friends slapped him on the back, saying, "Come on, Finnigan! Buy you a drink!" In the beginning there was nothing but a filling up with pride on these occasions when I observed my father and his public. But I know now I was witnessing the kind of surface "loving" and "adoration" which comes to the entertainer-artist by way of substitute for a profound and healthy loving on a one-to-one basis.

While my father was stick-handling himself through the intoxicating labyrinths of his hockey career, blending headlines with homage, we "Finnigan kids" were busy living our own young lives and trying to grow up. But I did have periodic vicarious glimpses of my father's other life which my mother in her pithy Ottawa Valley language always described as "living high on the hog" — his comings and goings to Chicago, New York, Detroit, in a private car with a porter; his name in heavy black on the sports pages declaring "Finnigan Scores Again!"; his talk of the Waldorf, the Royal York, the Windsor; his stories of an up-and-coming singer, Bing Crosby, of a Harlem jazzman named Fats Waller, of a Broadway musical called *Sonny Boy*.

From his voyages into the other world, my father often came home "in the clouds of the night" or in the dawn from his "Away" games because it was the team's custom to catch a sleeper right after the game from wherever they were, and then to travel all night to reach home. Sometimes in the small hours I would awake to hear the murmurings of my parents' voices, or the rustling of tissue paper.

The morning following my father's returnings we always got up with "Christmas" excitement in our hearts, for our father was a generous man with impeccable taste in clothes and would come home laden with gifts for my mother and for us. I can see the dresses for my sister and me, laid in layers of tissue paper, straight from New York's finest stores.

The vein of my father's generosity ran over into a fault. One day he took me to buy a pair of new shoes and instead bought me three pairs, one a chocolate brown pair by Hurlburt, no less, with gold eyelets and curly laces, so grand that, when I first got them, I used to stick my feet out in the aisle at school so that everyone could see them.

When it came time to buy me my first skates, my father bought the most expensive in the city. I can feel the leather in them yet; they were soft, black, almost figure-skating quality. The chrome in the blades was mixed with some other alloy which, in my mind, verged on platinum so that my feet on the ice netted the sun by day and the moon by night. I knew that no one on earth had ever had a pair like them. And certainly I knew that in the change shacks at the outdoor skating rinks there was no chance that I would ever get my skates mixed up with anyone else's. Whether it was because of my superlative skates, or because I was born with "hockey players' knees," I became a precocious hockey player, learning without any lessons or training to move on the ice in an unconscious imitation of my father's style.

My hockey career peaked in Grade Five at Percy Street

Ottawa Senators — like Frank Finnigan — sometimes cut a dashing image off ice, attired in the latest fashions, supplied by clothiers and furriers in return for their endorsement. Hockey was business even back in the Roaring Twenties.

School. It was a cold, sunny, brilliantly blue January noon hour in which my grade was playing off for the girl's championship of the school. To this day, I can recall the feeling of floating effortlessly up the ice, stick-handling my way through the entire opposing team (most of whom were still skating on their ankles and their asses), scoring time after time as the crowd, lined up around the boards of the outdoor rink, roared their approval. On one of

| Sunday, Mar. 18th

New York
'RANGERS'
vs.
New York
'AMERICANS' | # AROUND
~the~
CIRCUIT
With JACK FILMAN—MADISON SQUARE GARDEN | Sunday, Mar. 18th

New York
'RANGERS'
vs.
New York
'AMERICANS' |

CLANCY

THE HARPS THAT ONCE THRO' TEX'S HALL
—gave exhibitions of the airtight defensive game, have proven to the fans that their stellar team-work is equally effective under the new rules which call for more open-play. Off to a poor start in November, the Senators waged a heady, steady fight until they landed in the play-off position for the Canadian Group honors.

FINNEGAN

'Frankly' speaking,—the Senators are there,—with Frank Nighbor, Frank Clancy and Frank Finnegan turning in the brand of stuff that means a strong finish for the Parliament gang who step their best in play-offs and World Series. However, the club owners who are figuring their teams in the play-offs, seem to fear Eddie Gerard's Maroons. Boston wants nothing to do with Pittsburgh Pirates,—Bruins wont even speak to them.

Preceding Sunday night's City Championship clash between Rangers and Americans, the local Hockey Writers Assn. will name their choice for the most valuable player to his team of the two New York clubs. The Paramount Theatre Trophy is the prize and the contest has narrowed down pretty much to Normie Himes of Americans and Ching Johnson of the Rangers.

Play-off dates in both groups of the N. H. L. have been announced for March 27th and 29th, and from April 1st to 14th. The game is getting bigger, schedules running longer and Press Box …

Hope to introduce another 'home town' grad on the Senator's line-up tonight,—Alan Shields, No. 12 left-handed defenceman and winger, formerly of the Ottawa 'Gunners' club of the Ottawa Senior Amateur City League. The 'Gunners' were one of those friendly little cliques of puckchasers who got together during the War and have been turning out good teams ever since.

Kenora, Ont. and Regina, Sask. kids are cleaning up the western junior teams in their quest for the Abbott Memorial Cup, emblematic of the cradle championship of the prairies. In the meantime Toronto 'Marlboros' are smacking all the baby sextets in the East. Port Colborne, Ont. dumped Kitchener for the Intermediate O. H. A. title, which is about the same as Int. championship of the world in the amateur ranks.

As usual, the Maritime Province senior champs, Truro, Nova Scotia, Bearcats, didn't get beyond Montreal in their quest of the Allan Cup. Montreal 'Vies' must stop the Arnprior champs of the …

Shorty Green is plugging it thro' with three relief players on the bench,—making the best of a bad season's play in which his stars that he depended on faded before injuries or other troubles. Hockey writers have commended Shorty for 'taking' his setbacks and heartbreaks for the 1927-28 schedule with the few squawks registered to date.

Local Hockey Writers will also figure in the selection of the most valuable player to his team for the League-wide trophy offered by Dr. Hart of Montreal and the clean-play cup offered by Lady Byng for the puckchaser showing the best sportsmanship on the ice for the 27-28 season. Contenders for the numerous trophies have ordered special trunks to cart their silverware back home.

Jim Kelley, (Montreal Gazette), is the gentleman responsible for those long lists of British …

Referee Mickey Ion, is slapping fines on the boys right and left for 'insubordination' on the ice. Nels Stewart put on a comedy act in the Forum that cost the big bruiser 50 bucks. President Frank Calder and Referee-in-Chief Cooper Smeaton are backing Mickey in his house-cleaning of the wise-crackers who pull laughs from the crowds at the expense of the official in charge.

Canadiens will just about beat the scoring record of 115 goals made by Chicago Black Hawks last season. The present count for the Flying Frogs numbers 104 tallies to date and they have four games left in which to make up the difference. Their count of 'goals against' is of course far ahead of the Hawk 27 record which has 116 'fox passes' on the net,—Frenchmen have only 42 scores charged on the wrong side.

Hartford, Conn. and Newark, N. J. report progress in the erection of their 'Coliseums',—'Gardens' for next season's hockey …

Frank Finnigan was billed as hero wherever The Senators traveled — in Toronto, New York, Boston, Montreal, Detroit, Chicago, and even Pittsburgh.

these scoring rushes I went past the principal, a stately Mr. McNab whom my mother always described glowingly as "a scholar and a gentleman." As I passed him I heard him say, "Look at that girl go! She's just like her father!" This compliment offended me, I remember, for I was a girl in an age when girls were girls and boys were boys. I never played hockey again.

Ten years ago while researching a film on the history of hockey in the Ottawa Valley for the National Film Board, I had the occasion to encounter the continuing legend of my father, "The Shawville Express." I was a touring Maple Leaf Gardens with Dick Beddoes and King Clancy, my father's teammate with the Senators and later with the Maple Leafs. The "King" introduced me to an old trainer there who had been at the Gardens when my father played for the Leafs in the 1930s. He told a heartwarming story about my father.

"Ah, Frankie," he said, lighting up. "He used to come in well before every game and unwind the tape from around his hockey stick. Then he would take the skate-sharpener and sharpen the edges of his stick carefully, put the tape back on and go out and play. He never used more than one stick a year!"

Another time, while researching one of my oral history books along the Richmond Road outside of Ottawa, I met an old man who reminisced about seeing my father play for the Ottawa Senators. "Untrippable he was," the old-timer mused. "His balance was uncanny. They couldn't trip him — and they tried."

And then there was another old hockey buff in Ottawa who said to me, "Yes, he was a great one — but his pants always hung down!"

Some time ago while I was meeting with Gervais O'Reilly at Quyon, Quebec, he pulled out a rare newspaper photo of The Stanley Cup Winning Ottawa Silver Seven Team of 1905 and then began reminiscing about great Ottawa Valley players who went on to star in the N.H.L. — players like Frank Nighbor, Bill Cowley, Murph Chamberlain, and Frank Finnigan. "One of the great social events of my youth," Mr. O'Reilly told me, "was a dance on October 12, 1928 at the Shawville Theater — formal dresses, dance cards, a ten-piece band, the Royal Ambassadors from Cleveland, Ohio, no less. I can even remember some of the girls on my dance card — Aileen Morrissey, Aileen Gavan, Inez McLean, Annie McGarrity all from Quyon; Marjorie Clarke from Campbell's Bay, Ann O'Brien from the Island, and an Elliott from Shawville. But the highlight, the star event, was when

Frankie Finnigan, fresh from the Ottawa Senators, appeared at the doorway. Remember the Senators had just won the Stanley Cup that spring. We all almost fell back. And I remember he just stood along the wall with the boys — and he never danced."

And another time I went out to Stark's Corners, just back of Shawville towards Portage-du-Fort, to tape a descendent of the original settlement, M.A.O. Stark. The Stark house is a huge landmark brick set very high on a hill above the hamlet looking out over the Ottawa Valley across the river and into the Opeongo Hills.

Mr. Stark talked Shawville history and genealogy for a while, and then said how much he'd like to see my father again. "I don't get into town so much now I'm eighty-two and I miss meeting your father on the street there and talking to him," he said a little sadly.

"Did you ever watch my father play hockey when you were a young lad?" I asked him.

"Oh, heaven's yes," he replied. "Hockey was the big event. We'd hitch the horses to a cutter or maybe a sleigh and take some members of the family — it was a very large family of thirteen — but we would take some of them, the avid hockey fans, for five miles, in the winter, into Shawville to watch Frank Finnigan play. I'm six years younger than Frank so I would have been ten and he'd be sixteen. The Shawville arena of course has fallen down. But Shawville was one of the first towns in the whole Pontiac to have a covered rink."

Mr. Stark went over to his front window which looks down over Starks Corners and the fertile rolling fields of his ancestral farm.

"Yes," he mused, "I've seen him play right down here below on an outdoor rink in that field, play Portage-du-Fort, maybe when he was twelve, and Portage always was a rough, rough town — off limits to a lot of young people."

Then in 1981 Tundra Books of Montreal staged a reception in Petawawa for my first book about the history of the Ottawa Valley, *Look! The Land Is Growing Giants*, based on the legend of Joseph Montferrand, "King of the Ottawa River." At the reception, Sean Conway, MPP for Renfrew County, was a special guest who greeted me with the question, "Where's your father?" He happened to be in the crowd, and I pointed him out to Sean. "My grandfather always said he was the greatest. That's the book you should be doing," he said to me as he sat down beside my father. He spent the remainder of the reception engaged in good-spirited conversation with that other Ottawa Valley legendary hero, "The Shawville Express." I suspect the seed for this book was planted that day in Petawawa.

The Legend of "The Shawville Express" lives on today, even though my father died on Christmas Day 1991. For the two years previous to his death, he worked hand-in-hand with Bruce Firestone and the hockey enthusiasts who have returned the

Frank Finnigan was the last of the Ottawa Senators living when this portrait was taken by photographer Eva Andai of Shawville, Quebec. Something of his spirit — and something of the character of the old Senators — can be seen and felt here.

Ottawa Senators to the National Hockey League after an absence of nearly 60 years. When N.H.L. commissioner John Zeigler and the Board of Governors awarded an expansion franchise to Ottawa on December 12, 1991, my father shared the limelight with the new owners. "Without the support of Frank Finnigan," one governor was heard to say, "Ottawa wouldn't have been awarded the franchise." Frank Finnigan, "The Shawville Express," was scheduled to drop the puck at the Senator's first home game in October 1992.

Frank Finnigan's personal hockey career mirrors the course of history for the Ottawa Senators. Born in a small town cradled in the Ottawa Valley, he developed his skills and character on river ice before going down to the big city, like dozens of other players before him and hundreds more after him, to join the professional ranks playing in the N.H.L. The "Roaring Twenties" were glory years for Finnigan and The Senators with "The Shawville Express" dancing on skates to a championship tune wearing a R.J. Devlin hat in the 1927 Stanley Cup Victory Parade

Sporting the uniform of the new Ottawa Senators team while attending the N.H.L. Board of Governors Expansion Meeting in Florida in December 1990, Frank Finnigan lends his support and his image to the franchise.

down the streets of Ottawa. Finnigan starred. Headline after headline in *The Ottawa Citizen* and *The Journal* proclaimed his prowess and finesse — as well as the talents and courage of Alec Connell, Hec Kilrea, Frank "King" Clancy, Frank Nighbor, Harry "Punch" Broadbent, Cyril "Cy" Denneny, George "Buck" Boucher, Eddie Gerard, and their teammates.

The "Dirty Thirties" held no such glory for Finnigan and his teammates, however. Ottawa Senator owner Frank Ahearn disbanded the team in 1934, selling off local heroes like Finnigan and Clancy to the Toronto Maple Leafs, where they starred briefly before retirement. The Senators descended into the minor professional circuit of the Quebec Senior Hockey League until the team folded in the 1950s. Meanwhile, Finnigan descended into obscurity and even further into alcoholism. My father's near-miraculous release from his drug addiction in the 1950s now appears as the harbinger of the equally miraculous return of the Ottawa Senators to the ranks of the N.H.L. Frank Finnigan, "The Shawville Express," again became a star of the new Ottawa Senators in the two years before his death.

The legend of "The Shawville Express" thus spans two eras of hockey glory in Ottawa. From my father's perspective, using

As Frank Finnigan was always quick to remind everyone, the Ottawa Senators were once a proud team, winners of nine Stanley Cups before disbanding in 1933–34 — and will continue to be a proud team when they return to the N.H.L. for the 1992–93 season.

his memories and those of his fans, friends, teammates, and relatives, I have compiled this story of the Ottawa Senators. The story begins up the Ottawa Valley, in the cradle of professional hockey . . .

2

THE CRADLE OF PROFESSIONAL HOCKEY

"In those days the Ottawa Valley was the cradle of hockey. I think at that time the Valley developed at least fifty per cent of the hockey players in Canada."

— Frank Finnigan

That professional hockey was conceived in the Ottawa Valley was no accident. Geography, climate, character, and good old-fashioned wealth conspired to nourish what soon became Canada's national sport. The Ottawa Valley is a unique homogeneous area, as large as England, the watershed for the mighty Ottawa River and its twenty six tributaries stretching from Montreal to Bancroft, from Brockville to Timmins. Following the first waves of explorers, traders, and settlers into the St. Lawrence River Valley, subsequent newcomers flowed up the Ottawa to settle on both the Quebec and Ontario sides of the river.

Most Ottawa Valley settlers — chiefly Irish and Scots immigrants of little means — made their living from the land, scratching out a subsistence from farming during a short summer season, supplemented by winter work in the lumber industry, felling tall white pine, driving timber down river, sawing lumber at the many mills throughout the region. This industry was founded by families, the Gillies of Braeside, the MacLarens of Buckingham, the Boyles of Maniwaki, the Conroys of Aylmer, the McLachlins of Arnprior, the Barnets and the O'Briens of Renfrew, and J.R. Booth of Ottawa. The lumbering industry also fostered legendary lumbering giants of the Ottawa Valley like Joseph Montferrand

(Big Joe Mufferaw), Mountain Jack Thomson of Portage-du-Fort, Wild Bill Ferguson of Calabogie, Big Michael Jennings of Sheenborough, Cockeye George McNee of Arnprior, the Twelve MacDonnell Brothers of Sand Point.

Timber money was often instrumental in fostering hockey in The Valley — M.J. O'Brien, for example, founded the National Hockey Association and was the first team owner to try to "buy"

Toqued, furred, wrapped in buffalo robes, this merry group of young people might well be on their way to cheer their local hockey team on to victory.

An afternoon hockey game most likely, on Saturday or Sunday, being played on the Fort Coulonge rink and their opponents in the white uniforms have come up the line from Quyon.

The Stanley Cup when he formed the Renfrew Millionaires. And the heroic character the lumber giants assumed in legend was transferred to hockey heroes like Hockey Hall of Fame members H.H. "Harry" Cameron, F. H. "Hughie" Lehman, and Frank Nighbor of Pembroke; Edouard "Newsy" Lalonde and Cyril "Cy"

Denneny of Cornwall; referees M. J. "Mike" Rodden of Mattawa and J. Cooper Smeaton of Carleton Place; and founding owner J. Ambrose O'Brien of Renfrew and Frank "Cyclone" Taylor, enticed to play for the Renfrew Millionaires by O'Brien wealth and cunning.

Perhaps because of the long, cold winters with no shortage of water to freeze into ice rinks, perhaps because of the kind of

Father and daughter try out their improvised sail, created to hasten their skating speed over the smooth frozen surface of the Ottawa River.

Every hamlet, every village, every town, every mine in the Ottawa Valley had a hockey rink. This one at the Starelle Mine near Sudbury is certainly wired for night games.

"sporting" character the lumber industry created, the Ottawa Valley became the cradle of hockey in Canada, providing the various amateur and professional leagues — the Amateur Hockey Association, the Eastern Canada Association, the Canadian Amateur Hockey League, the Federal Hockey League, the National Hockey Association, and the National Hockey League after 1917 — with nearly 50% of their players between 1880 and

This old photograph is of Fort Coulonge's first hockey team and their supporters, many of whom traveled the long cold miles by horse and sleigh to Quyon, Shawville, Portage-du-Fort, to cheer their team to victory. Note the more affluent members of Fort Coulonge's "sporting people" in their fur coats and hats.

1920. The Valley also stocked the great Ottawa teams — the Rideau Rebels, the Ottawa City Hockey Club, the Silver Seven, and the Ottawa Senators — with some of their greatest players. During this era, the Ottawa Valley was a ferment of amateur hockey. Crossroads hamlets tried to equip and field teams to play neighboring hamlets and rivalries grew up between villages supporting pickup teams. Small towns built and regularly iced outdoor rinks, some with lights strung around the perimeter for night games. The speedy and reliable post office of those days delivered challenges to rival teams, and fans laid heavy bets. The sportswriter was born, reporting for small town weeklies and big city dailies. Governors-General in the Capital and Horatio Algers in the lumbering and mining towns of the Valley became promoters and financiers of hockey teams. Leagues were formed and re-formed; teams organized and disbanded. Cups were cast in pure silver.

Leagues sprang up like dandelions in June: church leagues — Roman Catholic, Presbyterian, Methodist — you name it; interclass leagues in elementary schools; high-school leagues; university leagues (McGill, Queen's, Toronto); an Upper Ottawa Valley

League; a Lower Ottawa League; inter-village leagues; inter-town leagues; inter-city leagues; inter-regimental leagues; county leagues. In Pembroke the highly popular Debating Club fielded a Debaters' Team, and in Ottawa the leading merchants began a mercantile team league, including the Ottawa Electrics made up of employees of the Ottawa Electric Street Railway Company.

In the beginning local merchants most often provided team

Quyon Hockey team, about 1906–07. Bottom row, LEFT TO RIGHT — Herby Moyle, Billy Boland. Second row — Frank Doyle, William Pimlott, Pug Pimlott, Angus McLean (later to run the Quyon ferry for fifty years), Pete Moran. Third row — Eddy Grant, Hilliard Walsh, Frank Kennedy.

sweaters and team equipment, as well as very scant traveling expenses, maybe tickets to travel on the train from Perth to Brockville to play there and come back the same night. It was a landmark experience for young men if there was ever entertained the thought of staying overnight in a strange and far-off hotel.

The invention of the fur coat with inside flask pocket was no accident. On outdoor rinks avid fans stood for hours on the snow and ice where screaming, yelling, and jumping was not only player inspiration but a manner of keeping warm in below zero weather. Whiskey was sustenance for fans traveling to games by horse and sleigh or on trains with little or no heat. "Mr. Renfrew," the late Les Fraser of the Fraser Men's Wear stores in Renfrew and Shawville, once told me of how, absolutely undaunted, hockey fans from Renfrew traveled by train to Ottawa and then for hours more by train from Ottawa to Montreal to see a professional game between the Ottawa Senators and one of the two Montreal teams, the Maroons or the Canadiens.

And recently at the Bonnechere Manor in Renfrew, Harvey Ferguson, a descendant of the first settlers along the Opeongo Line at the river-front near Farrells' Landing, described how he and his entire family used to bundle themselves up, heat bricks for the sleigh and for the game, cross the Ottawa River by ice in the enveloping dusk, nearly freeze rinkside as the bricks they often stood on cooled down — and all to see Frankie Finnigan, "the greatest," play for Shawville. Then, often in the pitch black, the temperature having plummeted, the Fergusons, huddled together for warmth, their faces frozen into silence, would make their return journey across the Ottawa through the untrammelled winds of that mighty River, over an almost imaginary "ice road" navigated by a driver and horses with all their experience handy and sixth senses alerted.

The Davises of Fort Coulonge, first settlers there along with the Proudfoots, the Jewels, the Frosts, the Coltons, and the Brysons, were renowned throughout the Valley as hockey players, fans, supporters, and organizers. The late Fred Davis, one of the family, told me this hockey story, entwined with horse-racing and what must have been some very challenging bicycling:

When I was a boy, Fort Coulonge was a great hockey town. One of the first covered rinks in the county was here; my dad owned it. But the townspeople, because they couldn't agree on what percentage my father should have, went onto the river and built an open-air rink in spite. So our great one, Harold Darragh, went to the Ottawa Senators.

Coulonge used to play Shawville, Quyon, even a team from Kazubazua. We would take a train to Ottawa and then get to Gatineau whatever way we could. A team of good horses driving a bunch can't go much more than six miles an hour, so you can imagine how long it took us to get to Shawville, Campbell's Bay, Quyon! The women were the coldest because they used to get fancied up for the games. They would warm up a bunch of bricks and put them in the bottom of the sleighs and cutters and stand on them. There was a terrible rivalry between Shawville and Portage-du-Fort; they were always fighting. I remember my mother telling me how one of the Toner boys from Portage had to hide in the basement all day because they were coming from

Shawville to get him. I don't know what he did the night before!

My father was a kind of jack-of-all-trades. He was slide master at the Coulonge Chute and he raced horses. That's how he met my mother. Near Portage-du-Fort on the road to Stoney Batter there used to be race track there. One Sunday my father went down with a good horse, a winner, and of course the women were all milling around him.

I got into race horses myself through Billy Sharpe, the blacksmith here. He was probably one of the greatest characters ever lived around here. And his father before him, the village blacksmith too. Billy was a great man with the ladies, a great man with the horses, a great storyteller. When he'd meet you on the street he'd always say, "Any choice news today, me lad?" Everybody had to go to Billy. Everybody sat around in Sharpe's. There was another old lad like Sharpe in Shawville — Harper Rennick, the blacksmith there.

I remember one great winter's day with Billy Sharpe when I was a young lad. At Quyon on the river they used to have harness races on the ice the same as they have now on the Rideau Canal in Ottawa. Billy Sharpe was going to drive a team down and then race. I was quite young and I had to beg my father and mother to let me go. When we got to Quyon there was a hockey game going on in the rink there. Billy Sharpe left me to hold the team and went to see what was going on. I remember he came out to me and said, "My God! There's a young fellow in there can play hockey!" It turned out to be Frankie Finnigan. Billy Sharpe won the race with his black horse, and he went home happy.

In the summertime, of course, the slides were all dry and we used to get on our bicycles and shoot down them for half a mile. You had to be able to put on your brakes, though, at the bottom!

In his memoirs, Edgar Boyle of Ottawa recalls with enthusiasm the social and sporting life associated with hockey in Maniwaki, the base for his family's lumbering operations:

Social life in the small villages was not very active in those days. There was not much time for it — working hours were far too long (seven to six). However, there were four regular places where everyone met at one time or another. They were the post office at mail time, the railway station at night when the Ottawa train arrived, the church steps after service on Sundays, and, in winter, the hockey rink. That was about the extent of it. There were no shows, no radios, very little card playing; actually very little social life.

There was a great rivalry between the two villages of Davidson and Maniwaki in sports. They played hockey and baseball, and played hard against each other. They also combined, under the Maniwaki name, to play against other Valley towns and also

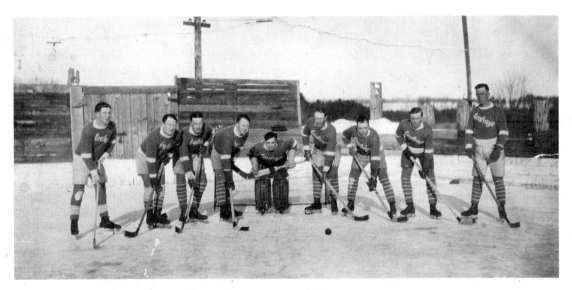

Fort Coulonge Hockey Team, 1930. Benny Duke, Tony Davis, Theo Spotswood, Ed Davis, Lionel Chevrier, Cuddy Harry, Frank Davis, Tommy Jules, Rossie Coll, Tommy Larmeau. This team actually traveled all the way down the Valley — by train, no doubt — to play Cornwall, Ontario.

against teams from Ottawa. They had a good baseball field, a splendid fairgrounds, and, even as far back as 1907, they had a very good indoor hockey and skating rink. The rink, which was in a substantial building, was situated on the Desert River Road, midway between the two villages. As a matter of fact, it was the first of three closed rinks built on the same spot. Two of them burned down.

I think it might be in order here to recall some of the more prominent players of that era. In hockey, there were the Gilmours (Billie, Suddie, and Ward), Jim Nault, Redmond Daly, Jim Quaile, Mike Lawless, Wally Lawless, Bob Mooney, Gray Masson, Lionel Bonhomme, Fred Rochon, Joe Gendron, *et cetera, et cetera.* The quality of hockey played in that era was of very high caliber. It was a notable fact that Billie and Suddie Gilmour had both played for the Ottawa Silver Seven, the world's champions of that day. The other members of the Maniwaki Hockey Team were relatively good . . .

Hockey at Maniwaki was perhaps more glamorous than the other sports. I believe one could divide the hockey of the early days into three separate eras. The first group, who played from about 1907 until about 1919, was comprised of Billie and Suddie

Unfortunately, other than "Maniwaki Hockey Team," there is no documentation for this photograph of players seated in front of a group of proud, sartorial men who must have been the team's backers, perhaps coach and manager. Whatever the date, Maniwaki has won and everyone is sporting ribbons and proudly displaying the championship cup.

Gilmour, Mike Lawless, Fred Rochon, Redmond Daley, Joe McFaul, Bob Mooney, and Tresor Godbout. Their competition was mainly from Ottawa city teams. The Valley teams of that day were must not good enough to compete. During all of this period Jim Donovan was the referee, and sometimes the visiting teams didn't get the best of the decisions. The second era, which lasted from 1920 until 1926, was graced by such players as Ward Gilmour, Charlie Logue, Jim Nault, Wally Lawless, Jim Quaile, and Lionel Bonhomme. This group, with the exception of Wally Lawless, had previously played senior hockey in either the Montreal or the Ottawa City League. I have forgotten to mention Gray Masson, who played for Maniwaki for four years. Gray, Jim Nault, and Ward Gilmour had previously played in the Ottawa City League. Jim Quaile had played with McGill University in the Intercollegiate, and Charlie Logue had played for Loyola College in Montreal. They were no mean group of hockey players and could entertain fast company. They had some illustrious years and brought great credit to the town.

The third era, with which I was associated, lasted from 1927 until 1934. Some of the better-known players in this group were Joe Gendron, Jim Quaile, Ken Taylor, Doc Luduc, Gerard Hubert, Joe Joanis, Truman Raymond, Leo Lacroix, Paul Valliancourt, Tommy Westwick, Bob Forest, Wally Lawless, Ray Lawless, Skip Britt, and Allan Lauriault. Perhaps the most successful year was 1933, when Maniwaki won the championship of the Gatineau, beat Shawville, the Pontiac champions, and then went on to meet Brockville, who were champions of the Ottawa and St. Lawrence districts.

Frank Finnigan also fondly remembered his early career as a hockey player in The Valley, recalling in this interview his first "away" game when the Shawville team crossed the frozen Ottawa River to play Westmeath:

When I was growing up in Shawville, there were no organized teams on all levels — peewee, junior, intermediate, senior, that sort of thing — the way it is today. But we *lived hockey* — and *without* any padding. Hockey on the creeks, hockey on the ponds, hockey on the rivers, hockey on the road — if necessary. We even flooded the Cowan's big black shed and made the first "covered" rink in Shawville. That was before Shawville built the first covered arena in all of Pontiac County. It held 300 standing up and was lit with coal oil lamps overhead. We used to shoot them out, partly for practice, and partly so the other team could see so poorly they'd lose. Of course, we cut off our own noses to spite our faces. But we were young and didn't know any better. Besides, we'd do anything to win. Anything.

Without any organized leagues, we were always looking to throw down a challenge for a game, any chance we got, to Bryson, Campbell's Bay, Portage-du-Fort, Quyon, anything within range because, remember, there were no cars in those days; players either went by horse and sleigh or by train — if they could afford it — and that was seldom. Remember, we are talking about times when many kids didn't have skates because their parents couldn't buy them and when even buying a new stick was a budgeting problem. That's how I learned to only use one stick a year and I continued that even when I was in the National Hockey League playing for the Ottawa Senators and the Toronto Maple Leafs.

I was only twelve, the youngest on the team, when the big challenge came from across the Ottawa River from Westmeath, Ontario, to play a game there. If you know your geography of The Valley at all, that meant taking the train up to Fort Coulonge, Quebec, crossing the Ottawa River by ice and then traveling into Westmeath. The Shawville team was called Cy's Pets, after Cy Hodgins who did some of the financing — Shawville was the center of a large prosperous English Protestant farming community — and most of the businessmen were hockey crazy. Besides, most of them were my relatives. We were the pride of Shawville, a very proud town anyhow, and the merchants had outfitted us all out in fine hockey sweaters with socks to match. Some of us even had the expensive fifty cent hockey sticks.

I remember my teammates so well — Hoddy Rennick, Albert Chisnell, Art Turriff, Archie Dagg, Lyal Hodgins, Rock Findlay, Clark Cowan, all dead now, except me. All fine fellows.

Well that January night in 1913 we were pretty excited, I tell you, as we got on that train all together at 7:15 sharp, headed up the Ottawa Valley to Fort Coulonge. A big dangerous journey for young lads, you know. Clark Cowan's mother wasn't even going to let him go. But then she was like that. Never let go. None of them married, you know. We had to pull him onto the train by one leg. She was holding on to the other. She even brought some heated bricks to the train to keep her son warm on this terrifying journey into the arctic of upriver. Poor Clark! He turned scarlet in front of the team. We felt for him — being sissified that way. But young boys are cruel too. After that we dubbed him "Precious" — and he had to beat some of us up for that.

Willie Hodgins, my uncle — all the Hodgins are related to me, you know, all fifty thousand of them now scattered across the country — went with us. He owned the hardware store in Shawville, and he was along to keep us all in line and to see that we had a safe journey.

At the Fort Coulonge station we were met by a flat sleigh and team of horses driven by a hockey buff from Westmeath come to pick us up. In the dark of the moonless night we drove through Fort Coulonge and out onto the wide, dark, deep Ottawa River to do a two-mile crossing to the Ontario side. It wasn't the first time I had gone to and from a hockey game in the dark night of the wintertime in The Valley. Sometimes it was so cold, you'd get off and run behind the sleigh to keep warm, to keep your feet from freezing before the game. Remember in those days we didn't have wind-proof, arctic-proof, weather-proof, rain-proof garb and gear. Just your long johns, a flannel shirt, and whatever kind of jacket your parents could afford, or that turned up in the stores in town that year. The worst part on a cold winter's night was the return journey after a game. You'd worked up a real sweat during the game — remember in those days we were all Sixty Minute Men — we had no subs — and then you'd get on the sleigh in wet, damp,

Shawville, out of all proportion to its size, was consistently renowned as a hockey town, perhaps because it was so well supported by its businessmen. This is a 1911 photograph of the Shawville Pets, backed by Shawville merchants. LEFT TO RIGHT — Frank Finnigan, Hoddy Rennick, Albert Chisnell, Art Turriff, Archie Dagg, Lyal Hodgins, Rock Findlay, Clark Cowan. Finnigan is only eleven in this photograph but is already playing with fourteen- and fifteen-year-olds.

sweaty clothes, and your teeth would start to chatter and you'd start to shake, and the chills would set in, and, even worn out from playing a whole game, the only way to survive was to get off and run behind the sleigh. Sometimes there were buffalo robes — if we were lucky — and you'd crawl under those and continue shivering. I often wonder how we didn't die of pneumonia. But we were young and tough, then.

This special night of the Westmeath game was, yes, during January, the heart of winter, but during a January thaw, and that warm, unnatural soft wind was blowing about us. And that poses all kinds of problems for crossing the Ottawa on the ice. It means melt. And sure enough, as we descended onto the river and began the journey across on the ice bridge, we found that there was at least a foot of water on the ice surface. Maybe two. Scary.

We grew silent and hung onto our hockey sticks tight, listening to the sleigh bells in the wind, and the jingle of the harness, and the muffled sound of the horses hooves, drowned in slush. The driver was silent, too, intent upon watching the ice bridge and keeping within the markers set up for travelers from the Quebec side to the Ontario side.

We thought of all the stories we had heard back home of ice bubbles and horses, sleighs and men going down. We thought of the drowning of the Downey Boys through the ice, all four of them. But we were young warriors going to war and, although we were scared into cocoons of silence, we knew it might happen to others but never to us.

When we got to the Westmeath rink, we quickly laced on our skates and jumped on the ice for a warm-up that was *really* a warm up. But the Junior team, for some reason or other, perhaps they were afraid of us — didn't show at all. So some of the townsfolk, feeling badly about our long journey and the let down, scrambled around town and picked up members of the Westmeath Senior team. Guys fifteen, sixteen, even seventeen. It was 10:30 by the time we got the game started. Naturally, we lost. But only by a score of 7-3. It was one o'clock by the time we finished the game, and the diehards went home to their warm beds.

Sweating, clammy, and tired, we climbed back onto the flat sleigh and drove back across the ice bridge to Fort Coulonge where we were billeted in the old Fort Coulonge Hotel, the Pearson, which has since burned down. Even hungry and thirsty, we were so tired we just fell onto the beds in our damp clothes. Uncle Willie forced us to undress and got us some extra blankets from the hotel-keeper.

But I was still so high from the game I couldn't sleep at first and lay under the blankets, trying to stop shivering and thinking of the ghosts in the room. For, you see, Fort Coulonge was a big lumbering town — it still is to this day — a big rough lumbering town, and I knew that all the lumbering giants like the Seven Frost Brothers of Pembroke, and Mountain Jack Thomson of Portage-du-Fort, and the timber barons like Gillies and Bryson and Fraser had all stayed over in this hotel. Jesus! I thought as I fell asleep, maybe Big Joe Mufferaw even slept in this bed!

That was my first "away" game. We were only twelve to fourteen years old. But we had become MEN over night. We had gone, all expenses paid, to meet the adversary and stayed at the Pearson Hotel. I didn't know then that years later I was to share space in the great hotels of North America with my teetotalling teammate Frank "King" Clancy, and with fans who were to become my friends, like multi-millionaire Harry McLean of "Mr. X" fame.

When I was a little older we had our revenge on the Westmeath Senior team. We went back to their town and beat them soundly. I cannot remember that winning score. I think in those beginning days I just remembered the scores of games we lost, and plotted return victories.

W. J. Conroy of Aylmer, Quebec, a descendant of the Conroy lumbering family, recalls another classic Ottawa Valley hockey rivalry, in this case between Aylmer and Shawville:

And Aylmer was a hockey town. I think of the well-known ones like Frank Finnigan; he was at Shawville. I played hockey up in Shawville myself and it used to be a rough place. They came down to Aylmer one time, a team from Shawville — they were all about six-foot-four inches, you know — and they came down here and they played the Aylmer Seniors, and they gave them a pretty rough time in Aylmer, you see. So we were invited up to Proudfoot's Hotel in Shawville, and it was a new hotel at the time. Well, the Seniors wouldn't go back; they wanted to know if we were crazy to go up there and get killed. So we picked up a bunch of the Intermediates. We were pretty young and stupid too. Shawville really worked us over.

After the game we went into the Shawville restaurant and we ordered ham and eggs and these bottles of pink soda pop for everybody who was in there. I don't know whose idea it was, but anyway none of us had any money because we were still in our hockey clothes, you see. We had rooms in Proudfoot's Hotel. So somebody started to sing in French, "Open the door and we'll all run out," and, of course, everybody from Aylmer understood, but the fellows up there in Shawville didn't. So all of a sudden somebody opened the door and everybody took off for the hotel and we charged into the hotel and ran up the stairs. We had some pretty fat players, you know, and I can remember one fellow ran under the bed to hide and the next couple of guys who came up jumped on the bed, and the bed broke and nearly decapitated the fellow underneath. Proudfoot wanted to put us out in the middle of the night. But, anyway, I remember in the morning we got out and went down to get on the train, and we all had our pads on and we were carrying our sticks and everything. We were still armed and we never undressed all night.

Behind the scenes, in villages, towns, and burgeoning cities the wealthy, powerful, and influential were gathered to raise money to fund their hockey teams, to buy equipment, to improve rinks, to pay travel expenses, to boost players salaries. We have only an inkling of the intensity of the betting on games in those days, for obviously most of it was unrecorded. But, on occasion, teams were accused of playing to lose because of bets that had been placed beforehand. When Haileybury met Cobalt for The Stanley Cup in the last N.H.A. game of 1910, famous mining magnate Noah Timmins, the Haileybury sponsor, was said to have bet $50,000 on the outcome. Haileybury won 14–9, and we have to presume that, in the manner of the rich getting richer, Timmins collected his bets.

This landmark game is worth evoking. At half-time the score was tied. Timmins burst into the dressing room of the Haileybury team and offered a thousand dollars to the lad who would score the tie-breaker and win the game, a game with surely one of the most bizarre endings in the history of Canadian hockey, as described by H. Roxborough in his book The Stanley Cup Story:

The tension in the arena was unbearable. Both teams had game-winning scoring chances but goalies Chief Jones of Cobalt and Billy Nicholson of Haileybury came up with brilliant saves. Finally Art Ross passed to Horace Gaul who shot the puck past Jones. Haileybury had won!

From the galleries crowded with Cobalt supporters, there came cries of despair. Suddenly from the weight of humanity, the railing collapsed; many fans tumbled fifteen feet to the ice and some were so seriously injured that they had to be taken to hospital on sleighs.

As if that were not climactic enough, the hysteria continued. Winning fans showered pennies, dimes, quarters, even dollars on the ice. The air was filled with money and the players were trying to catch their floating fortune on the fly.

But Billy Nicholson somehow had obtained a tub and any money iced in his vicinity was quickly snared and "tubbed." When he could find no more loot, and the sweat was pouring from his brow, he calmly turned the tub and its contents upside down and sat on it so that no one could dislodge him or the

The great Ottawa Senator, Frank Nighbor, right, in baseball garb, with Dave Behan, amateur sportsman and tireless worker with young boys athletic clubs in Pembroke. In Nighbor's day, before the advent of modern day methods of training and fitness techniques, summertime sports like baseball were a preferred way of "Keeping in shape." Nicknamed the "Pembroke Peach," Nighbor starred on five Stanley Cup winning teams and was the initial winner of the Hart and the Lady Byng trophies.

money. How much money he collected Billy never admitted. But there were guesses that he wouldn't have to work for a long time.

Those early years of the N.H.A. and N.H.L. were filled with colorful, eccentric players like Bad Joe Hall, and Harry Smith, who played for Cobalt and who used his hockey stick as much as a weapon as anything else. In a game between Cobalt and the Renfrew Millionaires, Larry Gilmour, who doubled as the team manager when he wasn't playing, was the victim of Harry Smith's free-wheeling stick. The situation worsened in the next game when Cobalt played against its arch enemy Haileybury. Players kept hitting the ice, recipients of Smith's well-aimed and foul blows. The Police Chief, Paddy Collins, was summoned to arrest Smith and take him to jail. In spite of Smith's below-the-belt tactics, Cobalt won 7-6.

Cornwall was another Valley town which contributed a wealth of outstanding athletes to big-time hockey in Canada, players such as Edouard "Newsy" Lalonde, "Cy" and Corbett Denneny, Carson Cooper, Perce McAteer, the Constant and the Penny Brothers.

"Hurl" and "Shinny" preceded organized hockey on the ponds and waterways of Cornwall. These games were founded on the principle of "every man for himself" as hundreds of skaters would collect on the ice to chase a rubber ball for hours at a time without any semblance of timing, rules, team play.

Adjacent to the old curling rink on First Street, Cornwall's first hockey rink was open air with two large trees growing out of

Born in Pembroke in 1895, F. H. "Hughie" Lehman (left) was an outstanding netminder for twenty-three years, thus earning the nickname, "Old Eagle-Eyes." He played on eight Stanley Cup challenging teams, but won only once with the Vancouver Millionaires in 1914–15.

H.H (Harry) Cameron (right) was born in Pembroke in 1890. During his career, he played on three Stanley Cup Champions — the Torontos of 1913–14, the Arenas of 1918–19, and the St. Patrick's of 1922–23.

the playing area. However, there exists no record of any player being seriously injured during play around them.

Early entrepreneur John Snetsinger built the first covered rink on the north side of Fourth Street near Pitt. Snetsinger's toboggan slide at the side of the rink carried tobogganers through a field in the rear of Gillies' Foundry, across Fifth Street and out onto Fly Creek.

This Ottawa Valley League Champion team from Pembroke included players W. Wallace, S. Shaugnessy, T. Jones, L. Kennedy, E. Howe, B. McPhee, J. Puff, L. Ranson — and almost as many executive members, namely D. Burns, W.D. McLaren A. Thomson, J.E. Wallace J.R. Grieve, S. St. James, H.J. Macrie, and President E.W. Cockburn.

Morrisburg was Cornwall's first hockey foe in lively games with Billy Peacock in goal and Billy Adams, Billy Turner, Arthur Mattice, Fred MacLennan, John Milden, George Pettit, Fred Degan, and James Cameer in the lineup. Stuart Rayside of Lancaster and Randy McLennan of Williamstown donned Cornwall uniforms during the holiday season when they were home from university. This team was good enough to hold down

Hockey in the Ottawa Valley was a sport not only for men. Shown here is the Pembroke High School Girls Hockey Team of 1921–22. Back row, LEFT TO RIGHT — M. Wilson, S. Thomson (Manager), B. Anderson, A.J. McDonnell (Coach), J. Jones. Front Row — N. Gourlay, I. Fraser, J. Wilson, S. Workman, D. Walker.

both the champion Winnipeg hockey team and the famed Montreal Shamrocks to tie scores in exhibition games.

Cornwall then joined the Ontario Hockey Association with Jack Hunter, Fred Degan, George Stiles, Harlow Stiles, Whitely Eastwood, Aeneas MacMillan, and Angus Allen making up the 1900-1901 team. In 1903 the same team was still in action with only one change made when Stronach Warwick replaced Fred Degan.

This team figured in two contests against the famous Wellingtons of Toronto for the Senior Championship of the Ontario Hockey Association. In the first of the home-and-home games, played in Toronto, Cornwall held the Wellingtons to a 3–3 tie. But in the second game, played at Cornwall, the Wellingtons won what old-timers called afterwards "some of the stiffest competitions ever witnessed in Cornwall." The Wellingtons defeated Cornwall by a 3–2 score and then lost the round to the Toronto team in the third game, 6–5. The Wellingtons thus won the John

Ross Robertson Trophy. For that contest John Ross Robertson himself had traveled from Toronto with the Wellingtons to see the playoffs in a place of honor in the upper gallery of the old Victoria Rink, seat of the Cornwall teams until its destruction by fire in 1933.

For some reason lost in the mists of time, Cornwall seceded from the O.H.A. and joined the old Federal Hockey League

One of Frank Finnigan's heroes C.J. "Cy" Denneny (left) was born in 1891 and played some of his junior hockey with the O'Brien Mine Team in the Cobalt Mining League. He played for five Stanley Cup teams and was coaching the Ottawa Senators in 1932–33 when they folded.

Edouard "Newsy" Lalonde (right), born in Cornwall in 1888, was one of Canada's outstanding lacrosse players of all time. A brilliant scorer, Lalonde was also one of the roughest players of his day in the N.H.L. Feuds between Lalonde and Quebec Bulldogs Big Joe Hall helped fill arenas.

where they played against such teams as Ottawa's Montagnards and the Montreal Wanderers. In succeeding years Cornwall won both the Senior and Junior Citizen Shields in the Ottawa Valley Hockey League. In the St. Lawrence League, Cornwall Canadiens carried off honors again.

In addition to the Dennenys and the Lalondes, among the Cornwall hockey aces who learned the game at home and then migrated to other towns and cities to make names for themselves in other leagues and higher places were Guy Smith, Donald Smith, George Penny, James Penny, William Penny, Arthur Kinghorn, Bill Coté, Percy MacAteer, George Harrington, George Anderson, Farrand Gillie, Fred Sugden, Mickie DeGray, Ernest Goudie, Leonard Goudie, Albert Lefebvre, Lindsay Langevin, Arthur Daye, Hugh Graveley, Malcolm Upper, Leonard Hurley, Aaron Watson, Jake Stacey, Fred Gillard, Whiteley Eastwood, William Provost, George Fitzgerald, Cyril Dextras, Eddie Aoslet, Ralph Tilton, Clarence Gallinger, Roscoe Lane, Charles Larose, Charles Laroche, Arthur Contant, and Joseph Contant.

The formation in 1910 of the Creamery Boys or, as they came to be called, the Renfrew Millionaires, probably was the peak event of early hockey in The Valley before the game moved to the big cities and took on its truly professional hockey league face.

At the turn of the century Ottawa Valley money began to turn its eye to hockey. Whether out of contagious hockey mania, eccentric millionaire's whim, or as a means of making more money, the mining O'Briens and lumbering Barnets of Renfrew began to whisper amongst themselves about forming a challenge team for The Stanley Cup. Kenora (Ontario), New Glasgow (Nova Scotia), Dawson City (Yukon) had all done it. Why not Renfrew?

Alexander Barnet, scion of the Barnet lumbering dynasty, came out from Ireland about 1840 on a sailing ship and settled at a hamlet back of Renfrew called Ashdad. There he attempted to set up a feudal system as the last Laird Macnab had successfully done down the road at White Lake and Waba. When Barnet's plans with both Irish and Polish immigrants didn't work out, he turned his entrepreneurial talents to timber; at the age of sixteen he took his first raft of squared pine to Quebec City where, with the profits, he bought his mother a Spanish silk shawl but presumably kept enough to plow back into his lumbering enterprise. Barnet worked his timber limits from 1890 until 1916 and became one of the major lumber operators in Canada with cutting rights all through the Ottawa Valley and mills at New Westminster, British Columbia. By the time Big Money in the Ottawa Valley was looking to invest in professional hockey, the third generation of Barnets was living on the amassed fortunes of its lumbering businesses, fortunes uncounted and probably inestimable until 1911 when income tax was ushered in.

In 1879 Michael James O'Brien, a Maritimer, walked through the bush to Calabogie Lake and there met a man named Jim Barry working in his fields with a team of horses. In the authentic manner of a true Horatio Alger, O'Brien had begun as a water boy for the construction gang working on the "Kick and Push" Railway line from Kingston to Pembroke and was looking at the contract to finish the line to Renfrew. He had walked up the already surveyed right-of-way from Lanark in order to estimate the lie of the land and the problems he would have to cope with laying the rail line. On the Barry farm he met more than he bargained for — his

M. J. O'Brien was born at Lochaber, Nova Scotia in 1851. He moved to Renfrew, began railway construction at an early age and later diversified into mining development in northern Ontario and Quebec, becoming one of the leading Canadian capitalists of his time. He was a backer of the famous Renfrew Millionaires.

In 1909 when the Eastern Canada Association was the only professional hockey league and Renfrew's application for admission was rejected, J. Ambrose O'Brien almost single-handedly organized the rival National Hockey Association and was instrumental in founding the Montreal Canadiens to play in the new league.

future wife, Jennie Barry. They were married in Renfrew at St. Francis Xavier Church, 1883. O'Brien, as a contractor, went on to build parts of the Intercontinental Railway all over Canada, including the North Shore Line of the CPR between Montreal and Ottawa, the K&P Line, and lines in the Maritime provinces. M.J. was away from home most of the time, but built Jennie a substantial house on Barr Street in Renfrew where she wished to stay. The servants were hired and the babies were born. Because Ottawa and Montreal were his business centers, M.J. began to use the Russell Hotel in Ottawa and the Queen's Hotel in Montreal as his homes away from home. His eldest son, Ambrose, was initiated at an early age into the mysteries of the O'Brien involvement in lumbering and construction, and later mining.

By 1901 O'Brien had begun to look to new challenges in mining. He had been appointed a commissioner of the Temiskaming and Northern Ontario Railway which then terminated at North Bay but was planned for extension northwards. Presumably this time spent in the north exposed O'Brien to mining talk and miners' meetings in Toronto. At one of these Toronto dinners, M.J. O'Brien met J.R. Booth, one of Canada's most famous financial entrepreneurs and "King of the Timber Barons," with whom O'Brien was later to become part owner of a large nickel property near Sudbury.

It was on one of these Toronto trips in 1903 where circumstances combined to make M.J. one of Canada's richest men, sometimes earning a million dollars a year. The full story of the O'Brien Mine at Cobalt has never been clarified. But it involved a fire ranger named King who sold O'Brien his Cobalt claims for $4,000 and a blacksmith named Fred Larose who sold his claims to the Timmins Brothers, the McMartin brothers, and David Dunlap jointly. The Big Cobalters, as they came to be called, O'Brien and Timmins fought a political-legal battle for years over the rights to the Cobalt silver mines.

Nine months after the legal dust had cleared O'Brien proceeded to become one of the richest men in Canada. Indeed, it has been said that if he had never invested anywhere else in the country, the O'Brien mine at Cobalt would have made him a millionaire many times over.

In the spring of 1907 a year or so after the Cobalt strike, the *Toronto Telegram* raised the ire of the populace of Renfrew, O'Brien's hometown, with stories on its sports pages.

"And now Renfrew talks of challenging for The Stanley Cup," the *Telegram* said, "All because they have won a fence-corner league championship." A further report went on to say, "Renfrew has challenged for The Stanley Cup. Now don't laugh. If you never lived in a country town you don't know how seriously these people take themselves." The fence-corner league referred to was the Upper Ottawa Valley League with teams from Arnprior, Pembroke, and Renfrew, and the small-towners were taking themselves very seriously indeed. Towns much bigger than Renfrew did not have

One of Renfrew's renowned characters, policeman Barney McDermid, accompanied by his faithful dog Spot, leads a parade down Raglan Street. Behind him is a carriage carrrying civic dignitiaries, followed by a military contingent of the First World War.

its array of millionaires and near-millionaires as residents.

On December 18, 1908, a meeting was held in Renfrew and the decision made to form a professional hockey team. A few days later a meeting in Ottawa reorganized the Federal Hockey League with professional teams from Renfrew, Cornwall, Smith Falls, and Ottawa (the Senators.) Thomas Low, a local MP and later a minister in a Mackenzie King cabinet, was Renfrew representative. Jim Barnet was chosen vice-president and Ambrose O'Brien, M.J.'s son, executive member. Bill O'Brien (not related) was chosen as the Renfrew trainer and Bert Lindsay, professional goalkeeper, hired along with Larry Gilmour, Ernie Liffiton, and Bobby Rowe.

Renfrew won the Federal League that winter but, for some reason or other, didn't challenge for The Stanley Cup. In March, 1909 when that team disbanded, only the four named originals were left to become the core of the new team when Renfrew made its grand entrance into big-time hockey the following season.

O'Brien tended to be a man of mystery, non-communicative

according to his family's memories of him, and never prone to leaving papers, diaries, records of his life, times, and fortunes. Indeed, biographers had to did deep to find out anything at all about his early years in Lochaber, Antigonish County, Nova Scotia. And certainly O'Brien's motives for backing a professional hockey team to bring The Stanley Cup to Renfrew are at the very least obscure. A new way of making money? Not likely for a man making millions out of his mining enterprises. A love of hockey? Perhaps. But Ambrose O'Brien said that his father never saw a hockey game in his life. A form of gambling heretofore not experienced? More likely as people like the Ahearns and Gormans of Ottawa could have told him a few decades later. In any case M.J. O'Brien hurled himself into making a championship team.

In November, 1909, his son Ambrose was on business in La Tuque, Quebec, when he got a momentous telephone call from the Barnets in Renfrew.

"There's going to be a big meeting in Montreal to form a new hockey league. Can you get there and see if you can get Renfrew in?" Ambrose was asked.

And it was true. The Eastern Canada Hockey Association had met in Montreal with five teams represented — the Montreal Shamrocks, Montreal Nationals, Montreal Wanderers, Quebec, and Ottawa Senators, the holders of The Stanley Cup at that time.

In a swift succession of November meetings in Montreal, Renfrew's application for a new franchise was refused and the Montreal Wanderers were cut out. Ambrose was sitting outside the conference room waiting for news when out of the meeting came Jimmy Gardner of the Montreal Wanderers and, swearing like a maddened hockey player, sat down beside the young O'Brien. The famous Montreal Wanderers had been chopped by the formation of a new hockey league, the Canadian Hockey Association with franchises going to the Ottawa Shamrocks, the Quebec Nationals, and a new club called All-Montreal.

After Gardner had finished swearing he turned to O'Brien and said, "Say, do you O'Briens have other hockey teams up North? Haileybury, Cobalt? Why don't we form a league? We have the Wanderers. And I think if a team of all Frenchmen was formed in Montreal it would be a real draw. We could give it a real French-Canadien name . . . " The two men tossed around the idea and came up with the name Les Canadiens. And so it happened out of anger and rejection that two Irish-Canadians from the little Creamery town in the Ottawa Valley known as Renfrew named and bankrolled the most famous hockey club in

French-Canadian sporting history, perhaps even in the history of hockey.

Events began to tumble over one another. Charlotte Whitton later always insisted that M.J. "Imjay" O'Brien and Alec Barnett, principal backers of the Renfrew team, didn't care about The Stanley Cup as much as they wanted to "rub Ottawa's nose in it for queering Renfrew's application for the Canadian Hockey Association." Whatever the myriad of reasons and motivations, *The Ottawa Free Press* reported a few days after the momentous Montreal meeting that "the biggest hockey grab in history was attempted earlier this week and so far as can be ascertained is still going on. The Renfrew hockey club is at the present moment after every member of the Ottawa team. Only fine organization and the looking-ahead policy of the Ottawa Club has prevented what might have meant the necessity of buying up an entirely new team to defend The Stanley Cup." George Martel of the Renfrew Club was put in charge of recruiting, and M.J. and Ambrose met personally with Ottawa players to try to lure them to Renfrew.

On December 2, 1908, at the old St. Lawrence Hall Hotel on St. James Street, Montreal, a meeting was held to name the new league the National Hockey Association and to formalize the existence of the Montreal Canadiens. Present at that landmark meeting were Doran, Strachan, Boon, and Gardner of the ostracized Montreal Wanderers; Ambrose O'Brien, George Martel, Jim Barnet from Renfrew; T.C. Hare from Cobalt; and Noah Timmins from Haileybury — an impressive group, indeed.

Following this meeting stories of player raids filled the newspapers, rumor having it that Renfrew had offered four Ottawa players — Marty Walsh, Fred Lake, Albert Kerr, and Fred "Cyclone" Taylor — $2,000 dollars each to desert Ottawa. "Stage money," cried out the Toronto *Globe*, seemingly unaware of the O'Brien resources or their propensity to follow through once they began something.

The Ottawa Senators retaliated by sending envoys around the country urging their players to stay with the team and offering good "under-the-table" Civil Service jobs in the off-season. *The Ottawa Citizen* reported then that Renfrew had raised its offers to $2,500 per man, with two-year contracts, off-ice jobs for any player who wanted them, all the money to be deposited immediately in a bank of the player's choice.

Throughout all the furor and controversies, true to the character of the O'Briens, Renfrew played it above board and honestly, and won the admiration of all involved, the press included.

1910 Stanley Cup championship game between Renfew Millionaires and the Montreal Wanderers. Hockey mania possessed
much of he Ottawa Valley. Every train to Renfrew brought in its
fans from Pembroke, Arnprior, Ottawa, Montreal, Brockville,
Eganville. When the special from Pembroke and the regular from
Ottawa both arrived at the Renfrew Station at the same time, the
streets were filled with people from the station to the rink.

Friday afternoon, the day of the match, the 1:40 train from
Montreal arrived at the Renfrew Station with a special car for the
Montreal Wanderers attached to the long line of regular passen-
ger cars. Half the town of Renfrew was there to look over the
team which had already won so many championships. " Never
before has there been such excitement in Renfrew as there is
today," reported *The Renfrew Journal.*

All afternoon hockey fans streamed in from the countryside,
some walking, some by horse and sleigh or cutter, from Burnstown, Springtown, Spruce Hedge, Black Donald, Goshan, Ashdad,
Haley Station, Adamston, Cobden, Mount St. Patrick, Dacre, and
all the farming communities in between. "The country people,"
The Journal reported, "were coming in loads from two to fifty!"

An hour after the arena ticket office had been opened all
reserved sets were sold. Even with the rink expansion O'Brien
had engineered and paid for, the new balconies almost dou-
bling capacity, it began to be apparent early in the afternoon
that not everybody who wanted to see the game could be accom-
modated. All seats were sold by 6:00 and it was Standing Room
Only after that.

Three to two betting after, the Renfrew Millionaires lost to
the experienced Montreal Wanderers 5-0. Montreal was presented The Stanley Cup and The O'Brien Cup, a massive trophy
made from Cobalt silver, valued in that day at $6,000, but far too
heavy to lift in triumph overhead. It now reposes in The Hockey
Hall of Fame.

The O'Briens had lost $11,000 on the first season and were
committed for $6,000 more in contracts for 1911–12. Only five
out of the thirty hard-won, hard-bought original players returned
for the second season, although Ambrose did help sign on Odie
and Sprague Cleghorn for the 1911 Millionaires team. Cobalt
and Haileybury dropped out of the league, the Big Time being
too rich for their blood and/or pocket books.

Renfrew never did win The Stanley Cup. Ambrose was finding less and less time for hockey as contracting work on M.J.'s

railway projects increased. Renfrew finished third in 1911 and then dropped its professional hockey league franchise. However, before they disbanded, the Renfrew Millionaires were invited to New York City's St. Nicholas arena to play-off with the Montreal Wanderers, Stanley Cup winners. On artificial ice, Renfrew won the game 9–4, and the New York press hailed the Renfrew Millionaires as "Champions of the World."

No small town in the whole Ottawa Valley ever attempted again to support and back, morally and financially, a pro team.

When I was first starting to do oral history in The Valley, my father told me that Cyclone Taylor of the Renfrew Millionaires was leaving his home in Vancouver to visit Montreal and would be staying at the Old Windsor Hotel there. Following a strong intuition, I phoned the hotel, spoke with the legendary Taylor, and made an appointment to go down the following day to interview him. In a three-to-four hour conversation, he graciously gave me the gift of his life story, which in its own way is a story of hockey in the Ottawa Valley:

So we played the Palmerston boys and, lo and behold, we beat them! I was in the front row all the way along and that cinched me with the Mintos, and I was there until I got to be Junior age, around sixteen, and then I joined the Listowel Junior team. And by the way, in 1904 Listowel won the Western League. We won the Northern League too. Played Barrie and we were even bumped up against the Kingston Frontenacs. And in all of

A Cyclone Taylor bubble gum card, today worth much more than its original one cent selling price.

Hockey great Cyclone Taylor played on two Stanley Cup teams — the Ottawa Senators in 1908–09 and the Vancouver Millionaires 1914–15. He starred, briefly, for the Renfrew Millionaires.

these championship games we played at home in Listowel. But the O.H.A., for some reason or other, decided we should play a "sudden death" game in Toronto at the old Mutual Rink, and the Listowel people were up in arms because they wanted to see this game. After all, they'd paid good money and supported us all winter. But the O.H.A. insisted on us playing the Beechgroves in Toronto and they beat us 8–6 for the Ontario Junior Championship. I think the trophy at that time was called the John Ross Robinson Trophy, and we missed it. Anyway, that game playing the Kingston Beechgroves in Toronto, the arena was filled with people and again I just happened to be — well, you have to be good some nights and not so good other nights — I scored nearly half of those goals. And that game in Toronto set me up. The teams then started to look to Listowel for a player.

I started out as a defenceman and became a forward. Yes, it is true that I wore a toque to cover my bald spot. I lost my hair on the back when I was young and I was sensitive about it. But lots of fellows wore toques in Eastern Canada because of the cold weather, and that would make a good enough excuse any time.

When I belonged to the Renfrew Millionaires, M.J. O'Brien spared no expense for us. They paid us good salaries and when we traveled he gave us the best, and the town of Renfrew entertained us. We were little gods, but the boys behaved themselves and we went into the finest homes in Renfrew and were welcomed. O'Brien spared no expense. Everything was lavish — Winnipeg goldeye — until the New York people bought them all, lock, stock, and barrel.

Yes, I was a "sixty-minute man." We all were in those days. I wouldn't want to make any comparisons with the players today. I can only say I wouldn't want to play in this game today. For one thing, you're only getting out there for two or three minutes. It suits them. They were brought up to it, and they don't know any better. But we were on for sixty minutes and we paced ourselves for that sixty minutes. And we could go! I've always said that any player between the ages of sixteen and thirty who can't play sixty minutes "*bang*" of hockey, there's something the matter with him. I know that if he's physically fit, it would be a joy. I know in my case it was a joy.

You paced yourself, just naturally, just the same as a man running five miles or twenty miles. He goes so far so fast and then so far at a different pace. You prepared yourself for that sixty minutes on the ice.

I don't think there was the violence in my day, but mind you, I remember in my day there were two players killed. I wouldn't want to give you the names because the fellow that killed one of them is still living in Ottawa today — that would be away back in 1904 or '05. Just a hit over the head; it was a lad from Cornwall. But we only had one referee in those days and he couldn't see everything. This hockey that's being played today, I don't know where it ever developed. Even little boys — I'm honorary president of the British Columbia Hockey Association, have been for some years — even those little boys are steeped with the idea of playing rough. They think it's alright. In some cases I think the parents and their coaches are as much to blame as anybody else. I've sat at little games there in Vancouver where you'll hear a mother scream, "Hit him, Billy! Kill him! Kill him!" Now, if a mother is talking like that to her children, well, it's got to stop.

We in Canada killed lacrosse by rough play — that's field lacrosse — and just the same they'll have to change their mode of playing in hockey. Hockey is such a splendid game: the skating and the skill and the speed. Anybody can play rough, they don't need to hit one another.

I played a lot of lacrosse, too, and I remember a game one Saturday afternoon in Vancouver. In those days there were no cars and very few people, except the rich, went to summer cottages, and the Saturday afternoon lacrosse games — especially the 24th of May holiday one — would draw enormous crowds. Well, this Saturday afternoon Westminster had come over to play us, the Vancouver team, and the game was just getting nicely under way with the place packed with yelling people, and some violence occurred — I can't remember what, though — our manager and owner, Mr. Con Jones, just pulled his team right off the playing field. Scores of people said they'd never go to see another lacrosse game. But when Westminster and Vancouver lacrosse teams played one another, it was nothing but a donnybrook, always a donnybrook!

And I feel hockey is in danger of doing the same thing. They could easily do it. There's people across Canada — and I venture to say the ladies don't want that kind of thing — oh no, it has to be stopped. They'll penalize those players until . . .

Of course, the salaries are a hundred times what we made. Conditions were different in my day when you could buy a pound of butter for seven or eight cents and eggs for three cents a dozen. But the salaries are still too high by comparison and it's going to end. It's ending already. The W.H.A. was responsible for that . . .

Newsy Lalonde, Lester and Frank Patrick, Joe Hall — they were the greats of my day and they compare very favorably with the greats of today.

I don't think the training has improved that much at all. And as for the equipment, we were just as well protected. Some of the teams now, sure they have half their team off half the time with hurt knees or smashed ankles. I never had an injury in all my years of professional hockey. I never had a wound worth putting me out of business even for a game . . .

I suppose at this age I could put down my philosophy of life. People speak of "self-made" men. Well, let's take my career, just the hockey. First, Toronto wanted me to go with the Marlboroughs. I don't know what made me go up to Thessalon; then, when I came back, the Wanderers wanted me to go to Montreal. But I often think if I had gone with the Wanderers, I would never have met Mrs. Taylor, and that was one of the greatest things of my life. I wouldn't have had these wonderful children that I have today.

What is that saying? "Man is destiny?" I don't think you are in charge of your won destiny. I think you're guided by your family or from Up Above. No, the saying is "Man is master of his own destiny." Well, I wonder what prompted me to make that decision about hockey? There was this inner voice that none of us can explain. But every move that I've made seems to have been to my advantage and to my pleasure, and I'd say to my success too . . .

I have fourteen grandchildren, and one grandson, he played this winter, and he's Junior A. The team he played with was Langley, which is about thirty miles from Vancouver. He went to school in Langley for the last two years. He was picked as the best all-round player in the league and there were five colleges in the States writing to him to go to them — and one of them was Michigan, where I played. They were very anxious to get Mark to go there, just out of, well, I guess out of the connection. But he's decided to go to Grand Forks, North Dakota; they're giving him a four-year scholarship. Some of them wanted him to play in the National Hockey League here, but he took our advice. He can have that four-year scholarship; he's only seventeen, and when he's finished he'll be twenty-one and he can still go and play in the N.H.L. That four-year scholarship is worth sixteen to eighteen thousand dollars, so that's one boy we've steered in the right way, and not by force — just by example, I suppose. With my grandchildren I'm very careful to make it advice, not instruction.

I'll tell you one of the nicest things that's happened to me lately. One of the television stations out of New York, they wanted to get somebody, an older person, the oldest person they could find — the oldest hockey player they could find — and when they phoned me and I said I was ninety-one years of age and that I had played hockey up until 1911, they said, "My God! You're the fellow we're looking for!" Now all I did, and it was one of the nicest things I ever did, I went out with Brian McFarlane — you know him? — and we skated around the ice, arm in arm, talking as we're talking now about hockey and things in general. People that saw it thought it was one of the nicest — well, I enjoyed it more than anything I ever did on television. And it was surprising the number of people that saw it and communicated with me and said, "Mr. Taylor, that was a lovely, quiet, homey little program." And it didn't last very long: seven minutes.

When I quit hockey, sure, I missed it, but at that time we had three little children and I was all tied up with family life. I missed it, sure, but you have to acquaint yourself with the changing conditions of your life. What have I got to look forward to? Me. At my age! Heaven, I guess!

Yes, I know they say I am the only man who ever scored a goal skating backwards. Well, let them say it, let them say it.

Miss Lillian Handford of Renfrew remembers The Millionaires and Cyclone Taylor in this light:

I almost got to see the game that Cyclone Fred Taylor was supposed to have skated backwards and scored the goal. Cyclone Taylor. Well, you see, my father sold pianos where Dr. Ed Handford's office is now — the Robertson Company from Ottawa sold pianos in there years ago. Well, Dad sold records as well in there, and the Renfrew Millionaires used to come in there in the afternoons when the Renfrew kids would be using the hockey rink and they'd listen to the records. Yes, the Patricks and the Fitzpatricks and Cyclone and all these men. I was always coming in from school and I always went through the store to see what I could see there. But, anyway, Dad had tickets for all the hockey matches, including the Renfrew Millionaires, and he and Mother used to go, and they used to put bricks in the oven to heat them and then take them to the rink to keep their feet warm. This night Mother was sick, and I begged so hard to be allowed to see them play and they wouldn't let me go, but that was the night I can remember my dad coming home and telling my mother that Cyclone skated backwards and scored a goal!

Charlotte Whitton always said that it was absolutely true and she could have remembered it, even been at the game, because she was a little older than I was and, besides, some of the Renfrew Millionaires boarded at the Whittons — her mother kept a boardinghouse. But you see, the Renfrew Millionaires were only a year or two there in Renfrew and they wouldn't really remember the people. They might have remembered my father, though, because he was always very nice to them and let them play the records. And they were all Red Seal records and Caruso and all high-class music, and they all just loved that music. They'd stay by the hour and play them.

Hero worship of "Cyclone" Taylor is clear in the name of this Renfrew Women's Hockey Team.

I remember my parents arguing about a proposed Renfrew Millionaires game in Cobalt. I know there was a great discussion as to whether my father could afford to go, take the trip. And, of course, hockey players were in and out of the shop so often, and he'd taken pictures of them all. I must say that the players were always very nice with you when you came in. Of course, I used to come into the store any time I could, but I got shooed through and up the stairs. They were good-looking young men. Anyway, he really wanted to go and see this game, and my mother persuaded him to go ahead. They won, of course, and he came back, thrilled to death. He'd got on the train to come home, the train was empty, and he was one of the first ones in, and on the side of his seat he found two twenty-dollar bills. He came home and presented my mother with them. She said, "Where did you get those? Were you betting on those games?" He said, " I didn't have to."

There were reserved seats in the Renfrew arena. They put them in when the Millionaires came. Before that, I think, it was just benches really, and everybody grabbed a seat where they could. But I must tell you a story that is sort of related to all this hockey. After the Second World War, my Uncle Alex was a great one for telling stories. He had two sons and a daughter, and the older son, Ken, was stationed in Ottawa for a little while and he wrote and asked me if he could come up to Renfrew and see me. Ken had never stayed in Renfrew and would like to come and

Lillian Handford's father made considerable income in portraiture, but photograph postcards were also a big part of his livelihood. Mr. Handford designed this Easter card using the Renfrew Millionaires as a big selling point. The card is addressed to Master Silas Reed, Ealing P.O., London, Ont., and says: "This is our good team of hockey players, the bunch who played in New York last Saturday night and won — score 9–4. Edward."

spend a weekend. My mother was dead by this time and Dad and Herb, my brother Doc Handford, and I were here. And there was a Pembroke-Renfrew hockey game being played. First of all, we couldn't get parked on Argyle Street at all, so we had to park a long distance from the rink and walk to it, all the way along I was saying "Goodnight" to people I knew and they were saying, "Good evening, Miss Handford," and then at the rink there were all sorts of friends and acquaintances talking to me, kidding me. So, we got into the rink. I had the tickets, so I was meeting them all, ushers and everybody. And when we finally got sitting down, cousin Ken said to me — he'd lived in Toronto all his life — he said, "Lil, do you know *everybody* in Renfrew?" And I said, "Well, not quite, Ken. Why?" He said, "Do you know you spoke to every single person you met all the way here?" And I said, "Well, I teach school here and they have all gone to school." That was the first thing that hit him. Well, then the game started! He said that he always thought his father had been making up stories about the Pembroke and Renfrew hockey matches. But you know, there wasn't one thing was left out in that game he saw that night.

We had a man in town called Bob Scott and he, at the rink-side, all night long, would yell out, "Get him! Get him! Get him!" You know, keep it up all the time the other team would have the puck. And we were sitting not too far from the penalty box, and hanging over the penalty box was a drunk with all the vocabulary and all the verbal abuse, and what those players sitting in that penalty box had to take was unbelievable!

And then this big Pembroke player fell on the ice and hit the back of his head so hard that it bled, and when they were taking him of the ice he left behind this trail of blood all across the ice, and it froze there, and when Ken came home with me he said, "I wouldn't have believed what I saw tonight. My father told us these stories about them being laid out and carried off the ice."

But everything happened at that game that night — you would have thought it had been staged for him. The crowd was wild. There was a good gang down from Pembroke. There were a couple of fights in the crowd. To the day he died, Ken never came to visit that he didn't say, "I'll never forget that hockey match you took me to in Renfrew!"

I interviewed Tommy Barnett in 1980 at his home in Renfrew, Ontario, shortly before he died. He was one of the last surviving members of the Barnett lumbering dynasty, a family which had had great influence in The Valley not only through its lumber operations but also as great breeders of fine horses and backers of hockey develop-ment and expansion:

We also had the Renfrew Millionaires, the great hockey team of 1910–11. Actually, the two chief financial backers of The Millionaires were my grandfather Barnett, who never went to a game in his life, and Senator M.J. O'Brien. And then there were the others who put up money as well. So much has been written but never any credit given to the other people who put in money. The books for the team were always kept in my grandfather's office; Mr. Hardy Cox was the treasurer and he was my grandfather's head bookkeeper. My uncle George Barnett, he was the president of the team, and Ambrose O'Brien was vice-president. And my uncle Jim Barnett, he was one of the chief backers of the team as well. And they all thought nothing of betting two, three, four, five thousand on a game in those days. Oh, I recall the late Dr. Bill Box of Renfrew saying that when he was going to school he was quite a good hockey player on the Renfrew collegiate team and he would be invited to go along to the games. My grandfather, father, and uncles would maybe take three or four young Renfrew fellows with them to a game in Cobalt — my uncles were interested in mining up there, as well as lumbering — and Bill Box told me about my uncle Ben winning five thousand dollars in one of the games up there. Well, five thousand dollars in those days was like fifty thousand dollars today . . .

One of the young men who followed the careers of those Ottawa Valley hockey heroes was Frank Finnigan, himself soon to become another hockey legend from The Valley:

I knew by the time I was nine that I was going to be a professional hockey player. Of course, we didn't have any radio or television then, but I used to save my money and buy every newspaper from Ottawa that I could get hold of. I wasn't very good at school, but I could certainly read the sports pages of *The Ottawa Journal* and *The Ottawa Citizen* at a very early age! The train used to come into Shawville at six every evening, and as soon as I would hear that whistle blow I would head down to Joe Turner's confectionary or Doc Clock's drugstore and get my papers. So would a lot of other people.

I read about Cyclone Taylor of the Renfrew Millionaires. They say he was the only man who ever really scored a goal skating backward. Joe Malone of the Quebec City Bulldogs scored forty-four goals in twenty-two games. I can remember I was impressed by that. There were all my Ottawa heroes: Eddie Gerard, Jack Darragh, Percy Lesueur, George Vezina, Gordie Roberts, Harvey Pulford, the Smith Brothers (Alf and Tommy), George "Buck" Boucher, Hod Stewart. And the others: Cy Denneny of Cornwall,

Didre Petrie of Montreal, Frank Nighbor of Pembroke, Larry Gilmour of Renfrew, Scotty Davidson of Kingston, Art Ross of Queen's University.

Eventually I played with some of my heroes like Frank Nighbor, Sprague and Odie Cleghorn, Punch Broadbent. And in time I got to know some of the greatest people ever associated with the early game — Frank Ahearn, Frank Selke, Dick Irvin.

The Shawville rink, one of the first in Western Quebec and scene of many of Frank Finnigan's first hockey victories. It fell down in 1972.

When I was young growing up in Shawville the whole world was a rink. A hockey rink, not a skating rink. When I first started to play hockey, I played on the ponds and on the crust. We'd have a big rain and it would freeze and make the crust — just the same as ice. Yes, it would be just the same as ice; it would carry a team of hockey players or a team of horses. And then we had the ponds and the creeks. When we got a bit bigger we had the small lakes, which we kept shoveled of in the winter. Then every second house in Shawville would have a little rink in their back yard. It wouldn't be too big but you could still play on it. The John Cowans on Back Street at the old *Shawville Equity* — they published that paper for a hundred years — had a great big summer kitchen and sometimes we would flood that and use it. It was the first covered rink! And then you'd have the streets to skate on when you'd have a rain and it would freeze. You played shinny on the streets in the winter and road hockey on the streets when the ice and snow was gone.

Well, then in 1913–14, Shawville got its covered rink — one of the first if not the first in the Upper Ottawa Valley. W. A. Hodgins, general merchant; Duncan Campbell, gentleman;

Chris Caldwell, hotel-keeper — they put up the money for the materials for the rink, but everyone in town gave their labor free. There was Standing Room Only for three to four hundred people. We even had night games. The first lighting arrangement was oil-burning lamps strung above the ice surface on wires. The lamps would smoke up, go out, and often be shot out by the players — sometimes on purpose to keep the other team from seeing too well when they were winning, sometimes just plain accidentally by a high shot. The Shawville rink fell down one day in the 1970s.

Now, covered rinks have some advantages, but not many. You have to wait for rink time these days, so you don't get nearly as much hockey as we did in my learning days. We just moved from one kind of rink to another — perpetual motion. If one pond wasn't good enough, we moved to a creek and so on. I played hooky from school all the time to play hockey and I wouldn't recommend that! I think everybody should get an education. I had a tough time.

We didn't have any fancy skates and equipment. I bought my first single-blade pair from Cedric Shaw for five dollars when I was thirteen years old; they were secondhand. Before that I played on double-enders. We were always collecting from the Shawville merchants for money for team sweaters. We had to supply your own hockey sticks. That was hard for me. The good ones, made of natural wood with clear shellac, were fifty cents each. The cheap ones were painted red to cover up the knots. We used frozen horse balls for a puck when we couldn't afford a rubber one. Most of the time.

By the time I was thirteen I was playing in the Pontiac League for Shawville against Campbell's Bay and Quyon. In those early days league size was limited by the number of miles a horse could travel per hour. We used to drive by sleigh to the games in Campbell's Bay and Quyon, three or four hours each way. We'd be in a lather of sweat after playing a full game and then out into the freezing night and the cold, cold sleigh. If we were playing Campbell's Bay — and had collected from the merchants of Shawville — we could catch the Push, Pull, and Jerk, get there in time for a game, and stay overnight at Smith's Hotel. That was the Big Time.

While I was in the Pontiac League we began looking for more competition, and we used to bring up teams from Ottawa for exhibition games, teams that were playing in the Ottawa City Senior League. Big excitement in town for twenty-five cents a ticket! There were four to six players on those early Ottawa teams who could have turned pro, if there had been enough teams to turn pro with. But there were only four teams in the N.H.L. at that time: Montreal Canadiens, Toronto St. Pats, Hamilton Tigers, and Ottawa Senators. Then the league expanded, the New York Americans took over the Hamilton franchise, and Boston Bruins came in.

Although he could have become a professional hockey player, J. Cooper Smeaton , M.M. (left) of Carleton Place chose his career as referee for more than twenty-five years in the N.H.A. and the N.H.L. Until his retirement in 1937 he was N.H.L. referee-in-chief. He was elected to Hockey Hall of Fame in 1961.

Born in Mattawa in 1891, M.J. Mike Rodden (right) made an impact on the sporting world as player, coach, sportswriter, and referee in football, lacrosse, and hockey. In 1944 Rodden became sports editor of the Kingston Whig-Standard *and until his death worked tirelessly for the establishment of Kingston's Hockey Hall of Fame.*

We were always looking for a hockey game, anywhere, any time, anyhow, in those younger days. We liked to go out to the smaller towns like Portage-du-Fort, Bryson, or Elmside and have an exhibition game. Of course we needed a livery team to get there sometimes — four dollars. So we'd go to W.A. Hodgins and he'd put down for so much. And we'd go to John Shaw — he was a storekeeper in town — and then we'd go to Chris Caldwell

— he had the hotel — and he'd put down for so much — and finally get enough to pay for the livery team and we'd be off.

Well, one of the referees who refereed in our league, Bill Smith of Ottawa, saw that I had possibilities. Word got around to Dr. Eddie O'Leary of Ottawa University, and he asked me to go down to Ottawa and play for Ottawa U. in the Senior City League against Montagnards, Ottawa, Munitions, and Victoria. You think that kind of thing only goes on today? Well, I played two seasons for Ottawa University, 1920-21 and 1922-23, at fifty dollars a game! Yes, the Coulsons — J.P. and his sons, Harry and D'Arcy, who owned the old Alexander Hotel and who backed the Ottawa U. team — they paid me fifty dollars a game. I was enrolled in the university as a "commercial student." But I never went to a class. That's true. You can see a picture of me yet in the hall of the old Arts Building at Ottawa.

I had some other interesting offers, too. When I was young and still playing amateur I had an offer to go to Pittsburgh and play on a kind of "scholarship" — they would put me through for a doctor or a dentist. It was a semi-pro league there, it wasn't a minor league, but I can't remember what the university was. They offered me pretty good money. I had the same kind of offer from Queen's University at Kingston — they would have paid me to play hockey there and put me through whatever degree I wanted. But I didn't have the education, you know, at all. Remember I quit school at Grade Nine.

Towards spring a team came up from Ottawa, the Royal Canadians, from Ottawa's Senior City League. Shawville played an exhibition game with them that night. When I went up to Gibson's Restaurant for coffee and sandwiches after the game, there was a telegram there for me from Frank Ahearn, owner and president of the Ottawa Senators. He wanted me to go to Ottawa the next day and talk contract. This was five games before the playoffs, mind you.

I went down to Ottawa the next day by train and met Mr. Ahearn and we talked contract. I signed the contract only an hour before I got into my new Ottawa Senator sweater, Number 8. It was a three-year contract for eighteen hundred dollars a year. I was a green kid from the country and he never held me to it, gentleman that he always was. The next year he upped it to thirty-five hundred dollars, then forty-five hundred, then fifty-five hundred, with bonus all the time. But he could have held me to it if he had wanted to.

It was a big jump from Shawville to the red, white, and black of the Ottawa Senators. I was nervous and didn't get my bearings at first. It was the playoffs, too, against the Canadiens. I suddenly found myself up against players who were as good or better than I was. No weaknesses in those lads — Frank Nighbor, Buck Boucher, Clint Benedict, King Clancy.

In those days The Ottawa Valley was the cradle of hockey. I think at that time the valley developed at least fifty percent of the hockey players in Canada. Even in the Western league there would be a majority of players from the East on the Edmonton, Regina, Calgary, Saskatoon, Victoria teams.

The roll call of legendary hockey players raised on the rinks of the Ottawa Valley goes on and on . . . Bill Cowley of Bristol, Ken "Cagie" Doraty of Stittsville, Bob Gracie of North Bay, Dave Trottier of Pembroke, Johnny Sorrell of Chesterville. Many of these players would travel up or down The Valley to join the professional ranks of the Ottawa Senators, merging their rugged Valley character with the finesse of native Ottawa players like Hall of Fame legends Frank McGee, Harvey Pulford, Frank "King" Clancy, Harry "Punch" Broadbent, Jack Darragh, Billy Gilmour, Harry "Rat" Westwick, Clint Benedict, Syd Howe, Tommy and Alf Smith, Gordon Roberts, Eddie Gerard, William H. "Hod" Stewart, Alex Connell, Frank and George "Buck" Boucher, Bruce Stuart, E.B. "Ebbie" Goodfellow, and Hector "Hec" Kilrea, to create some of the greatest teams in the history of hockey. Ottawa Valley boys would also stock the teams that challenged The Senators for supremacy . . .

3

THE CAPITAL CITY OF HOCKEY

"The guys were home . . . and the town was jumping with sporting men. Ottawa was a small town but it produced so many hockey players."

— Jake Dunlap

Soon after Confederation in 1867, Ottawa gained renown not only as the national capital but also as a "sporting town," with timber barons, military officers, government officials, wealthy professionals, and vice-royalty backing teams and participating themselves in cricket, rowing, rugby, horseracing, curling, boxing, lacrosse, toboganning, snowshoeing, and "shinnying" — as the precursor of hockey was called. Many Ottawa "sporting men" before the turn of the century were so-called gentlemen, with family names like Booth, Gilmour, Kirby, Carson, Devlin, Masson — even Lord Stanley, Governor-General of Canada from 1888-1891 and donor of The Stanley Cup, sponsored the Rideau Rebels hockey team on which his two sons, Arthur and Edward, played. From teams like the Rebels, the Capitals, the Victorias, the Bronsons, the Electrics, and the various clubs scattered throughout the Ottawa Valley emerged the players who led the Ottawa Senators — "The Silver Seven" — to three consecutive Stanley Cup victories in 1902–03, 1903–04, 1904–05, and then again in 1908–09 and 1910–11 prior to the founding of the N.H.L. in 1917. From 1917 to 1934 when the team was disbanded, The Senators would win another four Stanley Cups, in 1919–20, 1920–21, 1922–23, and 1926–27. During this era, Ottawa could rightfully be called not only the capital of Canada but also the capital of hockey. This chapter in the story of The Senators gives an impression of Ottawa "the sporting town" and "capital of hockey" culminating in the achievements of The Silver Seven.

An impression of the importance of sports in Ottawa social, political, and cultural life in the 1880s and 1890s can be gleaned from this account of the event of the winter season, described by C.H. Ireson in his recollections published in The Ottawa Citizen:

In those days Rideau Hall had two open-air skating rinks, two toboggan slides, and a covered curling rink . . . Governor and Lady Lansdowne gave two skating and tobogganing parties at Rideau Hall every winter, parties termed by the Governor-General as his "Arctic Ceremonies." In those days all members of snowshoe and toboggan clubs wore white blanket cloth coats, knickerbockers, bright-colored stockings, sashes and knitted toques. Rideau Hall colors were "royal" purple stockings and toques and red sashes. A collection of 300 people thus gorgeously arrayed on rinks all fringed with colored fairy lamps and festoons of Japanese lanterns produced a wonderfully festive effect. Supper was served in the long covered but unheated curling rink

Skating parties — like this turn-of-the-century costume ball — were one of the chief forms of entertainment for Ottawa's high society and vice-royalty.

where the tables were set out with silver branched candlesticks. The servants waited on tables in heavy fur coats and caps and the silver vases on the tables were filled with sprays of spruce and fir.

This vice-regal sporting tradition was continued by subsequent tenants of Rideau Hall. Lady Aberdeen, in a book co-authored with her husband the Governor-General, remembered her first winter in Canada 1982:

Our first winter introduced us to the delights of Canadian winter sports. It seemed to be a little disconcerting for our Canadian friends at first to find they had unearthed a Governor-General who was quite at home at curling and skating, and who had often used a sleigh at home.

But hockey on the ice was new to us and our children, and the staff entered into this sport with enthusiasm as also into the tobogganing from the high slide erected in the Government House grounds and leading right down to the Ottawa River.

I certainly thought I was not cut out for this sort of amusement but, in a rash moment, I gave Haddo (my son) a promise I would do anything he asked of me on his seventeenth birthday. To my horror I found I had pledged myself to going down the toboggan slide with him! I felt my last moment had arrived but it

Sir F. Middleton strikes a dashing pose in his extraordinary skating costume, circa 1889.

had to be gone through with. Under the children's careful tutelage I risked it time and time again and, in the end, enjoyed it as much as anyone.

Our Saturday skating and tobogganing parties with we gave weekly were a great feature of Government House life during the winter. All were invited to these parties who wrote their names in our Visitors' Book, and children were included, so the scene was

The Rockcliffe Park ski-jump, shown here in 1921, was a popular sporting scene until the 1950s.

a very gay and merry one, blanket coats and costumes with belts of many colors woven by the French 'habitants' being the correct attire, together with soft woolen caps and long woolen mitts.

Chocolate, piping hot, with whipped cream was considered one of the necessary accompaniments to these entertainments where everybody met and fraternized.

The most famous vice-regal booster of hockey as a national sport was Lord Stanley, whose two sons learned to play the game on the rinks of Rideau Hall. Lord Stanley sponsored the Rideau Rebels from 1889-1891, when the team challenged the Ottawa City Hockey Club for the championship of Canada. The Rebels lost to the City Club, which then went on to defeat a Queen's University and an Osgoode Hall team for the Cosby Cup and Dominion Championship. Meanwhile, The Rebels made a vice-regal tour of Ontario promoting the game in Kingston, Lindsay, Toronto, and Kitchener. Lord Stanley's great claim to hockey fame is, however, his donation of The Stanley Cup in 1891.

As reported in The Ottawa Citizen, *Lord Stanley, through his proxy Lord Kilcoursie, proposed the idea of a challenge cup for the champion hockey team in the Dominion during an awards banquet honoring the Ottawa City Hockey Club, as reported in the local papers:*

THE CHAMPIONS DINED
An Enjoyable Gathering of Admirers
of the Hockey Team

The members of the Ottawa Hockey Club will always hold dear to their memory recollections of the banquet tendered them last evening in the Russell House. It was under the auspices of the Ottawa Amateur Athletic Club. About seventy-five of the team's most enthusiastic admirers were seated at the table. The president of the association, Mr. J.W. McRae, presided with Mr. Russell, captain of the team, at his right, and Mr. Jenkins at his left. The vice-presidents' chairs were occupied by Mr. P.D. Ross and Mr. Desbarats. When all appetites had been satisfied, Mr. McKay proposed the health of the Queen.

Mr. Ross next proposed the toast of the Governor-General Lord Stanley, and in a few remarks referred to the great interest manifested in hockey by His Excellency.

Lord Kilcoursie responded, and read the following letter from His Excellency:

> I have for some time past been thinking that it would be a good thing if there were a challenge cup which should be held from year to year by the champion hockey team in the dominion.
>
> There does not appear to be any such outward and visible sign of championship at present, and considering the general interest which the matches now elicit, and the importance of having the game played fairly and under rules generally recognized, I am willing to give a cup which shall be held from year to year by the winning team.
>
> I am not quite certain that the present regulations governing the arrangement of matches give entire satisfaction, and it would be worth considering whether they could not be arranged so that each team would play once at home and once at the place where their opponents hail from.

Lord Kilcoursie then stated that Capt. Colville, who was at present in England, had been commissioned by the Governor to order the cup. It would be held here by trustees till the end of next season, and then presented to the champions. The reading of the letter was greeted with enthusiastic applause.

The president proposed the health of the Ottawa hockey team, which was drunk by their friends, who stood upon their chairs. The first of the team to respond was the amiable captain, Mr. Russell, who did great honour to his team in a speech that was full of humour, and which was heartily appreciated by all present. The other members of the team then spoke in the following order: F.M.S. Jenkins, H. Kirby, J. Kerr, W.C. Young, A. Morel, and C. Kirby. The last mentioned delivered his oration while mounted upon the table . . .

The president here read a telegram received from the Quebec team as follows: "Quebec regrets that she cannot send a delegate and do honour to the finest hockey team in Canada." The toast of the ladies, proposed by Mr. Russell, was responded to by Mr. Stowe and by C. Kirby and C. Bethane.

After the toast of the press had been disposed of, Mr. J.W. de C. O'Grady proposed the toast of the O.A.A.C., which brought the president and Mr. P.B. Taylor to their feet.

Speeches followed by Mr. Clarence Martin and Mr. Palmer, of the Rebels.

Lord Kilcoursie sang a song appropriate to the occasion and all joined in the chorus, which was as:

> *Then give three cheers for Russell*
> *The captain of the boys.*
> *However tough the tussle*
> *His position he enjoys.*
> *And then for all the others*
> *Let's shout as loud we may*
> *O-T-T-A-W-A.*

Lord Stanley (left), Governor-General of Canada, 1888–1893, sponsored The Rideau Rebels and donated The Stanley Cup to the nation.

*P.D.Ross(right), teammate of Lord Stanley's sons on The Rideau Rebels, was appointed a trustee of the Cup. He later became publisher of **The Ottawa Journal**.*

Mr. Garvin of the Toronto News and Mr. Colson followed with songs, and the pleasant gathering dispersed after singing the national anthem and *Auld Lang Syne*.

Lord Arthur Frederick Stanley's influence on hockey development in Canada did not limit itself to the donation of The Stanley Cup. In the 1890s the only fully organized league was the Amateur Hockey Association of Canada with the majority of its teams from Montreal, one of the several touted birthplaces of the game. Many of the Governor-General's staff were McGill University graduates, and when they moved to Ottawa to take government jobs they

Horse-racing on the ice of the Ottawa River, probably at Aylmer, was a popular spectator sport of the era.

A stalwart Ottawa Lacrosse Club pose for their team photograph on the field at Lansdowne Park.

brought the love of hockey with them. No doubt Lord Stanley longed to see an Ottawa team win his Stanley Cup. But Montreal maintained its dominance until 1902-03 when the Ottawa Senators, "The Silver Seven," began their domination.

During this period from 1891–92 to 1902–03, hockey mania seized Ottawa. Junior and Senior teams sprang from almost every neighborhood, sponsored by local businesses. While the Ottawa City Hockey Club, renamed the Capital Hockey Team, challenged teams like the Montreal A.A.A., Montreal Victorias, and Montreal Shamrocks for The Stanley Cup in the Amateur Hockey Association of Canada League, their farm team, the Young Capitals, were pitting their strength against such outstanding junior performers as the Electrics, Aberdeens, Jim Enright's

Young "Caps" Hockey Team of '96.
Back row, LEFT TO RIGHT—George Hyde, James Kimpton, Bill Sparks, Jack Tobin, Billie Powers.
Front—Jack Powers (of lacrosse fame), and Robert (Bob) Mulhall, who established a reputation for himself as an outstanding bike rider.

Victorias, Ottawa Seconds, New Edinburghs, a hard-hitting crew that sometimes came up The Valley from Buckingham, and a team bearing the banner of Garland's Wholesale and Drygoods House. The Garlands boasted some formidable young hockey players-in-training, such as Harvey Pulford, Forester McKinnon, Tom McNichol, and Tom Brown. The Young Caps produced such outstanding athletes as Bill Powers, Eddie and Paddy Murphy, and Bob Mulhall. Bob Mulhall also brought fame to the sporting city as a bike-rider in the days when bike-racing was at its peak and crowds surged through the gates of the old Metropolitan grounds at the east end of Pretoria Avenue to watch the race on one of the finest clay tracks in the country.

The Young Caps played most of their games in the old Dey's Arena on Laurier but sometimes played open-air against Enright's Victorias on the Nepean Street rink. A newspaper reporter in Ottawa one time asked one of the Young Capitals if he would recall a humorous incident from hockey wars of the period. The Young Cap replied:

There was nothing funny about it. In those days we played nearly two hours at a stretch without any relief. Few of the trams carried any spares and when a fellow went out to play a game he had to make up his mind that, barring serious incident, he was out there to the finish. The games weren't as strenuous as the brand of hockey we see now, but the long steady grind told on the players. Then, too, if there was any rough stuff we felt the full force of it because heavy padding was unknown. Even the goalkeepers had very little protection against flying pucks.

The Electrics ruled the Junior Hockey roost in Ottawa during the early nineties. The team was organized in 1892, the players for the most part being drawn from employees of the Chaudière Electric company, forerunner of Ahearn's Ottawa Electric Company. Though their existence was short lived, old-timers and hockey buffs always maintained that they were "the smartest collection of junior players that ever came down the pike." They won almost every game they played against other members of the Junior League at that time, the Ottawa Juniors and the Aberdeens. That they vanquished the Ottawa Juniors was impressive since that team boasted such outstanding players as Percy Butler, Charlie Spittal, and Martin Rosenthal.

During their first winter the Electrics won challenge games against both local and outside teams, including Perth and Carleton Place. In the winter of 1893–94 they joined the Ottawa City League and won the championship without losing a single game. The following winter the Electrics advanced by joining the Junior Amateur Hockey Association, then comprised of Montreal Hawthornes, Victoria Juniors of Montreal, Ottawa Juniors, and Montreal Maple Leafs. With Alf Smith on right wing they went on to become champions of the City League and champions of the Junior Amateur Hockey Association. Alf Smith turned pro with the Ottawa Senators and was with them for two Stanley Cups.

The Electrics played most of their games at Dey's Arena on Laurier. It is said that they virtually revolutionized hockey with a passing system which they developed to a new art and which Alf

Electric Hockey Team, 1893–94. Standing — A.H. Farley, B.H. Baldwin. Middle row — E. O'Neil, F. Nolan, Eddie Murphy, M.J. (Mike) Shea, Alf. Smith. Bottom — W.E. Dey, P.J. (Paddy) Murphy.

Smith continued on Silver Seven Stanley Cup teams when he played right wing with the great scorer Frank McGee at center.

Another team which served as seeding-ground was Enright's Boarders, later the Victorias, a team which in 1900 arose out of the enthusiasm of a group of ambitious youngsters who made the old Victoria Rink their rendezvous on winter evenings after working hours. They decided to organize themselves into a legitimate hockey team playing games against other Junior Sevens, both within the city and in outlying districts. They elected officers and decided to call themselves "Enright's Boarders," in honor of Jimmy Enright, owner of Victoria Rink and an active worker with and promoter of young sportsmen, particularly hockey players.

Jimmy Enright's first connection with hockey was in the sea-

and promoter of young sportsmen, particularly hockey players.

Jimmy Enright's first connection with hockey was in the season of 1894–95 when he was president of the club of St. Patrick's Lyceum, said to be the first team on which Alf Smith, of Silver Seven fame, ever played organized hockey. Besides Alf Smith, the St. Patrick's Lyceum team included other young lads who were slated to gain renown in the Sporting Town: George McGuire,

Enright's Borders, 1900–01. Back row — Alf. Young, Paddy McLaughlin, James J. (Jimmy) Enright, Art Throup. Front — Billy Bradley, H. (Bud) Harrison, George (Piggy) Dalglish, Eddie O'Leary.

Dolly Durkin, "Bunty" Templeton, Jimmy Egan, Joe Gorman, and Sam Armstrong.

In the season of 1897–98 Jimmy Enright was president of the Columbia Hockey club. It was during the season of 1900–01 that his "Boarders" began to make their presence felt in Junior hockey league circles, and three years later that they entered the Junior City League in competition with teams representing the YMCA, the W.C. Edwards Lumber Company, the Beavers, the Emmetts, and the Rialtos. At this time they changed their team name from "Enright's Boarders" to the Victorias.

Prior to entering the Junior City League, "Enright's Boarders" had made their presence felt up and down the Valley in games with Junior teams in Renfrew, Pembroke, Perth, Arnprior, Rockland, Carleton Place, winning the majority of these out-of-

clinched the championship with relative ease. That same year, 1903–04, they entered the Canadian Amateur Hockey League playdowns and won the cup in competition with Buckingham and Montreal teams. The following season they were again victorious, winning the same championship against Loyola College at the Montreal Arena by a score of 11–3. The Loyolas were considered to be the best of many Junior teams in Montreal, but Harrison, Throop, Young, and Shouldis, it was said, literally skated "rings around them and dazed them with their clever combination plays."

Other notable players, joined the championship Victorias in later years: Tommy Smith (Alf's brother), Jim McMullen, Billy Allen (more renowned as a boxer), Bob O'Leary, Fred Poereira, Eddie Hawken.

In time the Victorias got so full of self-confidence (perhaps so uppity) that they challenged the famous Silver Seven to a practice game in Howick Pavilion at Lansdowne Park. They didn't win but it is recorded that they put up "stiff competition" for the world famous Ottawa Senators.

The Bronsons epitomize the history of early junior hockey in the Capital City. Although not officially entered in any league they played against such "snappy outfits" as the Chaudieres, Mount Sherwoods, Dan McDonald's Hillsides, Aylmer Juniors, and the formidable Columbias, which boasted none other than Clint Benedict on its line-up, as well as Roy and Earl Rickey, both of whom played professional hockey later in Western Canada.

The Bronson's rink was at the corner of Somerset Street and Bronson Avenue in the spacious backyard of alderman James Peterkin, and one of its Juniors on his way up was a lad named Harry "Punch" Broadbent. On Peterkin's rink Broadbent developed the fine art of "elbowing" his way through opposing lines to become one of the speediest and most colorful forwards of the Ottawa Senators.

One night in the winter of 1903 the Bronsons decided to challenge the Columbias on their own rink on McLeod Street where the Museum of Man stands today. "Elbows" Broadbent flashed two hot ones into the net and the Bronsons defeated the highly touted Columbias. Broadbent and Benedict were to play together in professional ranks for the Ottawa Senators but that night on McLeod Street in 1903 they were pitted against each other as only young hockey players of ambition and motivation could be.

During the season 1902–03, when The Bronsons won every game they played, the parents and the neighbors of the victorious Juniors gave a splendid banquet in Peterkin's Hall, a means of showing their pride in the team and encouraging them forward to greater triumphs.

During this era, Ottawa University took its hockey very seriously, fielding usually six teams, each team adopting the name of its captain and equipping itself according to its own financial means. In the 1900s it was said that the Varsity frays attracted very little outside interest other than protest from nearby residents about the noise of the battles. But internally the hockey teams garnered the support of every student and every faculty member; and the rivalry was described as "so intense" that innumerable donnybrooks were enacted in the snowbanks surrounding the rink.

In the season of 1901–02 the Varsity team, captained by W.A. "Billy" Richards and having on its roster no less than Harry Smith of future Silver Seven fame, carried off the championship with a game played on Rideau Rink.

The equipment worn by these players was, to say the least, unpretentious and at the most innovative. The goalkeeper wore a very narrow pair of pads and perhaps an old baseball catcher's protector; the boys "at the front" stuffed university scribblers into their stockings, their only protection against flying pucks and sticks. Often there was only one precious puck per game and often good ice time was spent digging around in the snowbanks for the elusive puck. Sometimes more valuable time was spent while digging lost hockey players out of the snowbanks. The boards around the rink were only one foot high and many a "bodied" player literally flew into the surrounding snowbanks and had to be dug out.

From Ottawa University's championship team of 1901–02 two players, Billy Richards and W. A. Callaghan, were chosen for the Ottawa University team represented in the City League championship the following season. Of the pool of players on Ottawa University teams at the turn of the century, the majority entered the priesthood. Billy Richards, W.A.Callaghan, and J.J. Cox were also outstanding on some of the great football Varsity teams of that period; they were on the team that won the Dominion Football championship for Argonauts and, after he left Ottawa University in 1902, Richards also played hockey for McGill

University. Harry Smith was the only one who moved from Varsity to Professional rank with the Old Senators.

In an article in the Evening Citizen *of May 1935, Harry Smith, in his later years, told how he was given a "leave of absence" from Ottawa University:*

I would rather play hockey than eat in my younger days. One game a night wasn't enough; I yearned for more. Often I would play for one of our college teams between seven and eight o'clock at night, dash into my room and lock the door, pretending that I was settling down to my studies. But, as soon as the way was clear, I would jump out of the window and hike over to Dey's arena in time to play a City League game for the Aberdeens.

The college authorities got wise one night, had me up on the carpet and threatened dire consequence if the offence was repeated. It was and I got my walking orders.

When asked how he became so expert at "finding the net", Harry gave this explanation: "I used to go down on the Rideau Canal under the old Bank Street Bridge, put a tin can up on a post and practice shooting at it — like target practice with a gun. I used to keep this up for hours at a time until I was satisfied that I could find the vacant corners of a net without any difficulty." While playing with The Senators in 1905–06 Harry scored seven goals in one game against the Montreal Wanderers. After the

Ottawa City Hockey Club, 1895. Standing, LEFT TO RIGHT — P.D. Ross, Geo. P. Murphy, Chauncey Kirby, Don Watters. Seated — Jim Smellie, Alf. Smith, Harvey Pulford, Weldy Young, Joe McDougall. Bottom row — Harry Westwick, Fred Chittick, H. Russell.

match he was personally congratulated by Lord and Lady Grey who had been present for the game.

The University of Ottawa was not the only institute of higher learning to ice a team in the city leagues. From the turn of the century to the outbreak of the Second World War, Lisgar Collegiate

The rink at Model School, shown here in 1912 with Lisgar Collegiate in the background, was "home" ice to many Ottawa Senators in their youth.

Institute hockey teams regularly won Junior, Intermediate, and Senior City League championships. Operating under the belief that "a school which neglects sports will inevitably decline in spirit and attendance," Lisgar teachers instructed the likes of Hockey Hall of Fame members Gordon Roberts, Jack and Harold Darragh, Alex Smith, Harry "Punch" Broadbent, and Frank Boucher in the art of hockey. Other notable hockey-playing alumnae of Lisgar include Jack Fournier, Letham Graham, Jerry Davidson, Norman Scott, Stewart Christie, Eddie Cuzner, Carson Kendall, Grey Masson, Gordon Johnston, Howard Raphael, Paul Armstrong, Basil Frith, Tom Lowrey, and Tommy Westwick. Athletic prowess and academic achievement would seem to have co-existed fruitfully at Lisgar in this era.

During this era the Ottawa City Hockey Club, later called the Ottawa Capitals, competed in the Ontario Hockey Association League and then the Canadian Amateur Hockey League with considerable success, but not until 1902-03 was an Ottawa team able to win The Stanley Cup. At the start of that season, The Capitals were renamed The Senators, then nicknamed "The Silver Seven" in honor of the seven players on the team — Bouse

H.R.H. Princess Patricia and Major Worthington on "the small rink in the woods" at Rideau Hall, Ottawa, 1914.

Hutton, Arthur Moore, Harvey Pulford, Frank McGee, and the three Gilmour brothers, Dave, Bill, and Suddy. The league playoff between The Silver Seven and the Montreal Victories was tension filled, while The Stanley Cup challenge match between Ottawa and Rat Portage was somewhat wild, as Bill Galloway in his newspaper feature "Ottawa Senators: The Glory Years" recounts:

The Silver Seven and Montreal Victorias ended up the regular season tied and played off in a two game, total goals series which opened in Montreal on March 7th. This game ended in a tie. They played the second match in Ottawa on March 10th and Ottawa won 8–0. The ice was slushy and in no condition for a hockey game and was even worse when the Rat Portage (Kenora) team arrived in Ottawa to challenge for the Cup. The two game series opened on March 12th with ice conditions so bad that at one point in the game, the puck fell through a hole in the rink and could not be found. The teams stood around while 1500 screaming fans impatiently waited for another puck to arrive.

The rotten ice did not stop Ottawa who won 6-2 and again defeated Rat Portage 4–2 on March 14th.

A century-long tradition of tripping and slashing was begun during this period, and referees were dragged from the ice, bashed with sticks, hit with pucks. Indeed, play was so hard on officials that in a game between Rat Portage Westerners and the

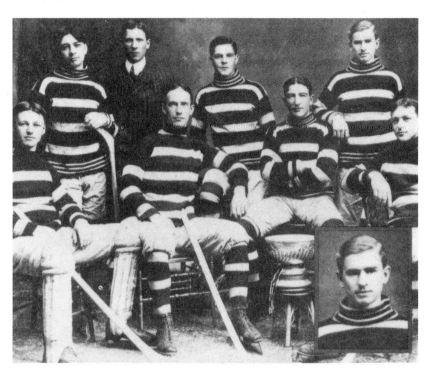

The Silver Seven, 1904–05.
Champions of the World and Stanley Cup winners. Front row, LEFT TO RIGHT — D. N. Finnie, goal; E. H. Pulford, defence; Alfred Smith, captain, right wing; Arthur E. Moore. Back row — Harry Westwick, rover;
M. H. McGilton, trainer; H. L. "Billy" Gilmour, left wing; and Frank C. McGee, center. Inset — Frank C. McGee scored 14 goals in a 23–2 Stanley Cup victory over Dawson City.

Ottawa Silver Seven the referee wore a hard hat to protect himself — the fans roared each time it was knocked from his head.

In 1904–05, The Silver Seven successfully defended The Stanley Cup from challenges by the Winnipeg Rowing Club, the Toronto Marlboros, the Montreal Wanderers, and the Brandon Wheat Kings, with Frank Patrick starring. Patrick's heroics could not overcome The Silver Seven, and before an audience of Lord and Lady Minto, at the Aberdeen Pavilion, the Ottawa team won the two-game series. That year The Silver Seven played in the Federal Hockey League, losing only one game, to Brockville.

Again in 1905-06, The Silver Seven accepted challenges from afar in their defence of The Stanley Cup. Dawson City traveled 4,000 miles, part of the way by dogsled, to play The Silver

Seven. Exhausted, they lost to what Brian McFarlane has called in his book, *One Hundred Years of Hockey*, "one of the greatest teams ever assembled." In the second game of the series Frank McGee set a record which stands to this day: 14 goals against Dawson city's seventeen-year-old goaltender Albert Forrest in a 23–2 game. One can only wonder how the renowned Silver Seven would have done if they had traveled 4,000 miles across ice

Klondike (Dawson City) Hockey Team, 1905–06. The Klondike squad traveled 4,000 miles to challenge The Siver Seven for The Stanley Cup at Dey's Arena.
Back row — Hector Smith, George Kennedy, Lorne Hannay, Jim Johnston, Norm Watt.
Front row — Albert Forrest, Col. Joe Boyle, Dr. Randy McLellan.
Not in photo — Weldy Young (manager), Dave Fairbairn, H. Martin.

and snow to play Dawson City on its home ground. The fatigue suffered by the Dawson City team was compounded by bad ice conditions. The Ottawa ice-maker, it has been said, slowed down the Dawson City team by flooding the ice with an inch of water, even though the temperature was well above freezing. Like race horses who do better on mud, The Silver Seven plodded through the slush to win The Stanley Cup for the third year in a row.

With this third consecutive Stanley Cup victory, the Silver Seven Senators set a record which stood alone until the Toronto Maple Leafs won three consecutive Cups in the late 1940s and the Montreal Canadiens, led by Maurice "Rocket" Richard, won five consecutive N.H.L. championships in the late 1950s.

One of the most colorful players with The Silver Seven was Harry "Rat" Westwick who served as captain on the team and played on the first Canadian all-star team selected by fans in 1905. Harry once gave this explanation of the origin of his nick-name, "Rat":

We played in Quebec this night in 1896 and a couple of days after we were back in Ottawa George Patterson Murphy, the president of the Ottawa Hockey Club, produced a copy of *The Quebec*

Harry "Rat" Westwick (left) was connected with Ottawa sporting activities for all eighty-one years of his life; with the Ottawa Capitals (lacrosse), with the Senators for three consecutive Stanley Cups 1902–1905, with the N.H.A. as a referee. His descendants continued to be associated with the Ottawa sporting scene.

The hockey career of "Peerless Percy" Lesueur (right) spanned fifty years but he gained his fame as goaltender for Ottawa Senators 1906–1913 including two Stanley Cup Championships, 1908–09 and 1910–11. He is credited with inventing the gauntlet-type glove for goalies and the net used by the N.H.A. and the N.H.L. from 1912 to 1925.

Chronicle in a store on Sparks Street where the players used to gather. It contained an account of the game and the hockey writer had really given us a going over. He called Harvey Pulford "The Bytown Slugger," Weldy Young was "a thug," and Westwick a "miserable, insignificant rat." After that I was "Rat" Westwick.

Bill Westwick, a relative of the "Rat," became one of the best sportswriters in hockey, covering the exploits of The Senators during the 1920s and 1930s as they struggled to match the achievements of The Silver Seven.

The 1906–07 Stanley Cup was won by the Kenora Thistles in a challenge match against The Silver Seven, and the Montreal

Wanderers in turn challenged for the Cup in 1907-08, defeating Kenora. However, the Ottawa Senators reclaimed the honors in 1908–09, easily defeating the Wanderers, with a young Fred "Cyclone" Taylor and legendary center Marty Walsh leading the team. The Senators lost the Cup again in 1909–10 to their old rivals the Montreal Wanderers, only to regain it the next season in 1910–11, with a team boasting the likes of Marty Walsh, Percy LaSeur, Jack Darragh, and Captain Bruce "Hod" Stuart. The Senators not only regained The Stanley Cup from the Wanderers, they defended it from further challenges by teams from Galt and Port Arthur. And at the end of the season, The Senators toured New York City with the Montreal Wanderers, playing several exhibition games in front of appreciative fans. The Renfrew Millionaires followed this same circuit, with the "hi-jacked" Fred "Cyclone" Taylor starring, a year later.

The Senators would not win The Stanley Cup again until the 1919–20 season, once the team had joined the N.H.L. — once the team and the game of hockey had turned from amateur status to professional.

The relative merits of amateur vs. professional hockey was often debated in these years leading up to the creation of the N.H.L. in 1917. A fascinating Ottawa Citizen *article, dated December 1909, entertained these arguments:*

A good deal of public curiosity exists as to what professional lacrosse and hockey players get in Ottawa, now that straight professionalism is an accepted fact. In the olden days of athletics — that is, of the period some twenty years ago, the players were supposedly amateur, but in quite a number of cases a 'divvy' was looked for at the end of the season and when a season was more than ordinarily successful this totalled to quite a respectable figure. There was no guarantee given as to the amount each was to get from the members of the executive, but the athletes expected to be fairly treated on the division of the surplus cash at the end of the season. It was understood that anyone who benefited this way would take a greater interest in the success of his organization.

Capt. Bruce Stuart of the champion Ottawa hockey team was asked what the players are receiving at present for their series. He replied: "I cannot say as to that. Each player knows what his own arrangement is, but managers of clubs are very much like heads of commercial establishments who usually prefer to keep their employees ignorant as to what their fellow workers are in the habit of getting. The man who plays hockey gets what he is worth to any club and therefore, there can be no fixed scale."

It is known however, that Tom Phillips, when with Ottawa, was reported to be getting $1,500 for the season, but it is certain that his salary fell far below that amount. In cases where a man's presence

Ottawa Hockey Club, 1908–09. Inside the circle and touching the cup, clockwise — C.B. Stuart, captain and rover; T. D'Arcy McGee, Pres.; L.N. Bate, Vice-Pres. On the circle, clockwise — A. Kerr, left; Fred (Cyclone) Taylor, center point; M. Walsh, center; H. L. Gilmour, rover; C.J. Bryson; P.M. Buttler; M. Rosenthal; P.J. Baskerville; N.C. Sparks, D.B. Mulligan. E. Dey, spare; Percy Lesueur, goal; T. Lake, point. Outside the circle, clockwise — M. H. McGilton, trainer; P. Green, Coach; Dr. S.M. Noble; H.M. Merrill, spare.

on a team is expected to assure victory, large sums have been paid. Art Ross, the captain of the Montreal Wanderers, is known to have received from Cobalt the sum of $1,000 for two matches against Haileybury. Tom Phillips of Kenora and Ottawa fame received $600 for two matches in Montreal. The ordinary man receives in the neighborhood of $600 for a season of twelve weeks.

By the time the First World War ended, The Ottawa Senators had joined the N.H.L. as a charter member. The City of Ottawa soon became the capital city of *professional* hockey during the glory years of the 1920s.

There have been four generations of Kirbys in the insurance business in Ottawa, one of them being the famous hockey player, Chauncey T. Kirby for whom J.R. Booth, King of the Timber Barons, struck a medal, still cherished in the Kirby family. I taped John D. Kirby, Chauncey T.'s son, at home in Ottawa less than a year before his death in 1990:

In the 1890s my father, Chauncey T. Kirby was playing hockey for Ottawa and I think it was the old Foulkes Arena, corner of Elgin and Laurier. The Stanley Cup was a challenge cup; it wasn't a league cup. You had to defend it every week.

I went to see a hockey match when I was old enough to go out in the evening — around 1911 — and it was a challenge to Ottawa who were holding The Stanley Cup and it was a challenge from Galt. They had come all that way to challenge Ottawa. And they got beaten. I was there and that was in Dey's Arena. All I can remember about it was it was a good clean game, no roughhouse at all, and I can remember that the goaltender for Galt was a fellow named Hay . . .

That Dey's arena, it seated over two thousand and the arena was always full. There was a crew of firemen walking underneath the stands with fire cleaners, chemicals to put out fire, smother it.

When my father moved to Montreal to work in the bank he played hockey for Montreal. Then he came back from Montreal in 1907 — he got fed up with the bank and he didn't play hockey anymore. He refereed.

There was another story that I want to bring in here. One of the last years he was playing hockey, the Ottawa team was on its way down to Montreal to play the Montreal Amateur Hockey Association and this was the last of the amateurism. Harvey Pulford wanted to be paid for playing with the Ottawa team in the game against Montreal. And this was announced when they got to Montreal. Chauncey T. Kirby was then on the management end of the team and C.T. said, "Fine, he wants to get paid. Well, he's not going to get paid and he's not going to play and he's not going to get back." And so Pulford didn't get the return ticket to go back. And that was the last of Chauncey's involvement with the hockey club, because it was a departure from the true amateurism that he believed in — "the Gentleman's Game" — where they bought their own uniforms, they bought their own skates, and they bought their own sticks, and often their own tickets to wherever they were going — although they had a fund usually of hundred dollars for that.

they were going — although they had a fund usually of hundred dollars for that.

My father refereed till about 1912. The Sims place where he was managing was open on Saturday night till nine o'clock and afterwards he went to the rink to referee. And he had done a day's work and he was pretty tired, I would say. Anyway, you know how the players and referee get messed up on the boards once in

"In the good old days" Ottawa had some whopping snow storms which brought the entire city to a standstill. Dave Gill, Manager of the Ottawa Senators and an executive with Frank Ahearn in the Ottawa Electric Street Railway, was renowned for inventing machinery to clear the tracks, like the one shown here.

a while? Well, one night they got mixed up and messed up with Chauncey T. three or four times. Anyway, when we came home — I dunno what the result of the game was — but anyway, my brother and I said to him, "You didn't have much luck on the boards, Dad?" And he said, "No." And one of us said, "Well, you really messed up a couple of plays." He never refereed again. When the criticism came from the two boys — from his own family — he signed off.

And, of course, the referees didn't get paid. They did it for love. But dad once got one hundred dollars and his transportation to go and referee a game in the Silver Mining League — between Cobalt and Haileybury. I saw Art Ross play at Dey's Arena. Art Ross was playing for the Wanderers. But, anyway, he said it was really for blood to play at Haileybury. And Ross said after the game they had to tie their skates and sticks, strap them together as weapons, and then swing them back and forth to fight their way through the angry crowd. But my father was the referee — all he had was his skates and blades to swing back and forth to defend himself! He got out of Haileybury as fast as he could. In fact, I think, he must have caught the train at North Bay which would be coming down to get into Ottawa around six o'clock. He never refereed up there again. That was it.

The medal J.R. Booth gave to Chauncey T. Kirby, center for the Ottawa City Hockey Club, is an eight-pointed star. The center would fit onto a bar that you'd pin on your coat in the form of a medal. On the back it says:

Champions of Canada
Presented by J.R. Booth, Esq. to
C.T. Kirby, Centre

By the turn of the century Ottawa, Hull, and the Alymer Road were dotted with mansions built by hockey enthusiast J. R. Booth, "King of the Timber Barons," and his family. This one on Metcalfe Street is now the Laurentian Club.

Other fellows who played on the team got medals at the same time. There was my uncle, Dr. H.S. Kirby, and there was Jenkins — now that's the famous curler, afterwards. There may have been a couple of Gilmours on it. P.D. Ross did some management of the hockey club, but he didn't play . . .

There's a very interesting thing about Cyclone Taylor. Now, Taylor went to New York once on an exhibition team with the Renfrew Millionaires to play the Montreal Wanderers, and they compared — he was getting a pretty good salary — and they compared the number of games he played in the season with a champion baseball player of his time and Taylor was making double the money per game that a baseball player was getting. You see, in those days hockey players never played more than Saturday and Wednesday nights.

I was around when the Auditorium was built and when The Senators were born and when they died, and I think — this is my own personal opinion — I think their demise was hastened by the location of the rink. Dey's Arena, where they were before, you got off at Laurier and Elgin on the Elgin street car and you walked a block to the rink. And also, you could get off at Canal Street and walk down Canal Street and come into the Rush End. Now the other part of the thing is that nobody in the name of God knew where Argyle Avenue or O'Connor Street was. O'Connor Street was a quiet street, you couldn't get through at Catherine Street — it stopped at Catherine and then the cars went out Bank Street and you had to catch Gladstone Avenue to get down to the rink, or it went through on to the subway before the next stop at

The Alexander Hotel and the Gilmour Hotel were two Centretown bars on Bank Street where athletic enthusiasists and hockey fans dallied and drank in the "Men Only" rooms. The Alexander was demolished in the 1970s and only the Gilmour building remains with its ghosts of Ottawa's hockey greats telling tales.

Pretoria. It confused people all the time. You'd have thought Frank Ahearn who owned The Senators *and* the streetcars could have said, "We'll put a stop here at Argyle so they can walk into the rink." I mean, after all, it was his money that was going down the drain.

We'd go to the City League as well because they had Ted Reid there, and also Wes Richards who played for the Shamrocks, and it was Jim McCaffery who used to manage that team then.

A pair of season tickets cost about $125.00. Wes Richards played for the City League Shamrocks team and then he went into the Senator organization during the golden years. He coached The Senators for one year, and I remember going to watch the Ottawa Senators in 1923–24. It was the first season Frank Finnigan played, and we had second row seats. He could really zing one and you'd feel the boards bounce.

really zing one and you'd feel the boards bounce.

Mrs. John B. Kirby also has fond memories of early Ottawa hockey life, which for her had a somewhat romantic aura about it:

I grew up in Ottawa in New Edinborough. I met John in

Another Ottawa born star of the early Ottawa Senators, Bruce Stuart (left) played forward for his home team on two Stanley Cup Championships, 1908–09 and 1910–11. Stuart once scored six goals in a game against Quebec.

H.L. Billy Gilmour (right) was born in Ottawa, 1885, and was a member of the famous Silver Seven for three consecutive Stanley Cup victories, 1902–03, 1903–04, and 1904–05. When the renamed Senators won the Stanley Cup in 1908–09, Gilmour finished the season with 11 goals in 11 games.

1922 or '23 on a mutual date. He'd just bought a new car and he met a young fellow friend of his in the Glebe and wanted to take him for a ride in his new car. And the young fellow friend said, "I know a girl down in New Edinburgh, let's go down and get a couple of girls."

I was a working girl by 1922. My very first job was at the age of fifteen. I took an intensive course of shorthand at Mrs. Rolls Shorthand School on Bank Street, about over where the National

how to type. So I took this course because my sister was working temporarily at the Japanese Consulate and she was going to have her first and only child. So she said, "If you learn shorthand you can have this job after me. It pays ninety dollars a month and you only work four hours a day. Ten to twelve and two to four." Consulate hours, you see. At the corner of Sussex and Rideau. So that was my first job. But when I met John in 1923 I was up in the Senate. I did one session, after the spring session. I worked for Sir James Lougheed who was the Conservative Leader in the Senate and he was an old man then. I met John, and he came round, and asked me to go to a hockey match — the only one I'd ever been to was Juvenile, you know.

But he took me to the Auditorium to see the City League, The Shamrocks. And we sat next to Mr. Seldon. The Kirbys had their regular seat there. We were sitting there a while and John said to me, "There's my father across the rink." I said, "I can't see very well." So Mr. Seldon handed his binoculars to me and I looked and there was this tiny man. Sure enough, in five minutes he was across the rink to meet "the redhead." His son had never gone out with a redhead before. But he knew what redheads were like because he had cousins that were five boys in the family . . . You can gather from this that I was a little on the flarey side.

When he took me to the match I had Oxfords on. It was wintertime and I wanted to look nice and I had long woollen socks on that ended here — of course we had long skirts. They were low, and John said to me, "You're coming out in the wintertime with those on?" But he had a car and he had the finest place to park the car because the Auditorium was at Argyle Avenue there. So we parked up on the Museum grounds somewhere and I had to pick my way in, and I only knew him about a week or so then. Well, we had met in September so it was a little more than a week, I guess. I know he remarked on me not wearing rubbers in the wintertime. So, he might have known what kind of a witch he got. That was our first date — a hockey game.

Phoebe McCord of Shawville, Quebec, stands out as one of the greatest storytellers in my experience. She really could tackle and enrich almost any subject, but here she describes — unforgettably — a riot in the Rush End in the early days of hockey in Ottawa:

The Kilreas of Ottawa were relations of ours. The first Kilrea, Jack, was an Irishman, pure Irish, over from Northern

Ireland. He got work in a lumber camp with my uncle, John Armstrong, a big handsome man. And John Armstrong brought Jack Kilrea home with him because Jack had no place to go. And then with his bride, Sara Armstrong, Kilrea moved to Ottawa and got work with J.R. Booth — oh, he was poorly paid — and he

Horse-drawn cars were Ottawa's first public transport.

This primitive vehicle (a 7 h.p. single chain drive Rambler) was purchased by Mr. L. N. Poulin in 1902, and in 1905 was fitted with an adjustable top for business purposes. Note the old-fashioned lantern-type headlights.

bought a little house on Laurier Avenue West. It's still there — just off Bank Street — and they had a little back yard. And Kilrea was having this large family. Fourteen they had, you know. Anyway, he was an Irishman and he was an Orangeman. And he rose on the Twelfth of July before sunrise. At the first gleam of the sun he would be out there in the back yard in his "couth." And he had a revolver and he'd be firing shots into the air and yelling, "Hurray for King Billy! Hurray for King Billy!" At the top of his voice and already drunk! Yes, he would already have had two or three good shots of whiskey. He collected whiskey for the Twelfth, the glorious Twelfth; he wasn't drinking beer that day!

And the police would come. In those days they were all Irish Catholics — not now though — and they would come and say, "Now, Mr. Kilrea, you mustn't make such a noise."

And Jack would yell, "Get out of here or I'll drill you full! Hurray for King Billy! Out of my backyard, you damn Dogans!"

And the police would say, "Kilrea, you are causing a disturbance —"

And he would shout, "Are you a Dogan?"

"No," the policemen would say, "we're Catholics."

And he would say, "To hell with that! You're all damn black dogans, every last man jack of you! Out of here or I'll drill everyone of you!"

And the policemen would go — partly because he was armed and partly because he was a fiercesome-looking man. He wasn't a big man but he was full of presence and he had yellow curls and a great yellow whisker. Another reason the policemen would go was because Jack Kilrea was the father of the later-famous Hec Kilrea of the Ottawa Senators.

Every Twelfth of July, Jack Kilrea petrified his neighbors. But the police stopped coming to his place on the Glorious Twelfth. "Oh, it's just Jack Kilrea," they would say when the complaints came in. "He doesn't shoot at anything. He just shoots up into the sky!"

Jack Kilrea was an Orangeman first, last, and always. For years the Kilreas lived from hand-to-mouth on Laurier Avenue. But then some of the girls got work and got married, and Hec was making all that money with the Ottawa Senators during the twenties and early thirties. And one Kilrea married a Jewish lady and when the first child was born her Jewish grandfather gave her a white mink hat and coat. It was the talk of the town.

The Rush End at old Dey's Arena in Ottawa was a section at both ends of the rink where you stood up all night. But that didn't matter. You were watching the Montreal Maroons play the Ottawa Senators and Aurel Joliat was playing. Oh my, that little wee Frenchman! Absolutely gorgeous! And my uncle Jack Kilrea was there, of course, in the Rush End, telling everybody around him that that was his son down there, big, blond Hec Kilrea. Jack would be having a few, maybe even had managed to save up some whiskey for the game, and he'd get bragging in a very loud

Roller skating emerged as yet another summer sporting event at the turn of the century. This is a Topley photograph of a 1907 roller skating crowd assembled at an Ottawa covered rink.

The bicycling craze which seized Ottawa in the Gay Nineties continued for thirty years until superceded by the motor car. This is a group of Ottawa cyclists taken opposite the summer cottage of Mr. E. Mial, Aylmer, Quebec, 1898. Alymer was a favorite destination for Ottawa boaters, skiers, cyclists, hikers.

voice: "That's my boy down there." And somebody would answer him with a vile insult, or slanderous French, and they would be into it. And more and more people would be into it, taking sides until the whole Rush End would be in a melee — everyone fighting and hitting and cursing and swearing, in both French and English! Oh, it was audience participation in the truest sense of the word!

The Charlie Conacher Cancer Research Fund two-hundred-and-fifty-dollar-a-plate fund-raising dinner is traditionally held in Toronto on St. Patrick's Day. To ensure my father's attendance at the 1987 dinner, Harold Ballard conscripted Jake Dunlap to be my father's escort. Jake drove him to Toronto, attended to his every whim in Toronto — I understand they even had a sentimental journey down Yonge Street and into the Maple Leaf Gardens — and then brought him home again safely. Although they are a generation apart, the time gap between Dunlap and Finnigan was bridged by incredible enthusiasm and detailed memory for the city of Ottawa in the days when it was the sporting hub of the country.

Such a sports-minded community provided fertile ground for the growth and encouragement of young athletes and for the perpetual increase of supporting fans, both of whom are so necessary to the development of sporting activities and organizations. I have always maintained that Ottawa was also the capital city of hockey for North America, and I was therefore not surprised when Jake Dunlap came to the interview with Frank Finnigan seemingly intent upon demonstrating the fact that at one time Ottawa was "the seeding ground" for hockey champions and the great teams of North America.

Jake Dunlap was born in Ottawa, one of the sons of Ann Elan and Henry Joseph Dunlap, originally from Cape Breton. He was educated at St. Patrick's College, Ottawa University, and Osgoode Hall, practicing law in Ottawa until his appointment in 1987 as Agent General to the United States for the Province of Ontario, based in New York City. An all-round sporting man, he played hockey as a junior for St. Pat's and as a senior for the Ottawa Senators in the Quebec Hockey League. His football career encompassed twelve years with Toronto, Hamilton, and Ottawa. After his return to Ottawa from his position in New York, Jake Dunlap, along with Val Belcher and Larry Brune, two football players from Houston, Texas, opened the very successful Lonestar Restaurant in

Ottawa, where, he used to say, "the men are men — and smell like horses." The Lonestar was sold several years ago, smell and all:

JAKE: Harold Starr and Carl Boucher, one of the famous Boucher brothers, got in and out of the bread business in Ottawa pretty fast. Carl usually worked as a printer for the *The Ottawa Journal,*

Alfred E. Smith (left) was the eldest of seven hockey playing brothers of whom only three achieved professional status. Born in 1873 he played with the Ottawa Electrics and the Ottawa Capitals before joining The Senators in 1895. He played right wing with Frank McGee at center for two Stanley Cup Championships in 1903–04 and 1904–05.

Thomas J. "Tommy" Smith (right) was born at Ottawa in 1885. Like all his brothers he played school and Junior hockey in Ottawa, then went on with The Victorias and The Senators. He twice scored nine goals in a game.

but one summer he and Harold Starr decided that they would go into the bread business. The very first day Harold loaded up the truck and headed up the Gatineau where, 'twas anticipated, he was going to make a fortune selling to all the cottagers as well as the regulars. Well, round about Wakefield Harold got into the hotel there, and somehow during a very long, pleasant afternoon lifting his elbow he traded his whole truckful of bread for a canoe. End of bread business . . . Remember Sid Howe? He had a sporting store in Ottawa.

FRANK: And his uncle had before him.

JAKE: I grew up in the Glebe on Second Avenue, and you know where Mutchmor School is on Fifth Avenue? Well, just west of Bank Street on Fifth there is a house and a hockey player lived in there, a good hockey player.

Gordon Roberts (left), a great leftwinger, was one of those rare individuals in his era who managed to play professional hockey while getting his medical degree at McGill University. He played for Ottawa in 1910 and while at McGill played six seasons with Montreal Wanderers. He later practiced medicine on the West Coast and played for the Vancouver Millionaires.

William H. "Hod" Stuart (right), brother of Bruce Stuart, played for Ottawa Capitals at the turn of the century before signing with the Quebec Bulldogs. He died tragically in a diving accident in 1907 at the height of his career.

FRANK: Pete Howe. Real shifty. Played for City League team, Rideaus or New Edinboroughs — Little Pete Howe, one hundred and thirty-five pounds.

JAKE: And Harold Darragh lived around there — Thornton or Ralph Street, near Lansdowne Park. Hero worship! We were full of it! Ottawa was full of hockey players in the summertime and we used to follow them around. What else was there to do? We read about them all the time in the papers, and then we'd go to the park and some of them would be playing hardball. And if we ever got a chance to meet one of them — well! I can remember Bill Cowley, walking home and seeing him — they lived in the Glebe on Powell Avenue near Bronson — and the odd time, you know, he'd go by and we'd all follow him down the street: "Geez, there's Bill Cowley!"

Of course, he was one hell of a hockey player. He "made" more wingers than anyone I can think of. I can remember talking with Lorne Duguid and I said to him, "If you see Bill Cowley, thank him. He kept me in the league." And Roy Conacher — Cowley *made* Roy Conacher the scoring champion one year. Cowley was the center-ice man and he'd pass it — he'd be fooling around and he'd get them in position and *bang!* into the net!

OTTAWA HOCKEY CLUB
Champions of National Hockey Association
1914 - 15

Cosy Dolan — Manager; Jack Darragh — Forward; Hamby Shore — Defence; Art Ross — Defence; Horace Merrill — Defence; Frank Shaughnessy — Manager

Angus Duford — Forward; Sammy Hebert — Goal; Alf Smith — Coach; Clint Benedict — Goal; Leth Graham — Forward

Eddie Gerard — Forward and Captain; "Punch" Broadbent — Forward

This old photograph of the Ottawa Hockey Club of 1914–15 contains many of the hockey "greats" in Ottawa who acted as role models for Frank Finnigan and, later, as hockey heroes for Jake Dunlap.

You know who I got very friendly with in Toronto was Cy Wentworth. Dead about three years. Nice fellow. He played defence with The Maroons. He was sales manager for Labatt's Brewery. And Bill Ward, who was assistant sales manager for Labatt's, and I lived in the Wentworths' house when I was going to law school in Toronto. So I used to see Cy, and Cy always used to talk about "Big Pete" Allen Shields. Cy used to tell me, "That's the toughest son of a bitch I ever met," meaning Shields. Shields went blind later in life.

FRANK: Harold Starr gave him an awful trimming at Harold Starr's hotel in the West End. Allan bothered him, really bugged him. Harold wasn't quarrelsome at all, but if he got something in his head like, "I think that son of a bitch insulted me," he'd go looking for him. Allen was an agitator.

JAKE: But last time I saw him, I was driving somewhere in the city and there was "Big Pete" Allen Shields on the corner. So I picked him up — he was living then in Britannia — and he was waiting for a bus and I went in and had a beer with him; he was going blind then.

FRANK: Well, there might have been a few old-timers who ended up on their uppers. Only a few . . .

JAKE: Fred Connor and Harry Connor — a hell of a good fellow, Connor Washing Machines. And Fred "Crew" Connor, he never played for the National Hockey League but he played for Rovers. But Harry Connor, he was doing so well, I remember, corner of Bank and Laurier, and he had appliances. Then they went into the Connor Venetian Blinds and they used to sell them up The Valley, all the hotels and the hospitals. Harry bought a place, they were doing pretty well, 27 Powell Avenue, and I can remember going in to see Harry there, and do you know what he drank? Burnett's White Satin. Oh Lord, he drank!

FRANK: Oh Lord! He drank a lot! Almost as much as I did — in my drinking days!

JAKE: Nothing at all to be sitting down at the store in the morning drinking Burnett's White Satin, both Fred and Harry.

FRANK: The Kilrea girls were good-looking. Well, they were blond, you know, and in those days to be blond, well . . .

JAKE: Kenny Kilrea was a hell of a hockey player, the youngest of the Kilreas. He was going to Glebe, he married a Simon girl, Simon the Furriers. Now old Simon had, I think, three girls: Julie, Frances (Frankie), and Sylvia. Frankie Simon, a beautiful girl, married Kilrea when they were only in Fifth Form. The Kilreas lived on First Avenue, then they divorced. They were only kids when they got married, eighteen and sixteen — Kenny and Frankie.

You know why the New Edinborough Canoe and Tennis Club was such a hangout for all the athletes in those days? So popular? I'll tell you why. They used to walk across the ice to buy beer and liquor in Gatineau Point and bring it back.

FRANK: Dave Gill was a great supporter of the New Edinborough Canoe Club and so was Jess Ketchum, old Jess . . .

JAKE: Frank, the reason you and I get along so well is because I'm Catholic and you're Protestant.

FRANK: Clancy and I never made any difference. And Alex Connell and Nighbor — I roomed with them and we never made any difference. And Buzz Boll was an RC from the West. I

Harvey Pulford (left) was outstanding in football, lacrosse, boxing, paddling, rowing, squash and hockey. Although born in Toronto in 1875, he spent most of his life in Ottawa playing Championship football for the Rough Riders, championship lacrosse for the Capitals, and championship hockey for the Ottawa Senators.

Born in Ottawa in 1892, H.L. "Punch" Broadbent (right) began his hockey career with New Edinburghs and Cliffsides before moving on to the Ottawa Senators for the 1912–13 season, scoring 21 goals. He was on four Stanley Cup teams — three with Ottawa and one with the Montreal Maroons.

roomed with him.

JAKE: Alex was my coach when I was at St. Pat's hockey. At the last he was soliciting business for a transport company, just a little job he had. Alex was such a gentleman. I can remember Kay, his wife.

FRANK: They had one little girl and she got in a dreadful accident down on Rideau Street. Alex Connell was the secretary of the fire department and Gray Burnett, who was our neighbor on McLeod Street, he was fire chief.

JAKE: I want you to try and name as many people as you can remember, because when everybody came home to Ottawa in those years from playing in the National Hockey League and the Western League, or the seniors or the semi-pro American league in the States, in the summer that was when things really lifted in Ottawa. The guys were home, they didn't have to play any more,

FRANK: Des Smith, Lionel Hitchman, Bill Cowley, all the Bouchers — four of them, Frank, Billy, Buck, George. Joe sold a correspondence music course, Carl didn't play hockey. Five, no, just four Bouchers — Bobby, yes, five. There were six brothers. Now get into the Kilreas: Kenny, Hec, Wally, Jack — he ran the camera shop — Brian played for Eddie Shore down in Springfield.

JAKE: Right next to Kilrea's Camera Shop was Stewart's poolroom. It was called "The Sewer" and all the gang played pool there. CPP Telegraph was at the corner.

FRANK: Crafty Crawford, Justine Bow, and then there was Ebbe Goodfellow, a hell of a hockey player, Harvey Rockburn, Ted Lindsay from Renfrew, the Cleghorns, Harold Darragh, Jack Darragh, Eddie Gerard, Punch Broadbent, Cy Denneny, Eddie Gorman from Buckingham, Newsy Lalonde, Les Graham, Des Smith, Roger Smith — his brother played for Pittsburgh same time as Lionel Conacher played over there before he went to The Maroons — Lew Bates, Eddie Finnigan, Joe Matt — went over to the States later — Jack McVicker from Renfrew went to The Maroons, Ray Kinsella, two Conn boys played for Toronto, Maddie Cullin, Quackinbush, Gordie Bruce played for Boston, Hank Blade, Tony Lecarie.

JAKE: All these guys that played pro, semi-pro flooding back into town, into Ottawa for the summer in the '30s. When April came, they all got together. "How are you going?" The camaraderie that existed at that time was wonderful, exceptional.

FRANK: Art Gagnier, Lionel Hitchman played for Boston. A lot of people say he made Eddie Shore as a scorer because they wouldn't go near Hitchman, defence, a tough son of a bitch, long reach, raw-boned, hard to go around — but he never carried the puck fast — a good blocker. Alex Connell, King Clancy, Clint Benedict, Bert McKinley — oh, so many!

JAKE: And Ottawa wasn't a big city then, about twenty thousand and you had that many players coming home every summer. Bill Touhey, D'Arcy Coulson, Harold Starr, Allen Shields, Gerry Lowry, all the Lowrys, Frank Lowry, brother of Tom Lowry of *The Ottawa Journal*, a great guy. Gerry Lowry told me one time that he was involved in a cup final and he threw a stick and they lost 1-0 and they never even put the puck in the net. You were automatically awarded a goal if you threw your stick in those days. Louis St. Denis, Gordie Bruce . . .

FRANK: We played ball, tennis, golf. They all had jobs in the government. We had leave. I got leave from Ottawa Electric, but I got paid all year. The Ahearns, Eddie Gorman — Buckingham.

JAKE: Aurel Joliat. You can imagine in the doldrums of the '30s, in the height of the Depression, suddenly all these guys swarmed back home. You can imagine what were they going to do. That's why some of them got into the bread business, or played ball over at Lansdowne Stadium, or went to The Whip, a place in Hull right next door to Madame Burger's. When you went over the Interprovincial Bridge on the right hand was the Empress Hotel, on the left was Beal's garage and the Regal. That was a great spot the Regal; all the guys met there Sunday morning. "Everything's legal at the Regal," they used to say.

FRANK: The Coulsons owned almost every hotel in Ottawa and Hull, them and the Barnabys. The old Alexander Hotel on Bank Street . . . they say millionaire M.J. O'Brien of Renfrew and the boys met there to form the National Hockey League.

JAKE: Could well have been, because the Russell and the Alexander were the two oldest hotels in Ottawa. The Barnabys fixed up the Gilmour.

FRANK: When I was playing hockey for Ottawa University, 1921, Coulson was backing the hockey club.

JAKE:: Ottawa University was an Irish university. Then the French came in. St. Pat's College was built for the Irish. St. Joseph's Church on Laurier Avenue is across from Sacred Heart. And where is the front door to St. Joseph's? Well, it's not on Laurier; it's at the side, because they wouldn't face each other directly. There was a fight between the Irish and the French . . .

FRANK: When I was there the two head priests were Father Legault and Father Cleary, one French and one Irish. And that was in the old building right on Laurier Avenue. And my picture, if they haven't taken it down, is still there.

JAKE: King Clancy's father, Tom, taught there when he was a young academic. And old Tom Boucher, father of all the Bouchers, ran a hotel, played football and after a game he'd get out on the hotel veranda in Lowertown and they'd all cheer him and he'd wave. He played for Ottawa University; it was in the big league then.

FRANK: A good Protestant that played for Ottawa U was Bob McCredie of Shawville. He played with Tom Clancy and Tom Boucher. King's dad got to be quite a drinker — like a lot of hotel keepers — and King's dad said, "Son, if you promise to never take a drink, I'll never take another drink." And that's why Clancy was a teetotaller.

JAKE: But lots of times people would think he was half-cut because he was such a cut-up . . .

JAKE: And there was Johnny Wilkinson. I think he played in Boston one year, but he played over in England a lot.

FRANK: At that time they had a league over there and a lot of fellows that were single went over there. They were not going to make the National Hockey League; there were only six teams.

JAKE: So they had the choice of playing in the City League and get relatively nothing or go to England.

J.P. Jack Darragh (left) at his peak was a member of the "Super Six" in a lineup with Clint Benedict, Cy Denneny and Sprague Cleghorn. He jumped from Cliffsides to Ottawa Senators in a championship year, 1910–11, and went on to win three more Stanley Cups. He never played for any other city but his home town.

E.G. "Eddie" Gerard (right) was born in Ottawa in 1890. He joined the Ottawa Senators in 1913–14 and became team captain in 1920–21. Winner of four Stanley Cups he finally retired in 1934–35 when The Senators were sold to the St. Louis Eagles.

FRANK: Oh yes, there was Leo Gravelle from Aylmer; Joe Matt from Buckingham; Bill Phillips from Smith Falls; Hank Stavenough, Arnprior; Lorne Anderson, Renfrew; and Larry Gilmour, Thaine Simon, and Roy and Jack Geisebrecht, and Harry Cameron of Pembroke . . .

JAKE: And Dave Martel, Morley Bruce, Roly Hurd, Sam Godin, Hib Mylks, Bob Boucher, all of Ottawa, and Murph Chamberlain of Shawville, and Johnny Sorell, Cornwall . . . And Connie Brown, Terry Murray, Hambly Shore, Harry Hullman, Spiff Campbell, Gene Chenore, Milt Halliday — all of Ottawa.

These players — all of Ottawa — went on to star with The Senators during the "Roaring Twenties" and the "Dirty Thirties," winning The Stanley Cup four times during the first decade of the N.H.L. The Senators became the true champions of the world, unrivalled in their achievement until the 1950s when the Montreal Canadiens would win five consecutive Stanley Cups.

4

THE CHAMPIONS OF THE WORLD

"It was nothing but the best for us, the best food, the best trav-eling, the best accommodation — the Waldorf Astoria in New York, the Leland in Detroit, the Congress in Chicago, the King Edward in Toronto."

—Frank Finnigan

When the National Hockey League was created in November 1917, the Ottawa Senators were a founding member, along with four other teams — Montreal Canadiens, Montreal Wanderers, Toronto Arenas, and Quebec Bulldogs. During the next decade, The Senators won the Stanley Cup four times — in 1919–20, 1920–21, 1922–23, and 1926–27. Senator great Frank Nighbor won the first Hart Memorial Trophy in 1924, presented annually to the most valuable player in the N.H.L., and the first and second Lady Byng Trophy in 1925 and 1926, awarded for gentleman-ly conduct combined with a high standard of playing ability. Senators Punch Broadbent in 1922 and Cy Denneny in 1924 won the Art Ross Trophy for leading the league in scoring. The"Roaring Twenties" were indeed the glory years of the Ottawa Senators, but long before the"Dirty Thirties" ended in World War II, The Senators had disbanded and the heroes of the capital city of hockey were dispersed around the league, sold to the highest bidder. Players of such high caliber as Frank Nighbor, Frank "King" Clancy, Clint Benedict, Harry "Punch" Broadbent, Cy Denneny, Alec Connell, Hec Kilrea, George Boucher, Harold and

Jack Darragh, Eddie Gerard, Allen Shields, Bill Touhey, Hooley Smith, Frank Boucher, Syd Howe, and Frank Finnigan would not wear an Ottawa sweater in the N.H.L. after 1933–34.

For the first seven years of their time in the N.H.L., The Senators were managed by Tommy Gorman, coached by Pete Green, and led on the ice by Frank Nighbor. Although The Senators strug-

Led by Captain Eddie Gerard, the Stanley Cup champion Ottawa Senators of 1919–20 included H. Merrill, S. Cleghorn, J.G. Boucher, M. Bruce, H. Broadbent, J.P. Darragh, C. Benedict, J. Mackell, C. Denneny, F. Nighbor — and executives P. Green, E.P. Dey, T.E. Ahearn, T.P. Gorman, F. Dolan.

gled through the 1917–18 and 1918–19 seasons, they returned to championship form the next season, winning the N.H.L. league title and defeating Seattle Metropolitans in The Stanley Cup, which was still a challenge cup at that time.

Bill Galloway recounts the Ottawa — Seattle series as follows:

Seattle Metropolitans journeyed East to meet Ottawa, at Dey's Arena, for The Stanley Cup. Dey's Arena had natural ice and the outcome of the series depended heavily on the weather. Ottawa won the first game on a soft ice surface on March 22nd by a 3–2 margin before a sellout 7500 fans. The second game on March 24th was again won by the Senators, 3–0, on a water covered rink. The third game on March 27th was a farce. With more than an inch of water covering the ice, Seattle came out on top,

3–1. It was decided to move the remaining game to Toronto's Mutual Street Arena where artificial ice was available. Seattle won the first game in Toronto 5–2 but were soundly defeated 6–1 on April 1st, 1920, and Ottawa left for home, clutching their sixth Stanley Cup.

Ottawa Senators Stanley Cup Winning Team, 1923–24.

Back row, LEFT TO RIGHT —E.P. Dey (President), Clint Benedict, Frank Nighbor, Jack Darragh, Francis "King" Clancy, Tommy Gorman (manager), Pete Green (coach).

Front row — Harry "Punch" Broadbent, George "Buck" Boucher, Eddie Gerard, Cyril "Cy" Denneny, and Harry Helman.

The Senators superiority on the ice and Ottawa's love for the team had been translated by the Gorman family into a box office success. Over 7,000 fans from a total Ottawa population of 70,000 regularly packed Dey's Arena on Laurier Avenue, paying $1.25 to $5.00 for a ticket. In 1919–20 there was even talk that Ottawa could support two N.H.L. franchises, and it was rumored that the Montreal Canadiens team would move to the capital. Hockey mania swept the city, such that even Parliament emptied out early on hockey night in Ottawa. *The Ottawa Citizen* reported on how The Senators drew fans from throughout the region: "Fifty coon-coated young bloods, Shawville's elite (rye whiskey flasks, no doubt, stuck in their inner greatcoat pocket) swept down to Senator games on the Push, Pull and Jerk from 'up the line.'"

The Senators won the Stanley Cup again the next year as their dynasty built. The team was led in scoring by Cy Denneny, who placed second in the league, two points behind Newsy Lalonde, his fellow Cornwall native.

As Bill Galloway reports, The Senators successful defence of the the Cup was unexpected:

The Senators finished a dismal third in the league in 1920–21 and were not given much of a chance to repeat as Cup winners when they met Toronto, in Ottawa, on March 10, 1921. Senators showed their old form in shutting out the St. Pats, 5–0. The teams went to Toronto on March 14th and again the high flying Senators emerged victors by a 2–0 count. The Senators headed West to meet the Pacific coast champions for The Stanley Cup.

The largest crowd ever to watch a hockey game in Canada to that time packed the Vancouver Denman Arena on March 21, 1921, to watch Vancouver Millionaires lose a squeaker to the Senators, 2–1. Ottawa won the second game on March 24th, 4–3, while the third game on March 28th ended in a 3–3 draw. Vancouver won the fourth game, 3–2, and the stage was set for the final contest on April 4th. Thousands of fans were turned away as The Senators eked out a 2–1 win and returned to a modest celebration in Ottawa with their seventh Stanley Cup.

Although Harry"Punch" Broadbent won the N.H.L. scoring championship in 1921–22, The Senators relinquished The Stanley Cup to Toronto St. Pats, who were becoming an arch-rival. In 1922–23, The Senators reclaimed the Cup, led by N.H.L. MVP Frank Nighbor.

The final playoff series, against Montreal Canadiens, was especial-ly memorable, as Bill Galloway reports:

The eighth Stanley Cup by an Ottawa team was won in 1923. The Senators bet out the Montreal Canadiens, who now had acquired the great Aurel Joliat, by a single point to win the championship. The Senators and Canadiens met in a two-game, total-goal series on March 7th in Montreal. Led by Clint Benedict, Ottawa shutout the Habs 2–0 in one of the wildest, dirtiest hockey games ever played in a Cup series. Sprague Cleghorn and Billy Coutu of the Canadiens ran wild, using fists, sticks, and elbows to injure and render helpless any player in a barber-pole uniform.

Both Canadiens players were ejected from the game. Canadiens general manager Leo Dandurand did not wait for the league to take action. He immediately suspended both players and they were not in the lineup in Ottawa on March 9th when Canadiens beat the Senators 2–1, to lose the total goal series by a single goal. Outraged fans demanded jail sentences and banishment for life from hockey for the two Canadien ruffians, but nothing

Ottawa citizens welcome home their 1923 Stanley Cup winners.

came of it and Ottawa headed West to meet Vancouver Millionaires for The Stanley Cup.

At the Denman Arena before a sellout crowd, Punch Broadbent of Ottawa scored the only goal of the game as the Senators won the first game, 1–0. The Millionaires won the second game on March 19th, 4–1, but lost the third on March 23rd by a close 3–2 score. The final game, on March 26th, saw the great Ottawa team outclass The Millionaires to win 5–1 and advance against Edmonton Eskimos who had arrived in Vancouver on March 24th and were awaiting the winner of the Ottawa-Vancouver series.

Ottawa defeated the Eskimos 2–1 in the first of a best two of three series played in Vancouver. The second game was played on March 31, 1923, and saw the great, Frank "King" Clancy of Ottawa play every position, including goal, as The Senators downed the Eskimoes, 1–0, to win The Stanley Cup. Ottawa goalie Clint Benedict had been given a two minute penalty for slashing and, as he headed for the penalty bench, handed his goal stick to Clancy, saying, "Here kid, take care of this place till I get back." King Clancy followed Benedict's instructions to the letter while Harry "Punch" Broadbent scored the only goal of the game. When The Senators left for Ottawa, Frank Patrick of The Millionaires called them "the greatest team he had ever seen."

The Senators arrived in Ottawa on a right, sunny day in April. They were accorded the biggest, civic reception ever given a Stanley

T.P. Tommy Gorman (left) was another one of Ottawa's early Renaissance sportsmen. He managed or coached seven Stanley Cup teams — three Senator, two Canadiens, one Chicago, and one Montreal Maroons team. Born in Ottawa in 1886 he was for many years Sports Editor of **The Ottawa Citizen.** *He is honored as a "Builder" in the Hockey Hall of Fame.*

T. Franklin Ahearn (right) was the pride, the power, and the passion behind Ottawa's great N.H.L. days of the 1920s. The stars of his time all held him in the highest esteem. His hockey losses were estimated at $200,000 but he said he never regretted a penny. He was born in Ottawa 1886 and died there in 1962. He, too, is a Hockey Hall of Fame inductee.

Cup team. Thousands lined the parade route, blocking Rideau and Sussex Streets at the rear of the Union Station as The Senators arrived by train. Fox-Movietone newsreel cameramen recorded the event for the theaters. There was no doubt, this Ottawa Senator team were worthy Champions.

At the end of the 1922–23 season, the high-flying Senators were sold by the Gorman family to a group of Ottawa businessmen headed by Frank Ahearn, whose father, Thomas Ahearn, owned Ottawa Electric and the famous Ottawa Electric Streetcar Line. Like so many entrepreneurs before him — lumber barons like J.R. Booth and mining moguls like M.J. O'Brien — and so many after him, Ahearn invested his fortune in his team, often risking corporate insolvency to sponsor The Senators. Thomas Ahearn was born on Le Breton Flats in Ottawa, worked as a telegraph operator for J.R. Booth, and became not only a highly respected businessman but also a well-loved Member of Parliament. To house their new team, the Ahearn's built a new 10,000 seat arena on Argyle Street called The Auditorium, which was well-served by Ottawa Electric Streetcars bringing fans to the ticket gates. They chose Dave Gill to coach the team and awaited another Stanley Cup.

The Senators lost to the Canadiens in the 1923–24 N.H.L. playoffs, even though The Auditorium was packed to overflowing with over 10,000 fans for the series. The Cup was won the next year by Victoria Cougars and then in 1925–26 by Montreal Maroons.

Shown here is the cover of the program for the final game of the 1926–27 Stanley Cup.

The program lists the starting lineup for the last Ottawa Senator team to win The Stanley Cup.

Civic Banquet
and
Citizens' Testimonial
to the
Ottawa Hockey
Club
· Champions ·
of the World
1927

Chateau Laurier~Thursday, May 5th 1927

Featured here are pages from the hand-printed souvenir program of the civic Banquet honoring The Senators.

Autographs

Frank Finnigan
John Gorman
Milton Halliday

George Boucher
Cyril Denneny
Alex Smith
Alex Connell
King Clancy
Frank Nighbor
S.E. Webber Porter

OTTAWA HOCKEY TEAM

❖

ALEC. CONNELL
"Bears his blushing honors thick upon him"

FRANK M. (KING) CLANCY
"I go, I go, look how I go—Swifter than arrow from the Tartar's bow"

GEORGE (BUCK) BOUCHER
"And he smote them hip and thigh with great slaughter."

FRANK J. NIGHBOR
"Here perhaps some seed is sown—The blood a Hercules might own."

CYRIL (CY) DENNENY
"I would applaud thee to the very echo that should applaud again."

REG. J. (HOOLEY) SMITH
"I am a man more sinned against than sinning."

HECTOR KILREA
"A merry man to all the maidens dear;
With captivating grace and golden hair."

FRANK FINNEGAN
"Eyes like the lakes of Killarney for clarity,
Nose that turns up without any vulgarity,
Face like a cherub and hair that is carroty,
Wow—you're a rarity, Finny me boy."

ALEX. SMITH
"Like some tall cliff that deigns to look upon this little world beneath."

JOHN J. ADAMS
"Oh! Jovial 'Jawn' how he dotes
Upon his daily Quaker Oats,
And everybody notes
The smile that won't come off."

EDWARD F. GORMAN
"Yet have I something in me dangerous."

MILTON HALLIDAY
"He wears the rose of youth upon him."

E. P. GLEESON, Trainer

B. DEVINE, Assist. Trainer   DONALD HUGHES, Helper

T. FRANK AHEARN
"This far our fortune keeps an
upward course,
And we are graced with wreaths
of Victory."

DAVID N. GILL
"There's nought in this wide World
pleasure so great
As to sit near a window and lift up
your feet,
Puff away at a Cuba whose flavor
just suits,
And gaze at the World twixt the toes
of your boots."

COMMITTEES

❖

CHAIRMAN
His Worship Mayor John P. Balharrie

TREASURER   SECRETARY
Mr. C. A. Gray   Alderman Wm. R. Low

BANQUET COMMITTEE
Chairman—Controller H. H. McElroy
Alderman D. A. Esdale, Alderman T. E. Dansereau, Alderman Samuel Crooks, Alderman
A. W. Desjardins, Alderman Aristide Belanger, Fred. Bronson, James Meagher
T. H. Clancy, H. W. Briggs, P. D. Wilson, Dr. S. M. Nagle, Dr. R. E. Valin,
P. M. Buttler, J. A. Seybold, Dr. H. L. Sims, E. W. Marshall,
Gordon C. Edwards, M. P., Alfred Eales.

FINANCE COMMITTEE
Chairman—A. H. Fitzsimmons
Controller Arthur Ellis, Controller Frank LaFortune, Alderman McGregor, Forman
Alderman J. A. Forward, Alderman J. W. McNabb, Alderman Jos. Landriault,
Alderman G. M. Geldert, Hon. Dr. J. L. Chabot, Hugh Carson,
C. Jackson Booth, C. A. Gray, Harvey Pulford, G. P. Harris,
W. Lyle Reid, T. P. Murphy, A. J. Freiman,
E. R. E. Chevrier, M. P., A. E. Corrigan,
J. G. McGuire, Dr. A. P. Davies,
Theo Lanctot, L. N. Poulin,
Jos. Laflamme.

PUBLICITY AND PRINTING
Chairman—Mr. W. Macdonald
Controller Ch. J. Tulley, Alderman Eric Query, Alderman George O'Connor, Alderman
E. D. Lowe, Alderman Robt. Ingram, Alderman Ernest Laroche, Alderman Gerald
Sims, Alderman J. W. York, C. J. Frowde, G. O. Julien, J. K. Paisley,
Major F. D. Burpee, Cecil Duncan, B. E. O'Meara, Ed. Baker,
George Church, Edward Phillips, George E. Booth.

GENERAL COMMITTEE
C. Jackson Booth, H. S. Southam, P. D. Ross, Hugh Carson, Hon. H. B. McGiverin,
Major F. D. Burpee, A. H. Fitzsimmons, E. R. Bremner, F. A. Heney, Norman W.
Wilson, A. J. Freiman, E. R. E. Chevrier, M. P., Gordon C. Edwards, M. P., Col. C. M.
Edwards, J. Ambrose O'Brien, J. A. Seybold, J. J. Heney, Jos. Meagher, P. M. Buttler,
Harvey Pulford, A. E. Corrigan, A. J. Major, G. Percy Harris, F. D. Hogg, Hon. Dr.
J. L. Chabot, William Foran, Dr. H. L. Sims, Dr. Andrew Davies, Geo. E. Booth, Harry
Rosenthal, Col. G. P. Murphy, H. W. Briggs, T. P. Murphy, A. F. C. Fiske, A. T. Anderson,
G. O. Julien, Basil E. O'Meara, Eddie Baker, N. G. Larmonth, Frank H. Plant, John Bain,
John Bingham, Dr. R. E. Valin, L. N. Poulin, John Gleeson, John Foley, W. F. C. Devlin,
T. H. Clancy, J. Bower Henry, J. K. Paisley, Clare Brunton, David Gill, Dr. R. H. Parent,
J. A. Pinard, M.L.A., A. E. Honeywell, M.L.A., E. S. Miller,
Mayor Theo Lambert, Theo Lanctot, J. P. Coulson, Joseph Barnaby, Leo Sauve,
Ivor Reece, W. Lyle Reid, T. A. Beament, W. H. Dwyer, Norman Smith,
J. J. Leddy, C. A. Gray, J. A. Machado, J. N. Brownlee, Cecil Duncan,
W. Macdonald, Fred Bronson, Elbert Soper, Chester Frowde,
and the entire City Council.

Not until 1926–27 did The Senators bring home the Cup again, as Bill Galloway reports:

The ninth and final Stanley Cup to be won by an Ottawa team came to Ottawa in 1927. The 1926–27 season saw ten teams in the newly expanded N.H.L. The league was divided into two divisions, the Canadian and the American sections. The Senators won the Canadian championship and met the Montreal Canadiens, led by Howie Morenz and Aurel Joliat, in the sectional final, with the first game in the Montreal Forum. Ottawa stunned the Canadiens by shutting them out 4–0 before 13,500 fans. Canadiens were odds-on favorites to win the Cup and were counting heavily on Howie Morenz when the teams returned to Ottawa to conclude the two-game, total-goal series. Over 10,000 fans jammed the Ottawa Auditorium on April 4th to see The Senators hold Canadiens to a 1–1 tie and advance to the Cup finals against Boston Bruins.

The Senators traveled to Boston to play the first two games of the Cup finals. The first game, on April 7th, ended in a 0–0 draw after twenty minutes overtime. Ottawa won the second game on April 9th, 3–1, and the teams headed for Ottawa to finish the series. The third game, April 11, ended in a 1–1 draw, setting the stage for the finale, in the Auditorium, on April 13, 1927. The fourth and final game was a fairly mild affair until midway through the third period when a series of fights broke out, eventually precipitating a riot, resulting in fines ranging from fifty to sixteen hundred dollars. One Boston player, Billy Coutu, was suspended and expelled from the N.H.L. for life and never played another hockey game in the league. President Frank Calder was praised by the media for his prompt action in punishing the perpetrators.

Ottawa did prevail in the final game 3–1, with two goals by Cy Denneny and one by Frank Finnigan. The victory was celebrated at a huge civic banquet, attended by political and sports dignitaries, at the Chateau Laurier. The Ottawa Senators hockey team would have little to celebrate between this 9th Stanley Cup victory banquet and the press conference called at the Chateau Laurier in 1990 to announce the "Bring Back The Senators" campaign.

The Senators have not won a Stanley Cup since 1927 and the team began a slow collapse into ignomy the next year as rumors of financial problems with the team's owners grew.

My father always claimed that Frank Ahearn was under pressure from Thomas Ahearn, his father, to get out of the risky business of backing an enterprise like a hockey team where profit was always at the mercy of the whims of the crowd. It was even suggested that old Tom wanted his money out. And so father and son were often in direct conflict, particularly since

This is the last Ottawa Senators team to play in the N.H.L., listed here in the 1933–34 General Motors Hockey Broadcast Guide.

OTTAWA SENATORS

THE Dominion capital has had its share of championship Clubs, but in recent years since the advent of big money hockey, they have not been so successful. This year's Club has indicated its strength, which may take them a long way. It is managed and coached by George Boucher, one of the old-time star defence players of the League.

BEVERIDGE, WILLIAM (Bill); 179 lbs.; 5' 10"; Home, Ottawa; 24; Goal. Amateur with New Edinburghs, Ottawa. Tried out with Chicago, 1929—signed Ottawa Senators season 1929-30 and loaned Detroit. Ottawa Senators 1930-31. Loaned to Providence Reds, Can.-Am. League, 1931-32. Ottawa 1932-33.

W. Beveridge

BOWMAN, RALPH (Scotty); 190 lbs.; 5' 11"; Home, Toronto; 22; Defence. Amateur Niagara Falls until 1933, when "pro" scouts picked him up for Ottawa. Thus far is being likened to Eddie Shore. A great hockey heart, he thrives on rough going.

Ralph Bowman

FINNIGAN, FRANK; 157 lbs.; 5' 8"; Born Shawinigan, Que., 1904; Forward. Amateur Montagnards Club. With Ottawa since 1924 except 1931-32, when he was with Maple Leafs. Considered one of the greatest defensive forwards in the game, and this year has a scoring punch.

F. Finnigan

— 20 —

HOWE, SID; 160 lbs.; 5' 10"; Born Ottawa, 1911; Centre. Amateur Ottawa Rideaus. Turned pro with Ottawa, 1929—farmed to London and Syracuse (International League) for couple of years. Ottawa recalled him in 1932-33. Hard worker—good play maker.

Sid Howe

LEDUC, ALBERT (Battleship); 180 lbs.; 5' 9"; Born 1904; Home, Quebec; Right Defence. Amateur 1922 Voltigeur of City of Quebec; 1923-24 Bank Canadienne Nationale, Montreal. Pro 1925-30 with Canadiens. A very colorful player who is living up to his high-powered nickname.

Albert Leduc

ROCHE, DESSE; 162 lbs.; 5' 7"; Born, Kemptville, Ont., 1899; Right Wing. Amateur with Earle on the M.A.A.A. Allan Cup team in 1929-1930. Turned pro with Maroons and traded to Ottawa last season for Wally Kilrea.

Desse Roche

— 21 —

SHANNON, JERRY; 170 lbs.; 5' 11"; 23; Home, Niagara Falls; Left Wing. Amateur Niagara Falls. An amateur who made big time in one jump. A smart, fast forward who has been scoring well this season. With Bowman and Kaminsky, Jerry is carrying the reputation of Niagara Falls Amateur Hockey to a new high level.

Jerry Shannon

SHIELDS, ALLAN; 182 lbs.; 5' 11"; Born Ottawa, 1906; Defence. Amateur with Montagnards, Ottawa, Spring, 1928. 1930-31, Philadelphia. 1931-32, N. Y. Americans. 1932-33, Ottawa. Colorful, two-fisted, fiery temper — loves trouble, but "Pete" is one of the most valuable defence players in the entire league.

Allan Shields

TOUHEY, W. J. (Bill); 155 lbs.; 5' 7½"; Born Ottawa, 1906; Forward. Amateur Ottawa Gunners. Pro with Stratford International League, 1927. Montreal Maroons owned him 1927. Ottawa since 1928, except 1931-32, when loaned to Boston.

W. J. Touhey

WASNIE, NICK; 171 lbs.; 5' 10"; 29; Born, Selkirk, Man.; Forward. The town of Selkirk also gave Johnny Sheppard, Harry Oliver and Joe Simpson to the N.H.L. Has played for Canadiens and N. Y. Americans, previous to his Ottawa connection this year.

Nick Wasnie

— 22 —

ROCHE, EARLE; 168 lbs.; 5' 8"; Born Prescott, Ont., 1901; Left Wing. Amateur with Montreal M.A.A.A. Allan Cup Winners 1929-30. Pro with Maroons 1930-31 and played with Boston before going to Ottawa last season in trade involving Alex Smith. Leading scorer of the league thus far.

Earle Roche

(Not Pictured)

VOSS, CARL; 160 lbs.; 5' 7"; 23. Home, Toronto. Although born in the States, his amateur experience was secured in Toronto with the Marlboros. Prominent in football and hockey while at Queen's University. Professional with Toronto Ravinas, London and Buffalo in the International League. Then to New York Rangers and Detroit Red Wings in the National Hockey League before being traded to Ottawa for Cooney Weiland.

KAMINSKY, MAX; 160 lbs.; 5' 10"; 21; Born Niagara Falls, Ont.; Centre. Kaminsky's entire amateur experience was secured in the Ontario League and most of it while wearing the colors of the Niagara Falls Cataracts. It is interesting to note that of the last year's Cataract team, Kaminsky, Shannon and Bowman are now playing heads-up hockey for the Senators. Max gives every evidence of being a great play-maker and has scored consistently since his arrival in the N.H.L.

HOLLETT, W. H. (Headline); 180 lbs.; 6' 0"; 22; Born North Sydney, Cape Breton Island. Hollett's experience in pro hockey has been most unusual. His ability to play lacrosse professionally convinced him that he could play hockey, so he bought some skates and tried. Last year he played in the Toronto Mercantile League, and this season was taken with the Leafs to their training camp at Kitchener. Farmed out to Buffalo, recalled by the Leafs to aid during Horner's suspension, and now loaned to Ottawa. It is predicted that he will consistently be in the headlines on the sport pages of Canada.

— 23 —

Frank was committed to building a winning team and providing them with nothing but the best in terms of salaries, bonuses, travel, and accommodations. The Crash of 1929 and the onset of the Depression did nothing to help Frank Ahearn, and during the 1931–32 season, he suspended operations, selling some players to rival N.H.L. teams, lending out others, with the hope of re-instating the team for the 1932–33 season.

FRANK FINNIGAN
St. Louis Eagles
Frankie Finnigan has been playing pro hockey since he turned with Ottawa in '24. Finnigan is rated the best back-checker right wing in hockey today. Scored ten goals and got ten assists for Ottawa in '33-'34. Was born in Shawville, Quebec, and has played all his hockey in Ottawa, except for one year when he was loaned to the Maple Leafs, winners of the Stanley Cup that season.

Once-proud Senators found themselves playing for the St. Louis Eagles in 1934–35 before that team disbanded the next season.

Frank "King" Clancy was sold to the Toronto Maple Leafs for $35,000, along with Art Smith and Eric Pettinger, though other star Senators — Frank Finnigan, Hec Kilrea, Alec Connell — were only loaned to N.H.L. rivals, before returning to Ottawa for the 1932–33 season. Significantly, while on loan to The Maple Leafs, Frank Finnigan helped his old teammate King Clancy lead The Leafs to a Stanley Cup victory. Ahearn ran the team for only one other season in Ottawa with a patched-up line-up that included rookie Ralph"Scottie" Bowman before transferring the entire franchise to St. Louis. The once world-champion Ottawa Senators became the St. Louis Eagles, a footnote in N.H.L. history.

An article in The Ottawa Citizen, *under the heading "Buying, Selling Hockey Players Big Business Now," gives a clear indication of Ahearn's motives in"liquidating" The Senators:*

Development and sale of high-class hockey players comes under the head of lucrative business.

Owners of the Ottawa hockey club of the National Hockey League, now sponsoring the Eagles in St. Louis, have sold nearly $200,000 worth of talent that, except in one instance, was home recruited and developed in the last few years.

The first big sale made by the club was made to Montreal Maroons, who paid $22,500 for the services of Reginald Hooley Smith, signed by Ottawa from Toronto Granites, Olympic champions of 1934.

Their next trade of major consequence was the sale of Frank "King" Clancy, dashing defence player, to the Toronto Maple Leafs for $35,000 and players. Clancy was picked up from Ottawa amateur hockey and developed on the Ottawa N.H.L. team.

The Ottawa club developed Hec Kilrea into a great left wing. Toronto bought him for $12,000 cash and players.

Sid Howe was signed to his professional contract by the Ottawa team in 1929, from the Rideau team of the Ottawa City League. Ralph "Scotty" Bowman was signed prior to last season from the Niagara Falls amateur team. Both were recently sold to Detroit Red Wings for $50,000.

This cartoon appeared in a Toronto Maple Leaf game program during the 1932–33 season while Frank Finnigan was "on loan" to The Leafs.

A few days later, Frank Finnigan, recruited from Ottawa amateur ranks and developed to professional stardom by the Ottawa club, was sold to Toronto for $8,000.

Ralph Cooney Weiland, secured in a trade from Boston, was sold by Ottawa for $7,500; Joe Lamb brought $5,000, when first sold to Boston; and the club got $3,000 for the veteran right-wing, Cy Denneny, another Ottawa product. These are in addition to minor sales and to the value of players secured in the various trades.

In later years, my father reflected upon the collapse of The Senators, trying to understand how the glory years of the "Roaring Twenties" became tarnished by the "Dirty Thirties":

After 1927 there weren't the people to support the team. In Ottawa in the mid-Thirties there were only 110,000 to 120,000 people. We didn't start to grow until after the war, 1945.

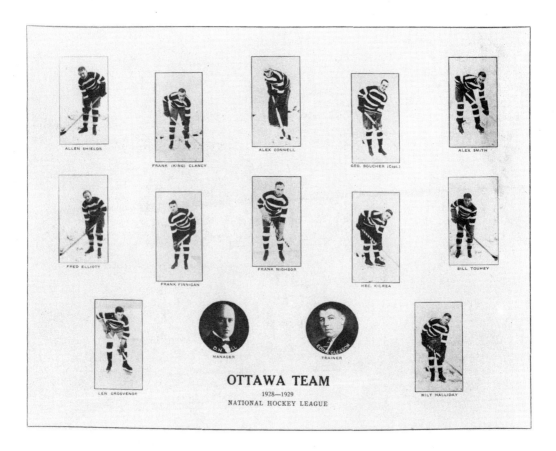

OTTAWA TEAM
1928—1929
NATIONAL HOCKEY LEAGUE

Holland Avenue — that's where the streetcar ended and that was the end of Ottawa in those days. In the Thirties there wasn't a whole lot of money in Ottawa and Hull — the Depression was on — the federal government, Ahearn's Ottawa Street Railway and Ottawa Electric companies, Booths in Hull — those were the big employers.

Instead of trying to strengthen the club by keeping players like Clancy, instead of trying to find some talented new players, they folded the club. They did sign on some new players but they didn't mature fast enough to save the team. Instead of us getting stronger after our 1927 championship, we were becoming like minor league team.

On the other hand, you couldn't expect Frank Ahearn to give entertainment to Ottawa and not break even. After all the Ahearns were big businessmen, and they just got fed up trying to make the team soluble, watching their money go down the drain . . .

St. Louis had a good rink. It was a big cattle palace and the ice surface was 220' by 100' (standard Canadian rink is 85' by 200'). There was a fence up in the stands; the black people sat on one side and the white people sat on the other side. They never packed the arena in St. Louis. Hockey was a new game. They tried a few games in Philadelphia and that didn't go over. Then a game or two in Atlantic City, but that didn't work there either.

By the end of the next season, the St. Louis team also disbanded. The Ottawa Senators name lived on, though, as the city iced a team in the Quebec Senior League . . . and dreamed of the day when a Senators team would again return to the N.H.L. and win a 10th Stanley Cup.

In another conversation, my father reflected upon these golden years which were to turn to dross as The Senators disbanded and his career reached a twilight phase:

The first year, 1923, that I played for the Ottawa Senators, we lost out to Canadiens. But my dreams came true in the 1926-27 season when we brought home The Stanley Cup to Ottawa. There was a big ceremony at the Chateau Laurier and the citizens of Ottawa gave each player an eighteen-carat gold ring with fourteen diamonds set in the shape of an O. A few years ago King Clancy's was stolen and Birk's borrowed mine to make a duplicate for him. On the Senators, King and I became great friends and some sports writers in Ottawa — Eddie Baker, *Journal*, or Bas O'Meara, *Citizen* — called us the Damon and Pythias of hockey. We became good friends and roomed together at the Royal York when we played on Toronto Maple Leafs, but it must have been difficult for King sometimes because he was a tea-totaller then.

I was having my troubles with Tommy Gorman, the manager of The Senators and part owner with Ahearns. My wife always said that it was because he didn't like me at all. But in actual fact Gorman was a real Roman Catholic and he was upset to find out that Frank Finnigan — with a name like Finnigan — was an Ulster Orangeman. For that reason, and because he had a lot of power in the Ottawa Senators then, he tried to undermine me by keeping me on the bench and not playing me very much. I joined The Senators in the spring of 1923, and even into the fall of the second season, he tried to bench me, but then Frank Ahearn bought out the Gorman shares, and when Gorman disappeared, I was on my way. Ahearn was far more interested in building a good hockey team than finding out the religious denomination of his players. But there was all kinds of troubles between the Roman Catholics and the Protestants in those days, and it was too bad. It was sad. But, I believe all that is gone today.

The Senators were pretty evenly split. Clint Benedict, Eddie Gerard, Jack Darragh, Punch Broadbent, Cy Denneny, myself — we were all Protestant. King Clancy, Frank Nighbor, Alex Connell — they were all RC's. Buck Boucher was on the fence. He married a Protestant and brought his family up Protestant so he took neither side. But we'd be arguing a little over some crazy thing and Buck would say to me, "Well, don't bother now. I'll write the Pope about it."

Frank Nighbor was an RC and we always roomed together. And then Alex Connell came on the team and Benedict went to Montreal Maroons. Alex was an RC and we always roomed together. We were good friends and really got along well. And Sunday morning, if we were in New York or somewhere in the States, Alex would always get up for church in the early morning, even though he was tired out from Saturday night's game, and he'd say to me, "You lucky buggar, you Protestant. You can lie here and have a good sleep and I've got to find my way to mass." No, religion never made any difference with us. And race never did either.

Once Gorman left, Frank Ahearn was in charge and we

became really good friends. The Auditorium and the Senators — that was pretty much Ahearn money but they had some shareholders. I couldn't say who they were. They were small shareholders who put in a little money. The Ahearns were taking a revenue off the streetcars — which they owned — bringing hockey followers not only to the pro games, but to the juniors and seniors as well, and anything else that was going on in The Auditorium, like boxing, skating, shows. They were taking a revenue off the streetcars to bring audiences again.

Frank Ahearn, I don't think he ever told me how he got interested in hockey. I think he just liked it as a boy and then he managed some hockey teams before he got into the N.H.L. He lost money every year on the Ottawa Senators. Ottawa, even though it was the cradle of hockey, wasn't large enough to draw big enough crowds to make money enough to keep a professional team. In those days the roads weren't ploughed in winter, so the crowds dwindled in bad weather. The Depression was on and the civil servants were poorly paid.

But even though he was losing money every year — and his father was grumbling about it all the time — Frank Ahearn was a perfect gentleman to us all, all the time. It was nothing but the best for us, the best food, the best traveling, the best accommodation — the Waldorf Astoria in New York, the Leland in Detroit, the Congress in Chicago, the King Edward in Toronto. And we always had a private railway car attended by porter Sammy Weber.

J.R. Booth's sons, J.R., Jr. (Bobby) and Fred — they were both playboys — used to be going down to New York often and they'd come into our private car and do magic tricks for us. They were really good magicians and they belonged to the Magicians' Association and were learning new tricks all the time.

The club bought the best tickets for us to the best shows. We saw Bing Crosby make his debut in New York at the Paramount Theater on Broadway and we met him after the show. Ever after that he was a fan of ours and used to come to the games and sit behind the players' benches and talk to us during the games, especially to Hec Kilrea and me. We saw Al Jolson in *Sonny Boy* and when he sang "Sonny Boy" everybody cried.

Sometimes the whole team would go to Harlem to hear the great jazz players, perhaps at the Cotton Club; we saw the Nicholas Brothers, famous tap-dancers, and we heard Duke Ellington, Lena Horne, Fats Waller, Cab Calloway, Count Basie. Calloway was my favorite.

Some of us would go into Jack Dempsey's bar after a game across from Madison Square Gardens. Have a beer and shake hands with Jack. He was finished boxing by then and he was the front man.

I used to love to tell my kids, or anybody else for that matter, that "I was in Sing Sing." Yes, Red Horner, Andy Blair, and myself, with two detectives, had the tour of Sing Sing when

Frank Ahearn at his summer place at Thirty-One Mile Lake in the Gatineau where he royally entertained his Ottawa Senators.

Hauptman was in Death Row and ready to walk the last mile for the kidnapping and murder of the Lindberg baby. I remember some of the prisoners were out on a field playing soccer but, most of all, I remember their cells — a bed two feet wide and a one-and-a-half foot space beside the bed. The floors were marble and that narrow walkway beside the beds was all worn down from men pacing like animals in a cage.

Chicago was a city in the grip of Al Capone and his mobsters. That was the time of Prohibition and speakeasies and bad liquor. Billy Birch from Hamilton and Lionel Conacher from Toronto — both then playing for New York Americans — and myself went into one of the hotels that was one of Al Capone's haunts, and we saw him there. It was a speakeasy with a dancing show.

In the Brunswick in Boston we used to meet Babe Ruth and Lou Gehrig on the elevators and in the lobby. Hec Kilrea, Alex Connell, Buck Boucher, King Clancy, and myself would talk sports with them.

Frank Ahearn used to have the team up to his summer place at Thirty-One-Mile Lake in the Gatineau. It was a huge island with main lodge, cabins, boathouse, icehouse. We boated, fished, played tennis, ate, and lived like kings. There was a cook, servants, handymen . . .

It's a funny thing but during my hockey career I played at the opening of three arenas. The first season I played for Ottawa

The advertisements in the programs for The Senators games appealed to both sexes.

Senators in 1923-24, that was the first winter the new Ottawa Auditorium was in business on Argyle Street in Ottawa. Then in 1927 the Ottawa Senators met the New York Americans in the opener at Madison Square Gardens. At the New York opening the crowds came in their evening dresses and furs, tails, and top hats. It was the first time we had ever played in a heated arena and we all nearly died of sweat. By 1931 when the new Maple Leaf Gardens was opened on Carlton Street in Toronto, I had been traded to Toronto, so I was there for that big opening. And I have been back for the celebrations at the Gardens of both the twenty-fifth and fortieth anniversaries. It's strange to walk down a red carpet on a rink where you used to break away . . .

The greatest character who lived at the Royal York Hotel at the same time I did was Harry McLean, the great railway construction man. He'd always stay there when he was on business in Toronto. McLean, you have to understand, was a giant. Except for Charlie Conacher he made the Toronto Maple Leafs look like midgets. He was about six-foot-five and would weigh about two hundred and thirty, something like Tarzan. No fat on him at all, raw-boned, all muscle, powerful to the end.

I don't know when he slept, but he would come up to our door at all hours of the night and pound on it until we answered. Yell, and pound, yell out, "Get up, you bastards!" We'd maybe have practice the next morning and we'd pretend to be asleep. But he'd just roar there until we got up — Conacher, Jackson, maybe myself. Nothing would do but we'd go up to his room. Sometimes he just wanted to drink — he always drank Johnny Walker's Red Label — but other times he wanted to eat. I have seen him order everything up to his room, all the food maybe, including oysters or a tank of lobsters. One time I remember he even ordered up the cook and had him cook the whole meal in his room. Another time he paid part of the Royal York orchestra to come up to his room and play for us . . .

I held my own for fourteen years with the "Great Ones" — Jackson, Joliat, Morenz, Clancy, Shore. To me, Morenz was the greatest. He was like a bird when he took off.

Yes, they used to say I was "untrippable." I had great balance. I was a very good right wing; Selke says it in his book. Looking back on myself, I can now honestly say I was a good stick handler, a good skater, a good defensive man in a tight spot. I was hard to get at because I always kept my shoulders forward, hard to hit, and I could hang on to the puck. I had two rules: it was my puck until I found the right place to put it; and never pass to a guy who is covered.

In 1937 I hung up my skates. I had played fourteen years with the best of them. In those days there wasn't the kind of training you get today. I was slowing down. I wanted to quit while I was up. I always said I would quit while I was up . . .

On August 19, 1987, I went to Quyon to interview the McArras family, who at the turn of the century had run the Norway Bay Ferry. Nobody was home, so I drove past Gervais O'Reilly's house, and there he was sitting out on his veranda looking for someone to talk with. Gervais is a fine fiddler and storyteller. I found him in a rare good mood:

I met Frank Finnigan not too long ago somewhere and I said to him, "What do you think of Wayne Gretzky as a player, Frank?" And he said, "Well, if we'd had him back in my time, we would have just heaved him over the boards."

Gervais then went on and told a superb hockey story about King Clancy and fellow Ottawa native Aurel Joliat, whom my father always considered a great hockey player, and certainly one of the greatest skaters who ever skated:

King Clancy really had it out for Joliat in this game and he had sworn that he was "going to get him really good." Of course, Joliat could skate so fast and stop and turn on the edge of a dime. So Clancy had missed him and missed him again, and it's getting on into the third period. So the next time Aurel Joliat came close to Clancy, Clancy headed straight for him to nail him. And Aurel, the little Frenchman, threw back at Clancy in a loud voice, "Come on, Clancy! You couldn't hit me with a handful of wet peas!"

Another time, W.J. Conroy of Aylmer told me these tales of Frank "King" Clancy:

King Clancy in later years came down to our tennis club in Ottawa, the Rideau Club, and I taught him how to play tennis. But I knew King before that. He used to come here to Aylmer and practice. He was older than I was, and he'd get onto the rink down there, and we'd all be skating around, and Eddie Gerard used to come up with him. He came down to the club and we got reunited. He was a hell of a nice chap.

King Clancy, he went around with Spiff Campbell. He played for The Rangers in New York and he was a great friend of Frank's. But he was a real booze hound and Frank was a teeto-

Frank "King" Clancy was perhaps the most colorful and likeable player in the N.H.L. during his playing career with The Senators and The Leafs. Advertisers rushed to gain his endorsement.

taller. He wouldn't touch it at all — or smoke. And he was always getting poor Spiff out of trouble. Spiff threw a party for them in New York and they were all drinking and everything and when they went to leave the party there was only one coat left. Somebody'd taken Spiff's coat and there was an undertaker's coat hanging there. Spiff didn't know what to make of it, he was so mad. Frank thought that was very funny.

So Spiff had to wear the undertaker's coat home. I don't know what it looked like exactly, or what the undertaker would be doing in the Club either. Maybe looking for business!

Frank Clancy didn't like the nickname "King." His father was called King Clancy. I don't know whether it was his real name or not, but he was known as King Clancy, and then it just fell to Frank, and some of us that knew him for quite a few years never got in the habit of calling him that. He didn't like it and he didn't make any fuss about it, but now and again he'd drop it, and he'd say, "That's my father's name. It's not my name."

He was quite a religious type, too, you know. There was a religious holiday in the summer in the Catholic church, and "King" was leading the parade down Bank Street, right in front. He wouldn't miss it; he was there every year. It was one of the big feasts and they had a parade. And he wouldn't miss that for ANYTHING! And Frank was very good to his family. His sister, she had a bit of trouble, and everything like that, and Frank looked after them, and the family down in Sandy Hill. Spiff Campbell never had a job after he quit hockey but he traveled all over the place with Frank, and Frank paid for everything. He was very good that way. After you'd finished hockey, you'd be lucky if you'd run into a Harold Ballard like Clancy did, but how many of them got that lucky!

Frank was one of the lightest defencemen in the N.H.L. We always said he was just as light in the head because he'd stand in front of the CPR train coming down the track and try to stop it, you know. He was that way. There wasn't an inch of Frank's body there wasn't a scar on. He was scarred from his neck to his feet. We'd be taking a shower at the tennis club and we'd say, "Where'd you get that one, Frank?" He'd say, "Wait a minute now, I think that was over in Chicago."

He never won a fight in his life. But as a defenceman, you know, his idea of stopping a guy was to stand in front of him. He'd stop the guy all right, but he'd land about twenty-five feet down the rink on his back — with another scar!

He was no good at tennis. He couldn't even count. I'll tell

you what he did to me. We were playing over at the Rideau Club in one of the city tournaments, a handicap tournament. That means that if you had a thirty or forty handicap, you had to win three points before you started to count. And you couldn't afford to drop a point, and, of course, every kid entered the thing and they'd get out there and they just batted all over the place, and if they happened to be lucky, you were down a game. And you played all afternoon to win, you see.

And Frank Clancy comes along as a referee, and I know he must have found out I was playing on one of the back courts, and he came over and he got up on this ladder and I played, I'll swear, three hours, beating a little kid that didn't know what the game was all about and killing myself. I got mad and I hit a drive and it landed far inside the line, you know. A pure fluke. Clancy says, "Out." Holy gee, what can you say? And he's sitting there nice and cool and everything and here I am running all over the court. So I won the match — anybody could have, I guess — and I came off and I said, "What the hell is the matter? Are you blind?" He said, "Why?" I said, "The one you called 'Out.' " "Oh," he said, "I knew you'd get that back." "Get it back!" I said. " I could have been out of the game by the time I got it back!" I had to play about four games to get that thing back. He was just having fun. Playing tricks really, eh?

When Pine Lodge at Norway Bay first started in the 1930s, Frank and Spiff drove my wife and me and friends of ours, Cracker Bell and his wife, up when they only had one cabin and the main lodge, but Frank and Spiff drove us up about two o'clock in the morning, so we hardly knew where we were, you know. And there was a great big bandsaw blade hung underneath the floor and they hit that with a sledge at about six o'clock in the morning for breakfast. And the whole building shook. Scared the daylights out of us! We didn't know what was happening. After that we used to go quite often. They had a nine-hole course; it was just like playing out in the back pasture, but it was a lovely spot.

I can remember when Frank used to drive down to Montreal from Toronto and he'd drive all night, and going down he drove so fast that he'd collect about four or five tickets on the way down. But he had to get there. I remember him telling us how many hours it took him and how many tickets he got.

For forty-seven years, until fairly recently, Charlie Kenny actively worked in a senior capacity in his family lumbering business, the McLaren Mills at Buckingham, Quebec. He has fond memories of the Boucher boys who played in this era for The Senators:

I knew all the Bouchers. They all had cottages on McGregor Lake, Frank and Buck and George. I spent more time with them than I did at home. I could tell stories by the hour; they were a great bunch. When they played with the Old Pros, they played baseball, hardball, in Ottawa. They played once a week. There was Wally Durand, George Boucher, Frank Boucher, Bill Beveridge, Boots Smith, Bill Cowley. When they'd go to the lake I'd go with them and I'd be their water boy there. I'd go several times in the summer. I didn't get home very early, there were many stops on the way. The last one was at Perkins Mills. Of course the drinking didn't bother me — I was only a kid then. I used to stay up at the cottage with my older brother and a shanty cook. Dad and Mother only came up weekends, so they didn't know what time it was when I got in with Bouchers, but it was a late night for me. I had great fun though.

It was different in those days, you know. They used to have a canteen — a little hotdog stand on the beach at the end of the lake — and as kids we went down there every night until three or four in the morning. I never saw liquor. I really didn't. We'd have a soft drink. Now, today, kids don't know how to entertain themselves. We'd have a hotdog and build a campfire and sing songs. Frank Boucher, Sr., lived right across the road and he'd come over, and he had a fellow from New York that stayed there a lot with him and they'd play guitar for us. They'd bring a drink, but I never saw the kids, and I'm talking kids of seventeen or eighteen or nineteen, with a drink. George Boucher used to tell the story of Alex Connell borrowing Frank Ahearn's good 'coon coat, a beautiful thing. Connell took it down to the tailor's and had it altered to fit him. Ahearn was a big guy and when he tried to put this beautiful 'coon coat on again — well, you can imagine!

George was coaching hockey in St. Louis one time and a fellow wired the toilet seat and one of the big guys came out and sat on it from out of the shower and it gives him a jolt and jee! It nearly kills him!

Old Frank used to talk about Ching Johnston. Two minutes to go before the game he would say to Les Patrick, "You're not going to play me," and he would drink everyone's beer, and go back to the dressing room just before the game and he'd take all their false teeth and he'd put them in different glasses — one over here and one over there — and switch them all around. Of course, in those days they'd had so many teeth knocked out, they had no protection, that they were all probably wearing false teeth. And there would be pandemonium before the game as they tried to find their own false teeth! Another time they were

Born in Ottawa, 1901, Frank Boucher (left) was a member of another hockey-playing family — George with Ottawa, Gilly and Bob with Canadiens, Frank with Vancouver and New York Rangers. He won the Lady Byng Trophy so many times he was finally given permanent possession of it.

George Boucher (right) was a great halfback with the Ottawa Rough Riders before he joined the Ottawa Senators in 1915 to become an outstanding defenceman. His team won the Stanley Cup four times. He ended his playing career with the Montreal Maroons and Chicago Black Hawks but returned to Ottawa to coach the Senior Senators to an Allan Cup victory in 1948–49.

catching a train at Chicago to get to New York that night right after the game, and he went in to the dressing room early and cut all their pants off at the knees. And they had to go like that!

Dad always went to Ottawa for hockey games when The Senators were playing. He had six tickets right in front of the Governor-General's box, on the boards there. Bill Beveridge was goalie and there was Allen Shields, there was Ted Leach from Niagara Falls, there was Kiminsky, there was Shannon, and Bill Touhey with the comb. Oh cripes! He never came on the ice that he wasn't combing his hair! He'd have a little comb and he'd step on the ice and he'd be combing his hair. And the two Roaches were there when I used to go, Des and Earl Roache. Old

Frank Boucher and the two Cooks were playing for The Rangers there, and then when the Quebec Senior League took over, I had seats there but I moved up one row behind the box because it was different pucks then. As long as the Senators were there, I used to go to every game. I never missed one.

Frank and George and Billy Boucher, they were really a very sporting family. Then I think there was a brother Carl that lived in Aylmer. One time Carl's wife sent him down to the corner store in Ottawa to get a loaf of bread and a pound of butter and he never came back. George was playing with The Rangers then in New York, and one day at practice he looked up and he saw Carl in the crowd. He was with Ringling Brothers! And George talked Carl into going home, and when he went home he arrived in with a loaf of bread and a pound of butter. He'd been gone nine years! Carl had run away with the circus.

One time there was a guy going all around here saying he was Billy Boucher. I was just married and came in and he said, "I'm Billy Boucher." I said, "Oh, that's good." So he told me that he had come down to Buckingham and met a bunch of the guys in the Palace Hotel and had overspent and hadn't enough left to get him back to Ottawa. He said, "Could you lend me ten or twenty bucks?" I knew there had been a guy going all over the country, including Montreal, imitating Bill Boucher, and he was said to know more about the Bouchers than Bill did.

"Oh," he said, "you're a friend of George's. You're always at this place at McGregor Lake."

I said, "Well, I haven't got any money on me, but are you going to be around for a while?" He said, "Oh yes." So I said, "I've got to go to the bank after my dinner. If you want to wait until two or two-thirty and come back, I'll give it to you."

I got on the phone and I phoned Bill Boucher because I knew him. He coached the Aylmer Hockey Team when I was a manager of the Junior team here. And Bill said, "Can you keep him there?" I said, "Well, he's not supposed to come back till two-thirty." He said, "I'll be right down." So he brought that big police-man in Ottawa, a detective — he's dead now — Bill Hobb's side-kick.

I said, "I watched where he went and he went into the Palace Hotel. I think he's till there." So they went up and they arrested him. Well, the Ottawa police couldn't arrest him because they didn't know him. But he passed bum cheques and he always imitated Bill Boucher and they put him in the jail here. Bill was boiling and he wanted to go in. "Let me go in there.

Give me ten minutes with him and then you can have him." They nailed him. That's a long time ago.

J.D. Dunfield of Ottawa, in October 1992, looked fondly back on the Ottawa Senators of the early 1930s:

I lived on the corner of Metcalfe and Waverly, which was about four short blocks from the old Auditorium. I believe the Old Ottawa Senators must have often played on Saturday nights because I was not allowed out on the weeknights while going to school.

With my small weekly allowance and the profits from the sale of the *Saturday Evening Post*, I was able to purchase the 25 cent "rush-end" standing room tickets. If you arrived about an hour before a game you could usually find room to stand up against a steel hand-rail about half way up the end zone at the south end of the rink.

This was the best position to secure the odd hockey puck that ricocheted up into the stands. Thank goodness the players did not use the"slap" shot in the 1930s as there was not any protective glass around the boards.

Of course, the goalie did not wear any face mask and the forwards and defence might have had Eaton's catalogues under their stockings for shin pads.

The care of the ice was labor intensive. After each period three men would come out with long-handled brooms which had faggots or twigs tied around the end of each pole, with a wide sweeping motion the three men would work their way from one end of the ice to the other end, after which the small ridges of snow would be pushed down to one end with handplows and shoveled into a trap-door behind the goal posts just off the ice surface.

There were only six teams in the N.H.L. in those days and Ottawa was in the "Big League." At one time Montreal and New York City had two teams but it was generally a six-team league. Player trades were not common and you could remember the names of most of the players on each team. Ottawa was the cradle of hockey talent with the Finnigans, Kilreas, Cowley, Beveridge, Connell, etc., filling the rosters of many teams.

Budge Crawley, the great Canadian film-maker, once told me of an encounter with three Ottawa Senators off ice that forever changed his life:

I was just a little gaffer about ten when my father (he was chief accountant for lumber baron J.R. Booth) decided that my table manners had improved enough to allow him to take me out to dinner. At that time the Tea Gardens was the place to dine in

During his 1927–28 year with the Ottawa Senators Alex Connell set a goaltending record, registering six consecutive shutouts. He was known as the "Ottawa Fireman," partly because he worked with the Ottawa Fire Department and partly because he "put out the fire of opposing marksmen."

Hector "Hec" Kilrea starred for The Senators in the late 1920s and early 1930s before joining teammates Frank Finnigan and Frank Clancy with The Leafs. He was said to be "a merry man to all the maidens dear."

Ottawa. I discovered that the pre-dinner rolls were unlimited and was well into my seventh or eighth when a big fight broke out on the balcony above between the Ottawa Senators (my father identified them: Frank Finnigan, Harold Starr, Harold Darragh) and the Chinese men who owned the restaurant. At first they used their fists. One of the Chinese men came right over the balcony and down on the tables below. Can you imagine that! Real cowboys and Indians! Then the Chinese men went into the kitchen and came out with their red-hot pokers. I don't remember much after that. I suspect that the restaurant diners cleared out and that my father led me away. But I know now that that was the beginning of my film career.

From as early as I can remember my mother was a loyal fan of I. Norman Smith, both as a writer and as a representative of a paper with integrity. She clipped out and kept many of his great Saturday "Window" editorial page pieces which appeared in The Journal. *Although she never spoke it, she must have been pleased when the late Tom Lowery hired me on the at* The Ottawa Journal *as a general reporter. I, too, in my turn cut and clipped some of the best of I. Norman Smith and the other day, in the manner of those coincidences which are not really coincidences but which occur in so much of my life, while working on this hockey chapter I opened an old file and there fell out Smith's tribute for the passing of Tom Lowrey from the Ottawa scene, November 7, 1981. Smith's reminiscences moved me deeply and his closing paragraphs made me wish that I might have been party to, or even overheard, the great sports talk that went on in* The Journal *editorial offices in those days:*

Early Sunday evenings after a big Ottawa sports event a wholly sober talkfest took place at the far end of the big newsroom. Grattan's (O'Leary) favorite perch was on the coil by the window; others nabbed chairs, sat on desks, or in a standing-room-only situation, held up a wall.

According to the year there would be Tom (Lowrey), Baz O'Meara, Walter Gilhooly, Bill Westwick, Bryan White, Eddie McCabe; outsiders like Father Armstrong, [Mayor] Stan Lewis, Jim McCaffrey, and a Gorman. We told our wives we had to go down to check or write something, and sometimes we did. But really it was to get together in the hope we might once again listen to the sights and sounds of Dey's Arena and hear tales of

King Clancy, Jack Dempsey, Frank Amyot, Eddie Gerard, the fabled Mike Mahoney — and even of sports writers. But about that time the night staff claimed it needed the newsroom to get the morning paper out.

In the winter of 1988 it was far too late for me to gather together such famous hockey buffs or to try to recreate a milieu in which such rich sporting talk would be inspired. But I did manage to gather together some men from different walks of life, and different age groups with a wide knowledge of the sport: Roy MacGregor, sports writer and columnist for The Citizen: *Bob Wake of Carleton University, a hockey buff for sixty years; and the two Finnigans — Frank, "The Old Pro Alive," and his son Frank Jr. In this "hot-stove" conversation, they bring back to life the glory years of The Senators:*

FRANK SR.: Eddie Shore — quite a hockey player.

FRANK JR.: He was big. He was good and he was tough and he was Mr. Hockey. He was very much like Bobby Orr. He could stick-handle, carry the puck — same as a forward.

FRANK SR.: All our defencemen in those days could carry the puck the same as a forward. When the puck went into our end the defence didn't wait for a forward to go back and pick up the puck. They rode out, they broke out themselves . . .

FRANK JR.: Remember, you could pass as far as your own blue line. Now, the defencemen, they don't want them carrying the puck too far — so it's a different game. No doubt Orr was as good as I've ever seen. But Shore was TOUGH. Bobby Orr wasn't what you would call rugged — Shore was MEAN.

FRANK SR.: "Here comes Shore." My game plan was to check him down my wing — the same as everybody else. But he'd probably come down — the way Orr used to — and score just the same as Orr would. But Shore was AGGRESSIVE.

ROY: Frank, if you had to check Eddie Shore and you grabbed a hold of him, how quick would they be to call a penalty?

FRANK SR.: Well, not the way they call them today. They seemed to let a little more go in those days. There was more bodychecking in those days. Today if they grab your stick, they get a penalty for it. In my day I might have grabbed the odd stick . . .

FRANK JR.: That's where they brought in that rule: only two steps before charging . . .

FRANK SR.: Red Horner could carry the puck just as well as a forward and oh, a pretty big fellow . . .

BOB: I saw him play a game against Canadiens in Montreal and Canadiens had fast-skating forwards. They were beautiful to watch. And every time they got down past the Toronto blue line, Red Horner would just wrap his arms around them — and the referees let him get away with it.

FRANK SR.: He got away with a lot — knees and stuff, too, you know. Yes, he did. He was really one of those rough hockey players

J.J. Jack Adams (left) was an outstanding player before he became one of the N.H.L.'s innovative executives. He was with Ottawa's Stanley Cup winners in 1926–27; then went on to put Detroit Red Wings on the map, as coach, manager, developer of the farm team, and Gordie Howe.

Another Ottawa great, Clint "Benny" Benedict (right) spent seventeen years in the N.H.L. playing on four Stanley Cups, three with Ottawa and one with Montreal Maroons. Born in 1894 Benedict moved into senior ranks while only fifteen years old. He was the first goalie to try using a face mask.

— that's what stood out for him. It wasn't that he was as spectacular as Hap Day or King Clancy . . .

FRANK JR.: But he kept them honest, Dad. That's what you got to have. If you let them run all over that rink, you are in trouble.

FRANK SR.: The only way they will play honest is to let them make the rinks bigger — another twenty feet wider, twenty feet longer.

FRANK JR.: Oh, Dad, you're exaggerating! You couldn't make them that much bigger. It's true they are making hockey players bigger — big as basketball players — but still . . .

ROY: But I want to know about not wearing helmets, not wearing masks.

FRANK SR.: They should have in my day. I protected myself. I skated pretty low and they hooked, you know, up that way, and got me.

FRANK JR.: When I was playing, some fellas were wearing helmets, in the '50s.

One of the N.H.L.'s colorful tough guys, Sprague Cleghorn (left) had a truly chequered career, playing alongside Cyclone Taylor with the Renfrew Millionaires and with Ottawa's Stanley Cup greats in 1920. When he joined The Canadiens in 1922 he took on a vendetta against Ottawa. Many brawls resulted.

Frank Finnigan's admiration for his opponent Aurel Joliat (right) knew no bounds and grew with time. The "Mighty Atom" or "Little Giant" was born in Ottawa but played for the Canadiens on a line with Howie Morenz and Bill Boucher. He played on three Stanley Cup teams and was on one first and three second All-Star teams.

FRANK SR.: I remember back in the Senior City League days there were fellas that played for the Hull Volants and the Hull Canadiens — they wore helmets, not all, but some.

ROY: Charlie Burns that played for Detroit, he had a steel plate in his head, and he always wore a helmet. And then there was a goaltender in your day, Frank, Clint Benedict.

FRANK SR.: He got an awful hit — one of the Canadians — a puck.

ROY: Interesting. You're saying they should be made to wear masks. But I can't help thinking that in your day, when you had a guy in a corner and you had a real good chance to nail him, something would go up in your mind and you'd say, "I can't really hit his head, or his face." Would you think that?

FRANK SR.: You'd think that. Yes. I never thought of swinging a stick. In those days, very few did.

ROY: Sprague Cleghorn — didn't bother him to swing a stick. Hooley did. Playoffs against Boston.

FRANK JR.: What happened when Hooley Smith was suspended that time? He was suspended for ten games. Quite a blow. Ten games out of a thirty-five-game season. Now they'd get ten years. Must have been a pretty vicious blow.

BOB: Frank, could you skate faster than Hec Kilrea?

FRANK SR.: No. Well, maybe if I got under way, faster. On the Ottawa River, for instance. I could skate with any of them. But Hec broke fairly fast — and he was a terrible skater.

BOB: In Montreal, between the periods, they used to have these races. Remember? And Hec Kilrea won that.

ROY: What would other players have said about you? What would they have said Frank was so good at?

FRANK SR.: Well, I was known as Fearless Frankie . . . Selke said I was the "Coaches Dream."

ROY: Where does the "Fearless Frankie" come from?

FRANK SR.: I was, well, I guess I played pretty aggressively . . .

FRANK JR.: I always heard that Dad was always very hard to knock off his feet. Dad always used to say, "I skated low with my feet wide."

BOB: How did you get the name "Shawville Express."

FRANK SR.: Well. I used to play for Montagnards and for Ottawa University and I used to come down on the PPJ (Push, Pull, and Jerk) to the games. When I played for Ottawa University I was in the Commerce course — they signed me on there — it was all Irish then. The French were only starting to come in and they were battling . . . and I took courses there. I'd touch the typewriter keys a few times and open the odd book because we had to do that in order to — or they would have called us "tourists." And we couldn't play for Ottawa University unless we were "going to school." Lionel Chevrier was my center ice player for Ottawa U at that time, and Ladoucoeur from Hull was my left-winger.

ROY: For the University of Ottawa. You got a degree then? You had to learn typing. Did you learn to type?

FRANK SR.: They'd just give us a piece of paper the day we came down and we'd copy that. We got sixty dollars a game for that . . . Arnprior wanted me to go over to play for them. They were going to force me on territorial grounds. But Dave Gill was then the head of the Senior League Ottawa and District, and Gill was manager of New Edinboroughs. So Dave said, "No, he'll play in Ottawa. That's the closest Senior League. Arnprior is only Inter-

Ottawa University team in Ottawa City Hockey League, 1922–23.
Top Row, LEFT TO RIGHT — J.P. Coulson, Rev. A. Garry, J. Reynolds.
Second row — G. Bolam, A. Lajeunesse, G. G. Lafrance.
Third row — A. Ladoucoeur, L. Chevrier, F. Finnigan.
Fourth row — W. Desu, G. Soubliere, H. Findlay.

mediate and he's beyond that. A step back." So he protected me. Then I went to Montagnards and that was the year The Auditorium was built, 1923. They gave me a thousand dollars and then they paid my up and down expenses on the train and my expenses for a room — we stayed at the old Russell at that time. So then when I went with Montagnards the next year — I was two years with Ottawa University — Dave Gill, head of Senior Amateur Hockey, said to me, "I'd like you play for New Edinboroughs but I know you've been getting so much from Montagnards. But we can't match that, so you go ahead and play for Montagnards." The butchers on the By Ward Market were putting up the money for Montagnards.

Montagnards, Champions of the Ottawa and District Hockey Association, 1923–23. Bottom row, LEFT TO RIGHT — S. Seguin, Trainer; J. Harnett, Chairman, Sports Committee; E.P. Belanger, Sec. Trea.; Dave Lafreniers, Second Vice-pres.; George Fraser, Chairman House Committee; Leo Bourguignon, Trainer. Second row — R. Huard; J.B Guenette; First Vice-Pres. Third row — Frank Finnigan; V. Scott; A.E. G Bourguignon, Pres., J.E. Morris, Manager, and Coach; Gene Chouinard, W.F.J. Pratt. Back row — J. Brennan; E. True; H.E. Reaume, Captain; A.D. Devenny, Ed. Gorman.

FRANK JR.: The old Montagnards Club was on the corner of Cambridge and Somerset, a sporting club with a license. You bought a membership, two dollars, and you went there, and had a beer and shot the breeze. When I played Junior for Montagnards, we were not allowed to go there but the Seniors were. Mr. Rip Riopelle was the manager of the club then, Rip Riopelle, personnel manager of Air Canada now. He was quite a hockey player — Senior here — and he had a cousin, Howard Riopelle played for Montreal.

FRANK SR.: Old Tom Murray of Barry's Bay was a good friend of mine. His whole ambition was to play baseball, turn pro. Catcher. He was a good catcher but, well, baseball wasn't a Canadian game. At the time he had Bill Skuce pitching for him, in the Ottawa City League, but he also used to go up and pitch at Barry's Bay for Tom.

ROY: He must have been an amazing physical specimen, Tom Murray. He was one hundred and still going . . . Nelson Skuce over at *The Citizen* also is a great pitcher.

BOB: Any of you guys ever get chased out of town after a ball-game?

ROY: Oh, I've had police escort to the cars.

BOB: In Chicoutimi they used to put us on a high-bodied truck. You know, during the game a little excitement, a little ugliness . . .

ROY: It happened in the Arena. It wouldn't happen where Frank played — on such high levels — as he says, "I played with the best" — but where it's not good hockey, there would be terrible fights and the police would come.

FRANK SR.: We never had any fights. We used to have referees come up from Ottawa, but then our league bust up during the First World War. I was only fourteen when I was first playing in the league with guys who were sixteen, seventeen, eighteen. Shawville, Quyon, Campbell's Bay, Fort Coulonge, Portage-du-Fort. Shawville was the only place on the line that had a covered rink, do ya see?

One of the many hockey players who came out of Ottawa to star in the N.H.L., Ebenezer "Ebbie" Goodfelloow(left) was born there in 1907 but only played amateur with Montagnards before going on to his long successful career with Detroit Falcons and Red Wings. He was on All-Star teams, won the Hart Trophy, captained the Red Wings for five years, and was on three Stanley Cup teams.

Ralph "Cooney" Weilands' (right) hockey career took him from Seaforth, Ontario, where he was born, to the Ottawa Senators, 1932–33, to Boston for the Stanley Cup Championships of 1928–29 and 1938–39, to Detroit for a year, and finally to Harvard University as coach.

The first money I ever earned was when I was thirteen and Quyon paid me to play against Fitzroy Harbour for money under somebody else's name. I was under age, only about a hundred and thirty pounds, so I had to take somebody else's name for Quyon. Ten dollars. And Quyon lost. We were playing against men. They came across on the ice to us. There was no power plants in those days, so it was safe crossing in a car. The ice isn't sitting on top of the water, so it cracks and goes down if you try to cross with a car or a team of horses. It was easy to maintain a nice road in those days.

BOB: There couldn't have been as many fellows as good as you playing at thirteen. I'm curious how you got so good. There were no teachers, no coaches . . .

FRANK SR.: Well, I played all the time on ponds and on the streets. No coaches. I guess I got better and better all the time. And we used to play on small rinks and you had to be a good stick-handler to get around — no room, no ice surface . . .

And I was playing with fellas a lot older than myself. You learn from them. You improve. I was playing with fellas ten years older than myself. Even on the ball team, I was playing with guys ten years older than I was. Dougal McCredie was ten years older than I was, Clarence Caldwell was ten years older than I was . Bill Cowan, Larry Hynes, Hilton Findlay, Clifton Woodley, Charlie Bowan, they went to play with Ottawa University too. But at that time you had a pretty fair Intermediate league; Pembroke, Arnprior, Carleton Place, Perth, Smiths Falls — they all had pretty fair hockey clubs in those days, and all Senior clubs were in Ottawa, a league at Minto Rink and then at Dey's Arena another league, and then they played off . . . All we did was play hockey in the winter.

BOB: But there was no talk about how the game should be played. You just went out and did it.

FRANK SR.: That's right. You had a coach or a manager, you know. But what did he know?

FRANK JR.: He changed the lines.

FRANK SR.: And in those days he didn't change too many lines!

FRANK JR.: And opened the doors . . .

FRANK SR.: That was just before the seven-man hockey went out. Around 1912 I guess the Silver Sevens were playing seven-man hockey. I never did. Johnny Quilty's dad played seven-man hockey — Bobby Quilty — a Silver Seven.

By the time I started to play for Ottawa the manager and the coach were in place. Managers didn't have to be a star to be a coach. The same in baseball — if you understand the rules and know the game, some fellas become a coach. In my day P.D. Green was coach when I first turned pro, then Alec Curry, then Newsy Lalonde, then Dave Gill. He was both manager and coach. The thing with a coach is he can't tell you what to do. He can change the lines but if you're on ice playing your line he can't tell you "pass that puck." You know it before you get there. You know what

All Star "Stars" in the Ace Bailey Benefit Game, 1934 at Maple Leaf Gardens. Back row — Chuck Gardiner, Red Dutton, Eddie Shore, Allen Shields, Bill Brian, Lionel Conacher, Ching Johnson, Nels Stewart, Frankie Finnigan. Second row — Larry Aurie, Hooley Smith, Jimmie Ward, Lester Patrick, Leo Dandurand, Bill Cook, Howie Morenz, Aurel Joliat, Herb Lewis, Howie Morenz Jr.

you're going to do. You've got your mind on it. The coach can tell you this and that, but you don't hear when you're on ice. We had practices, but again the coach didn't do a hell of a lot. He would get you to go up and down the ice, and maybe take a man off so you could play short-handed. Keeping in shape in those days was up to yourself. There was always somebody coming up who could take your place, so you kept yourself in shape. If you hit the dope or the liquor on the day before a game, you were only hurting yourself. Lots of fellows in the older days, before my time, some of them hit the bottle pretty hard before a game, and of course they didn't last so long. The odd fellow would smoke but not to excess. It kills your wind. And you know that. You were your own judge of when you were in shape. If you couldn't do that, you wouldn't make the team. That's why we all played baseball and tennis and hardball, even golf, in the summer to keep in shape.

BOB: I'm curious about the fact that what you're saying is that all this was done on some kind of basic innate talent you must have inherited. You weren't taught. I wanted of ask you whether when you were playing hockey or even practicing, or even before the age of thirteen — this may sound foolish — but did you think about what you were doing?

FRANK SR.: Yes. I always wanted to make pro. When I would get the paper and see the Smith Brothers and Bruce Stewart and his brother and Punch Broadbent and Cy Denneny, and Frank Nighbor and Eddie Gerard and Buck Boucher and Jack Darragh . . .

BOB: There was none of this stuff of the older player taking the

The Senators of the early 1930s were fondly portrayed in a series of cartoons in the Ottawa newpapers.

younger player aside and giving him advice. I'll give you an example. Remember Billy Dineen — he's a coach now — and his brothers are playing in the N.H.L. now? And the story I got, rightly or wrongly, was that one of the things they couldn't break Bill Dineen of doing was that when he came down to the defence, he always cut outside. He never cut inside and this meant that he got shoved to the corner by the defenceman. Now, the guy who was telling me this story told me that Bill Dineen was told many times *NOT* to do this, but he could never break the habit.

FRANK SR.: Your coach could tell you things, but if you didn't have the ability to learn from that — well — if you didn't learn how to go in on this side and this side and mix it all up and cut in different sides different times, then you fox him, and then he knows you aren't always going to do the same thing . . .

FRANK JR.: Bill Dineen from Ottawa went down to play with St. Mike's after he finished with St. Pat's, and when he was finished playing with St. Mike's he played with Gordie Howe, so he had a pretty good teacher. If he could learn anything, he could certainly learn from Howe.

BOB: How old were you when you began to learn all these things you're telling us now?

FRANK SR.: It would be a couple of years after I turned pro. You get a little smarter. But if you haven't the ability to improve yourself, you just don't make it.

FRANK JR.: You didn't have the time either, Dad. You were only playing thirty-five games a year then, so you had to learn fast.

Now they play eighty, and the practice sessions that you'd have then compared to now — you learn a lot from watching other people, too, you know. You watch somebody's technique and then you try to copy it, see if it works for you . . .

BOB: Did you have specific game plans in your head? Did you say, "Here comes Morenz and with him I have to do this and that?"

FRANK SR.: Sure, with Morenz I always had to be a couple of strides ahead of him, and I'd go up, and I'd try to run with him, because if I started with him, then I was soon thirty feet behind! And he always came down my wing — the left-hand side — and he played center ice and he'd go back and he'd come down at a terrific pace. He was an awesome skater, he'd go so fast. So, anyway, he'd go back after making that rush — if Toronto had Morenz today he'd get them out of their own end — anyway, he'd go back and say "Give me that puck!" And he'd come down again, and gain maybe the third time. He was terrific. But I always put him into center and Nighbor had this poke-check —

they haven't got anyone in the league today who can check like that — but, anyway, I'd shove Morenz over to Nighbor, and if I didn't pick him up, Nighbor would with his poke-check, so he would have to go through the defence then . . .

BOB: How did you get from Montagnards to playing pro hockey?

FRANK SR.: Well, of course, they were always looking me over and then I was playing in The Auditorium where the Ottawa Senators

were playing, and I looked pretty good — I was twenty-one — so, anyway, they called me in Shawville.

BOB: Well, so far we've gotten out of you what it is that you were noted for. So let's try statistics.

FRANK SR.: My best year would be around twenty-one goals. I was up in the first ten for three or four years. Morenz, Joliat, they were ahead of me, of course. I was an average scorer — no, maybe a little better than that. I might have been called a really good defensive player . . .

FRANK JR.: When Dad went to Toronto he was brought there more for defence — they had a big line "Kid Line" in Conacher-Jackson and Primeau. Dad was taken there to bolster a defensive checking line.

FRANK SR.: We had Bailey who got hurt: Shore took the feet from under him. We had Harold Cotton and Harold Darragh on one line and for penalty killing we had Andy Blair, Bob Gracie, and myself. The Thoms-Boll-Finnigan Line came later. The Kid Line was such a scoring line — they were dynamite.

ROY: Would you be there the night Ace Bailey was hurt?

FRANK SR.: No, I wasn't. But I was there the year before, on loan. Ottawa Senators disbanded for a year and I went to Toronto, then back to Senators. They got money to go again, and then they folded and I went to Toronto.

BOB: I was a kid up North in Chicoutimi when Ace Bailey got hurt and I've seen this argued by sports writers — Toronto's Andy Little — and he said he really didn't know what happened. I wonder if you have any impressions because this was a horrendous event.

FRANK SR.: There was a little melée, shoving and pushing in the center of the ice. I wasn't there, but they have told it to me often, and I've had people try it on me to show me how it happened. Anyway, Bailey was standing there, and a few others in the center of the ice, and Shore came up and just took the feet from under Bailey, and he went up in the air and down and hit the ice and fractured his skull. Shore didn't intend it but that's what he did. He intended to give him a flip. Bailey never got over it. He was time-keeper at Toronto for years, and he coached. He just couldn't play hockey again because he has a plate in his head. He was lucky there were great brain surgeons in Boston at the time.

FRANK JR.: Tim Daly, the old Maple Leaf trainer at Maple Leaf Gardens, he said that you "only used one stick a year." And he said, Finnigan would come in and unwind all the tape on his stick and he would sit down — this was a pre-game ritual — and he would sharpen his stick! Now why did you do that?

FRANK SR.: Well maybe I wanted to take a little piece off the toe of the stick because sometimes I wanted to pull the stick up fast in a game and, if that little tip wasn't taken off, the puck would go under it. So when you went to take a pass in close to your feet, if that little toe wasn't the right shape, the puck would go under and you'd lose it. I used a jackknife and then wound the tape all around again. Maybe I used one stick a year, but they lasted a lot longer then. They were good sticks. They were good sticks. They were all one piece but sometimes you'd get them that they weren't balanced, so I did a little carpentry on them — my father was a master carpenter, you know. I think they were made of ash.

And Alex Connell, he was a pretty good RC, and we used to generally eat together at the Waldorf Astoria, that was the old Waldorf, not the new one — and we'd have filet mignon, stuffed oysters, and strawberry shortcake — in training before the game, you know — and we'd have a stay-over in New York because we would be maybe going to Boston two nights hence. And it would often be Friday and after we'd eaten the steak I'd say to Connell, "Jesus! Alex, this is Friday! You shouldn't have eaten any of that." And he'd say, "You son of a bitch, you should never have mentioned it!" A great goalie. Hainsworth and Ted Benedict too. When they were making up the new Montreal Maroons, Punch Broadbent went down there and Ted Benedict, too, and he got hit very hard down there. That's when he started wearing the mask. Eddie Gerard went down and he was coaching them; Sprague Cleghorn hit Eddie Gerard across the throat there with his stick and Gerard lost his voice forever. Gerard was quite a defenceman for Ottawa.

BOB: I was in Montreal when Howie Morenz ran into the boards at the back of the rink, broke his leg, went in to the hospital, and died. And there were two stories that I heard. One was that he died because of the effects of the broken leg, which sounds odd, and the other one was that his friends brought so much alcohol into the room to him that he died of that.

FRANK SR.: I think that is right. I can't be sure. I was at the funeral in Montreal Forum — that is where he was waken — center ice — thirty thousand people filed past, and from what I can understand, maybe he had a few drinks and had a blood clot.

ROY: What was it like to be famous in those days?

FRANK SR.: People always used to like to say they knew me. But they didn't know me at all.

ROY: But they wouldn't write you up the same way — like "Frank Finnigan has a drinking problem." As a journalist in those days they wouldn't write that kind of stuff, the way they would today.

FRANK JR.: No, because Frank Finnigan would probably be down to the paper the next day and shove the paper down their throat.

ROY: It was so different then. The press wasn't so close, and they wrote you up as a hero. And the young kids in the rinks, they'd know who you were from your face.

FRANK SR.: And they had the gum cards and the cigarette cards.

ROY: There was a conspiracy of silence, of respect. But not today — oh, I used to cover sports . . . I was at a game when Phil Esposito came running after Earl McCrae. Earl had said before, "Roy, don't go near Esposito. He's mad at sports reporters." And I was going to the restroom and Earl was right behind me and Esposito saw him and came charging up with his stick and Earl ran out of Maple Leaf Gardens as fast as he could go and I never saw him again . . . What do you feel when you watch a game now?

FRANK SR.: I like it now but I think it was better in my day. Today it's a business. But I think there were better hockey players on the teams in my day they could take a pass, give a pass, play anything — there are so many teams today that hockey's watered down the size of the roster for each team, twenty-five players, four lines, six or seven defencemen, changing the lines all the time. You had three lines in my day, four defencemen, a couple of utility players.

FRANK JR.: In your day seventy-five per cent of them were excellent hockey players. Now you're getting fifty per cent maybe good players, and the rest are "grinders." Ten on each team are first rate; the rest are grinders.

ROY: We've gone from sixty-minute men to guys who are only on for three minutes. How much would you play?

FRANK SR.: If your line started, you'd play around twenty-six minutes.

ROY: There's only a couple of men in the N.H.L. who would have that amount of ice time.

FRANK SR.: That's if your lines started. A fellow has to be on at least three or four minutes to even find himself in the game.

ROY: There's another point. What value is a twenty-four-second shift? You have to be on for a longer time to be of any use.

FRANK SR.: You can't be on for two minutes and never get a chance to touch the puck . . . Aurel Joliat played for Montreal Canadiens all his life. Morenz at center and Joliat on left wing. Joliat was getting a little bald and he wore a black cap; I used to, just for fun, hit him and knock his cap off. He didn't like it, but you had to slow him down a little, and that was the only way to do it. He could turn on a dime and he'd come back at you — he wasn't a bit afraid — guts, I call it. No, you could hit him pretty hard and he wouldn't quit. No, he'd come back.

BOB: When I came up here in 1925 from the Saguenay Valley you were playing then, Frank, and I remember you. Being eleven years old then, I was memorizing the names of all the N.H.L. hockey players. Well, Chicoutimi is an isolated area and Shawville is an isolated area, but out of my country — that is the Lake St. Jean district — there has been George Vezina, Johnny Gagnon, and one of the Lamarands. Now we could skate from October to March, so how come only four players from Lake St. Jean? And the Ottawa Valley has produced so many hockey players you can't count them. And incidentally you don't get them any more.

FRANK JR.: The towns were closer together and they went on the train, and lots of times there were men ready with horses and sleighs to put some young lads on with some hay, and get them to games — hockey-nut men. Campbell's Bay and Coulonge and Shawville fought for years, and Quyon . . .

ROY: That's the key right there. The towns have to hate each other.

BOB: I know I'm the only one from the Saguenay Valley but we had all that too. When the Chicoutimi team went down to play Jonquier, they had to get the police every time, to get the guys to the train to go back to Chicoutimi.

FRANK SR.: Here in the Ottawa Valley you have so many towns together able to reach each other, all within a hundred miles of each other, or less. And all kinds of train connections. From Chicoutimi you could only get to Quebec City and Montreal. Before I started playing for Ottawa University they came up to Shawville. They had heard about me — "pretty fair player" —

The late Mrs. Ira Merrifield with a cherished sculpture of her late brother, Hib Mylks of the Old Ottawa Senators. The Merrifields were the first settlers at Beeechgrove, Quebec, up the Pontiac.

and they had the Sons of Ireland down in Quebec City and they offered me real money to go down there and play for them. And they came up to Shawville in big limousines — Landreville's taxi had them then — and they came up from Ottawa to Shawville to sign me up. I didn't sign but three years later I went down and played for Montagnards against the Sons of Ireland.

BOB: In those days that was wonderful hockey — as good as the N.H.L., they say. Punch Imlach was playing for Quebec Aces.

ROY: Did you have a master plan for your hockey career? It sounds as though it just went from year to year.

FRANK SR.: Well, you know, you play in there for fourteen years like I did, but you know retirement time is coming two or three years before it happens — the twilight zone. A lot of the fellows they missed the old slap on the back and the crowds, unless they got into something or had a trade, and a year or two after they got into the alcohol. Like me.

BOB: Were you ever really hurt?

FRANK SR.: A charley horse, that's all. An osteopath, one of the first in Ottawa, eventually cured that. Down on Elgin. I had good pads on but he hit me hard — Red Horner — he only hit me once and he never did it again. After that, I knew how to fake him. I'd give me the puck over there or hang on to it, or go around, or give it over this time and next time hang on to it. But he'd always take two or three strides to hit you, so I could make him make his move. I never deliberately hurt any player. I might have taken the wind out of a fellow, maybe by hitting him. I always hit with my rear. I'd turn and bodycheck with my rear — maybe into their midsection and they'd lose their wind. I never broke any bones and I never did stick work. Yes, I cross-checked but only to protect myself. Not like today where it's deliberate cross-checking — and never called.

BOB: This makes a picture of you in some ways. My recollection of hockey in your time was that it was not a time of mamby-pamby hockey. Yet you may be suggesting that there was different kinds of ethics, that there were certain things you just could not do.

FRANK SR.: I never used my stick on anyone. I never carried my stick high. If I saw a player coming and I knew he was going to stick one into me, I'd put my stick up to protect myself. I think most of the players of my time were the same — more body-checks in my time but not putting into the boards as they are today — cross-checking, sticks up.

We seldom had pitched battles the way they do today. I remember one night in Ottawa Buck Boucher was down on the ice and Cleghorn, who was a tough customer — and he was a big man, too — anyway, Cleghorn kicked Buck. And of course Cleghorn had no use for Ottawa because years and years ago when they went out West to Vancouver to play — he was playing for Ottawa at the time — and something happened in the play-offs out there. Ottawa got rid of him, sold him to Montreal Canadiens. It was said Cleghorn had taken a woman on the train and some of the other players were taking their wives. And Cleghorn sent her ahead out to Vancouver on another train and met her there. But it was a scandal to the other women, breaking the moral code. But, oh, Cleghorn cut them all — Gerard, Nighbor, Cy Denneny — with his stick.

BOB: You haven't answered the question about how many fights Frank Finnigan got into. We know that King Clancy got into hundreds of them and lost them all.

FRANK SR.: The night of the Conacher banquet, just before he died, Clancy said, "I always had somebody behind me. I used to start them all. But I always knew I had Finnigan right behind me. I just pulled out of the road."

Well, I did hit Cleghorn one time. And he went down. Oh, he was treacherous. Oh, he was tough. If we had been in a room, he'd probably have taken me — but on the ice — I got in the first lucky punch. You know, the funny thing is if you have your glove on and he has his glove on and you take a swing at the fellow, you slide so much and he slides so much, you have no real footing for a fight. But if you take your glove off, he'll feel it.

The Patricks were big, and Conacher, just used to take the New York Telephone Book and tear it in half. One time he took Harold Cotton and held him by the ankles out of the Lincoln window right over New York City — that's how he lost his hair. Conacher was just like Tarzan. He could drink a twenty-six-ounce bottle of liquor and down it like a Coke. Lionel Conacher was as big as Chuck. The Conacher brothers were about two hundred and twelve pounds, no stomach on them at all, all muscle — just like Harry McLean . . .

There would be few hockey tales to tell like this about The Senators during the "lost" years between the disbanding of the N.H.L. team in 1933–34 and the return of the team to the professional ranks in 1992–93. Still, a Senator team played on, joining the amateur ranks of the Quebec Senior League, contesting for this league championship and The Allan Cup. And despite the collapse of the N.H.L. franchise, the spirit of the nine-time Stanley Cup winning Senators proved indomitable, perhaps even inspiring the motto, "We won't back down," adopted by the management of the new N.H.L. Senators as they won back the franchise.

5

THE LOST YEARS
OF THE SENIOR SENATORS

*"So fans in Ottawa were watching better hockey actually in the
Quebec Senior League than they'd be watching in the N.H.L.
during that period . . ."*

— Howard Riopelle

Although The Senators left the N.H.L. in 1934, the team played
on in the Quebec Amateur Hockey Association, Senior League,
until the late 1950s. The team was not just a pale imitation of its
N.H.L. predecessor; indeed, many of the N.H.L. Senators played
with the Senior Senators, either leaving the N.H.L. team which
had picked them up after 1934 to return to Ottawa, like Eddie
Finnigan, or returning to Ottawa in their twilight years, like Syd
Howe. Ex-N.H.L. Senators like Alex Smith and George "Buck"
Boucher coached The Senators, who were owned during much of
this period by Jim MacCaffrey. The Senior Senators also produced many players who went on to play in the N.H.L, like Larry
Regan who played many years for the New York Rangers and then
coached the Los Angeles Kings in their early expansion years.

Regan starred with the 1948–49 Senators who won The Allan
Cup, defeating the Edmonton Flyers in the East-West finals. His
teammates included Eddie Embery, Stu Smith, and goaltender
Legs Fraser, all coached by "Buck" Boucher. Several years earlier,
during the war, Ottawa was home to two armed services teams
which won The Allan Cup — the 1941–42 R.C.A.F. team, led by
the famous Boston Bruin "Kraut" Line of Schmidt, Bauer, and

Dumart; and the 1942-43 Ottawa Commandoes, featuring the likes of Louis St. Denis, Denny Kilrea, Kenny Reardon, Bingo Kampman, led by the Mac Colville-Aleck Shibicky-Neil Colville Line, and coached by Dick Irvin. Although many of these players were N.H.L. stars before they enlisted, others came to fame while serving in Ottawa playing for these teams.

Ottawa Senators, 1948–49, Allan Cup Champions. Front row— Larry Regan, Bill Watson, Eddie Embers, Jack McLean, Lade Cheek, Stan Smith, Unknown Trainer. Middle row — Alex Smart, George Greene, Jack Irvine, Ray Trainor, Bobby Copp, Fred Murphy. Back row — Frank Mathers, Conny Tudin, Butch Stahan, Legs Fraser, Emile Dagenais, Buck Boucher (Coach).

The years between the collapse of the N.H.L. franchise and the Second World War were tumultuous for the Senior Senators and especially for those Senators who were sold to other N.H.L. teams. Frank Finnigan's younger brother, Eddie Finnigan, joined the Senior Senators at the beginning of the 1934-35 season and led the league in scoring until the St. Louis Eagles called on his services. Before his professional career was over, Eddie would play for three teams that collapsed under him — St. Louis Eagles, Boston Cubs, Rochester Americans — before returning to Ottawa to play for the Senior Senators again. In a recent interview, my Uncle Eddie reflected on his tumultuous career:

Like my brother Frank I started to play hockey in Shawville. They had a church group there and they played in the old arena. When I was twelve or thirteen, we moved to North Bay, and I played up there in the Park League first, then Junior City League, and then for the North Bay Trappers when I was fifteen. I came down from North Bay to Ottawa when I was fifteen. In 1928, I played for the Shamrock Juniors, and I went on the Ottawa Senators negotiation list. I got five hundred dollars a year on this negotiation list for the professional Senators. That was under the table. I was supposed to be amateur. I was on that list for, I guess, about three years.

The Shamrocks won the championship in 1928. The next year I played for Rideau Juniors, and they won the championship in 1929, and then in 1930 I played for Rideau Juniors again. They were in the playoffs against Primrose and it was a matter of how many goals we were going to beat Primrose by. The Cowleys played for them — both Bill and Dan. And the first game Primrose beat us 3–1 and their goalie kicked out more shots than any goalie you ever saw in your life. Anyhow we laughed about it and thought, "Well the next game we'll give them a real hiding." So the next game we beat them 2-1. At that time it was total goals to count, so they won by one goal.

And then Rideau Seniors came in to the playoffs, and they were allowed to pick up Juniors, so they picked up myself and Bobby Walton. We played for the Rideau Seniors and we won the championship for the City League in 1930. After that — I'd be eighteen — after that we played against Hamilton. Two games, one in Ottawa and one in Hamilton, and we were tied and we had to play the third game and it was booked in Montreal and we played in Montreal in the Forum. We were beat out by Hamilton by one goal. That's the night I lost my big front tooth. We were playing overtime and I was skating down the ice — beat the defence, beat the goalie, staggered into about ten feet from the net and shot, missed the net, with nobody in it! It would have tied the game.

So after that game I got the offer from the Montreal Maroons to come down and have a tryout. If I didn't make it for the Maroons, I was going to play for the Montreal Royals and they'd get me a job in Montreal. Well then the Ottawa Senators picked me back up again. Yes, Ottawa stepped in and said, "Hey, Finnigan's our property. You've no business touching him. You've no business offering him a contract or anything else." In other words this is why they put you on a negotiation list. You'd almost think at that time — Toronto did it too — and you'd almost think at that time that they're holding you if they need you and if they want you then they'd take you; if they don't — well, nobody else can get you and make a better team. Dog in the manger. They claimed at one time that Toronto had eight hundred players on the list.

So I had to go back to Ottawa then. I played Senior City League with Rideau Seniors who won the championship that year, and then the next year I played for New Edinburgh and we won the championship that year.

Eddie Finnigan of Ottawa, Frank's brother, was also a talented hockey player who played for the Ottawa Senators in the Quebec Senior League.

The next year, 1933–34, I played for The Senators in the Quebec Senior League. Then I played professional with St. Louis Eagles. I was there the last two months of 1934. St. Louis disbanded and that threw all those players on to the market. I was picked up by New York Americans and I went to their training camp in Oshawa. I was there for two weeks but took trouble with my hamstrings and I could hardly put on my skating boots or anything else and I was lame. Anyway I missed practices, and what have you, and I didn't make their club. They went back to New York and I was sent to Rochester where they had just started up a club. But the New Americans never played a game — they went bankrupt before they opened a season. That threw all those players on to the market.

Then I was picked up by Boston. Frank was there playing for Toronto Maple Leafs and I was playing for Boston and some nights I was playing against Frank. Well, I didn't play against him exactly. I was playing on left wing at that time and Nick Metz was the man I was to cover and having all the trouble with. I talked to Frank and I said, "I can't skate with that Nick Metz. He's too damn fast for me." "Well," Frank said, "make sure you're out in front of him and skate ahead of him and watch him. If he moves

Eddie Finnigan followed in brother Frank's footsteps and went down to St. Louis to play for the Eagles. Now in his eighties, Eddie could only remember some of the names of the people posed in this photo taken in the St. Louis arena. "Back row, LEFT TO RIGHT — Claire Brunton, manager; Buck Boucher, coach; Pete Kelley; Irv Freud; Ayrs; Gerlais; ? ; Carl Voss (later New York Americans); Joe Lamb; ? ; Eddie Gleason, trainer; ? . Front row — Bill Beveridge; ? ; ? ; Brydson; Teddy Graham; Bill Cowley; Eddie Finnigan; ? ."

in, you move in. *Don't* let him go by you. Get out in front of him and make him tired."

Yes, yes, Frank knew how to deal with him. So then we went back to Boston and I played about two games there, and we were going on a road trip, and I was rooming with Bill Cowley then, and we went to the train station to go on this trip — it was a four-or-five-game road trip and I said to myself, "If I get on this road trip I'll show these lads that I can play hockey." And we were at the station all ready to go when suddenly they were running around yelling, "Finnigan!" "Finnigan!" "Where's Finnigan?" Eddie Shore had hurt his knee and he wasn't able to make the

trip so they were taking defencemen off the Boston Cubs —
that's the second club for semi-pro for Boston playing out of
Boston — and they were taking defencemen off the Boston Cubs
to help out in Shore's place, so they were leaving me behind to
help the Boston Cubs. So then I was with the Boston Cubs for the
rest of that season. At that time there was Porky Dumart and
Bobby Bauer, Flash Holland and Jack Portland were on defence.
And I finished the rest of the season with them. We missed out
the playoffs by one point.

The next year the Boston Cubs disbanded. I was still Boston
property and I was to go to Providence. It was sixty dollars a week
plus a split of the gate receipts. Less money. Half the money. I
think my original contract with Boston was four thousand dollars
if you played for the season in the N.H.L., and if you "went
down" it was either two thousand or twenty-four hundred. I
didn't go. So then I got a letter in Ottawa that I was suspended
from playing anywhere. I was Boston's property. I couldn't play
for anybody else. And nobody else would take you if you were
Boston's property. I was untouchable.

And the same went for other clubs. There was like a
"Gentlemen's Agreement." And I stayed home and I didn't have
an amateur card so I couldn't play. But I played for Cranes
Printing and played for the government team and some exhibition games.

I must have been out for about two years and Cecil Duncan
was head of the Canadian Amateur Association and he was here
in Ottawa, so I got my amateur card back after two years. Then I
played for The Senators in the Senior group again. Every game
that I was going to play, I was dressed and everything and I didn't
know whether I was going to play or not because the N.H.L. were
raising a hell of a fuss about me getting my amateur card back
and being allowed to play. But I played that season, anyhow.
Then Cecil Duncan was replaced by a man out West — I don't
know his name — from some college out there and he became
head of the C.A.A. chain. I got a letter from him telling me that
my amateur card had been revoked and I couldn't play any
more. Then Boston came here to some kind of exhibition game
in The Auditorium and I went over to Bruin's manager Art Ross
and told him the circumstances. He said, "Very well. I'll fix it up.
I'll contact them and you'll get your amateur card back." So he
did and I got my amateur card back.

I played for Hull after that and they won the championship.
And we went down to St. John, New Brunswick to play for The

PLAYER'S CONTRACT

AS PRESCRIBED FOR THE

National Hockey League

The ....

Of ....

WITH

I hereby certify that I have, at this date, received, examined and noted of record the within Contract, and that it is in regular form.

President National Hockey League.

Regular Contract:— ....

Approved .... 192...

☞ IMPORTANT NOTICE TO PLAYERS AND CLUB PRESIDENTS ☜

Every player before signing a contract should carefully scrutinize the same to ascertain whether all of the conditions agreed upon between the Player and Club President have been incorporated therein, and if any have been omitted, the player should insist upon having all the terms, conditions, promises and agreements inserted in the contract before he signs the same.

NATIONAL HOCKEY LEAGUE

PLAYER'S CONTRACT (REGULAR)

Articles of Agreement between the HOCKEY ASSOCIATION

OF ST. LOUIS INCORPORATED ....

of the City of .... St. Louis ...., in the { State / Province } of .... Missouri ....

a club member of a League known as the "National Hockey League," party of the first part, hereinafter called the Club and

.... D. Edward Finnegan ....

of the City of .... Ottawa .... in the { State / Province } of .... Ontario ....,

party of the second part, hereinafter called the Player.

Witnesseth:

That in consideration of the mutual obligations herein and hereby assumed, the parties to this contract severally agree as follows:

1. The club agrees to pay the player for the season of 19 34-35 beginning on or about the 8th November, 1934.

day of .... 192..., and ending on or about the 19th

day of .... March ...., plus play-off and Stanley cup games at the rate of $ 3900

.... for such season; and an additional sum at the rate of

$ 100.00

for such season said additional sum being in consideration of the option herein reserved to the club in Clause 10 hereof; said additional sum to be paid whether said option is exercised or not, making the total compensation to the player for the season herein contracted

for $ 4000; the amount payable for the balance of the season being

$1000, and if the player is transferred to a minor league club he receives a minor league salary, but notwithstanding anything contained in this contract the player shall not be transferred to a minor league before one month after the beginning of the 1935-36 season.

Eddie Finnigan's 1934 N.H.L. contract with the St. Louis Eagles.

Allan Cup. Played against them and we were beat 3–1. Came back here to Ottawa and they beat us here in Ottawa also. At that time they had Legs Fraser in the nets. Anyway, there was a group of them and they came up to Ottawa after that and played for The Senators here.

Then after that I played for Spencerville. Alex Woods was the goalie here in the City League. They were looking for a couple of men so he and I used to go down — the referees all came from Ottawa here so the referees would take us down and we played at Spencerville. We got fifteen dollars a game and in the playoffs we got twenty-five dollars a game. I think we were in three or four playoff games. After that, the last year I played for Renfrew. I'd be thirty-four that year. We got six hundred dollars for the season for playing for Renfrew. After that I decided to hang them up.

Several years ago I was invited to speak to the students at a school Nepean. It was there that teacher Lee Witt said to me, "You must get to 'Rink Rat' Eddie Albert," and he was indeed a fund of stories about hockey — and many other things, too. At his home he was joined by long-time friend and hockey buff, Jim McKnight.

Born in 1911, Eddie Albert was hanging around The Auditorium, seat of the Ottawa Senators, by the age of fourteen, doing odd jobs, watching Herman Proulx make hockey sticks, absorbing the hero talk.

Eddie's tales and Jim's commentary paint a picture of hockey life in Ottawa after The Senators left the N.H.L. to play in the Quebec Senior League during the late 1930s:

EDDIE: We lived on Eccles Street. I lived right next door to Stewie Evans that played with the Detroit Red Wings. He used to hit a tennis ball against our house all day long. It would drive my mother nuts. Right beside St. Agatha's School. Right around the corner at 492 Bay was Jimmy McCaffrey that run the football team and the hockey team. Charlie Hulse lived across the street from us. In the next block up was where Lorne Green was born. He was born Lawrence Greenberg, his father was a shoemaker. He'd be, let's see, I'd say about No.116 or 118, a big brown house on Florence Street. Then right at the corner was the Ankas. Nora Anka. There was a big family of thirteen or something; they were originally from Perkins Mills on the Quebec side. Nora would be Paul Anka's aunt. Paul Anka's father owned the general store on Laurier Avenue. He and his two brothers, Johnny and Maurice,

tion was the section at the opposite end to the Rush End and the Hull gang, that's where they all sat. They were all up there yelling, "We love oh la, we love oh la." That was the green. And the red where the vice-regal box was in the center ice, and the players' box. And then on the right of the reds was the blue. And

Pop Irvin (left), a utility defenceman with the 1934–35 Senators, played alongside Maynie Peterkin, Stan Pratt, Jack Wilkinson, Tag Millar, Jules Cholette, Charlie Hulquist, and Rod Lorrain.

Vince Godin (right) played for coach Dr. Wes Richards on the 1934–35 Senior Senators against rival teams in the Q.A.H.A. — Royals, Canadiens, LaFontaine, McGill, Victorias, and Verdun.

that was the middle class up in the corner. And then they could stand a thousand easy there around the back of the rink. It was like when you got to the last row of the actual seats in the rink there was a very high fence and you could stand behind that. And I used to go and steal the Coke cases from the guys that had the concessions the time I was there. We used to sell them for two dollars to the guys from Hull that would bring the girlfriend over and she was too small to see over the rink. We used to sell them the Coke cases at two bucks a piece. Oh! Really a rental! They didn't want to take them home. And that was in the Depression when nobody had a job. And we'd go out of there with ten or fifteen dollars.

I think there was more people came over on the streetcars from Hull to see the games at The Auditorium than came from Ottawa. So these mobs got off the streetcar and it a wonderful spirit, eh? There was that wonderful smell, too, of rink and skates and liniment and brine. They used to put the brine in the pipes to freeze them. If you had a bad cold, you just went down to where the icemaker was and opened the door. No more cold, it would clear your head like that.

JIM: The thing I remember most is Hec Kilrea used to win the races. He used to race Morenz around the rink, and Morenz was touted as being the fastest skater in the business, and Hec beat him all the time. I remember Clancy running down the ice on his skates carrying the puck.

EDDIE: He was not a fancy skater. Well, he never started to skate till late in life. Do you know another thing about Clancy? He could only go round the back of the net one way. He couldn't take the puck and cross his legs that way, the left to the right. But he could cross his legs from the right to the left. So when he got the puck he always had to go around that way. He couldn't go around the other way. That's how he used to do it. Course it was a totally different game, eh? They had no red line and you'd carry the puck out. You couldn't shoot it out like they do today — not to center ice — and you also had to carry it in. You couldn't shoot it in. That's why they were such good stick-handlers. Nobody can stick-handle today.

JIM: The War really depleted the hockey ranks. I mean there wasn't great hockey then, there couldn't be. That's why guys like Richard scored those fifty goals. But your great scorers you have, like today, you've got Gretzky with all the points and you had Hull, eh, and then before him you had Richard — like total goals and assists. You know who the top man was with the most goals and assists up till 1947? Bill Caplin. And do you know who he beat out by one goal — who was top scorer with the most goals and assists? Syd Howe from Ottawa. Hockey was better in those days. I liked it better. The present people would say, "Oh, no. You don't know what the hell you're talking about." But they never saw it, so they can't make comparisons . . . And they had no real training like they have today. No real physical training. In those days they never had to take their medical, they just went out and played. And some of them held full-time jobs too.

When I was with the Quebec Senior League my mother was a widow — my father died when I was a kid, eh? — at the time I worked in the dressing-room with the team and I'd go to Jim McCaffrey who was the owner of the Quebec Senior League team and also of the Ottawa Rough Rider Football Team. He was with the Ottawa football team in 1926. So I'd say, "I need some money Jimmy." He'd say, "Go to the Ottawa Electric building and see Wes Brown. And I'd go in and I'd say, "Jimmy sent me, Wes. I need some money." He'd say, "How much do you need?" I'd say, "I dunno, twenty bucks." Twenty bucks was a lot of dough, you know. He'd write me a cheque for twenty dollars and then he'd say, "Go to the girl there in the wicket." That was the cashier on Sparks Street. And I'd go over there and he'd wave his hand and she'd hand me the twenty bucks and I'd sign the cheque.

For working around the rink. A Rink Rat. Taping sticks. I started when I was fifteen. It wasn't really a job. I was the one, it was my job in that respect. The kids would beat the shit out of you to get the job. Everybody wanted it. It was a sort of a prestige thing to work with the highest hockey club in the city. And go to Montreal on the train with them and to Quebec City. And Cornwall, we used to go to Cornwall by bus. That's when Senators was not professional not N.H.L., 1938, '39 . . .

EDDIE: Old Herman Proulx's little cubby hole was here where he sharpened the skates and displayed the sticks that he had made, but his factory — you went around the corner, and you went up a wooden ladder, and you went up through a hole and then he had the huge big plant where he made the sticks with big lathes and cutters. That was afterwards CFRA.

They never broadcast in those days. They never even sold programs. In the old city league they used to have big wooden things on each side of the rink with shamrocks and all the players and their numbers written on it.

And they say Foster Hewitt was the first guy to broadcast a game, but I'm sorry to tell you that it was one of my namesakes that broadcast a game before him. His name was Frank Albert. That was before Foster came in. What year? 1923. Oh I listened to the games in the late twenties, but it was a crystal set with the earphones.

JIM: Dr. Gilbert was broadcasting it, I would guess. He was the first one with a radio station in Ottawa. That was CKCO. It wouldn't have been Tommy Shields? Tom used to do football.

EDDIE: He used to write too. He was sports editor for *The Citizen.* Coached the old Senators in the Quebec League. The press box was right behind the players place. The players used to sit here and the penalty box was here and then the press box was a separate section right up here. And this is where they'd come out from the dressing rooms and come onto the ice . . .

JIM: Nobody gets hurt today. In those days if Sprague Cleghorn decided to take somebody apart they came apart.

EDDIE: And of course they didn't have all this equipment. There was no such a thing as a helmet. They had little shoulder pads because they didn't want to burden themselves down, and their pads were bamboo cane with a piece of felt along the front. But if they wanted to get in a fight, they'd just hit you with the stick.

It was more quick and decisive then. It wasn't these long drawn out things where everybody gets into it, and it's a brawl, and nothing happen to anybody. Today the odd guy might get a little scratch if the guy can get his helmet off. I remember — and I know I keep going back to the Quebec League that I remember — but a lot of guys in that league later played in the N.H.L. — and I remember this guy Lemay — he was going into the corner and this big guy — oh! a tough son of a bitch of an Irishman — came in with his —

JIM: That was Mr. Brennan from Quebec Aces — he was with Mike McMahon.

EDDIE: And I remember Lemay going into the corner, and I don't know what Lemay did — one little thing — and Brennan went — it was just like a snake's tongue coming — he went wwwhhaaacck, wwwhhaaacck, like that with his stick. Eight stitches here and six stitches here. There was no helmet. He just went wwwhaack wwhaack to the head like that, and all we saw was blood.

JIM: There was another time too, Eddie, he got Lemay going into the — in those days there was no glass around the rink it was all that mesh stuff — and Albert Lemay had a pretty prominent proboscis shall we say — and Brennan caught him going in there and Brennan just made sure he went all the way and Lemay's nose went right through the mesh. He pretty near killed him.

EDDIE: His nose was sticking through the mesh like this. Oh yeah, there was lots of crazy things happened. And in Quebec City they used to spit through the mesh at you. A lot of lumberjacks would come down from the bush eh? Sunday afternoons? We played there Sunday afternoons and all the big lumberjacks would come — all half-cut with the big boots and the plaid shirts and they'd get around the back there and an Ottawa player going in — cccr-rrunnccch! Bring it right up from here, right in their face you know. You know what the players did? They'd turn around and give it back to them.

JIM: Louis St. Denis used to have his neck just covered in spots there from guys throwing ballbearings and stuff at him.

EDDIE: They'd hit him with ballbearings and stones and apples and that. Louis took two pounds of stuff out of the back of his net after a game one time that they had thrown at him. The goaltender with Ottawa, Louis St. Denis. He lives in Arnprior today.

We've got to relate this properly. He was the goaltender and guys in the Rush End used to throw — maybe they could even use slingshots I dunno — but these big ballbearings and bolts and everything and they'd throw them at him and they used to hit him on the back, 'cos all he wore was a baseball hat. No stuff like that today, you know. When this stuff would happen, it would hit, and it would fall, and all they used to do was they'd take it with their goal stick and push it back into the net, eh? He used to save it all up for the whole game and one time he took it out and it must have weighed two pounds. This was in Quebec City. It was wild. And the players always made sure they had their stick at the

Joe Cooper (left) and Kenny Reardon starred on The Allan Cup winning Ottawa Commandoes of 1942–43. Front row — Jerry Cooper, Ted Saunders, Polly Drouin, Louis St. Denis, "Sugar" Jim Henry, Johnny Inglis, Vince St. German. Back row — Mac Colville, Alex Shibicky, Ned Colville, Joe Cooper, Walt Murray, Kenny Reardon, Alex Smith (Coach). Missing — Jack McGill, Gordie Poirier, Kenny Kilrea, Gordie Bruce, Eddie Slowinski, Bingo Kampman, Jake Brunning.

end of the game because, once the game was over, all these big lumberjacks would jump on the ice and all the guys went off with their stick like this. Lances forward. Just waiting for somebody to come near them. There was some wild hockey in those days. But I think there was some awful brawls. Jean Pucey — he played with The Canadiens team — they barred him for life.

JIM: And then Pucey went to The Rangers.

EDDIE: They fired him for life because he really hurt somebody.

JIM: And there was nobody could bury a stick in you any easier than Punch Broadbent. I think Frank Finnigan could say that.

EDDIE: And elbows too. That's why he was called "Old Elbows." He was the original Gordie Howe, you know. Howe was great with the elbows. Punch was first. I knew Punch pretty well 'cos when I was a kid he was our insurance agent. He sold insurance and he used to come around to the house all the time. In those days you paid them ten cents and they came every week and you had these twenty year policies, ten, fifteen cents, and a quarter on the kids. And Punch used to come around. I knew Cy Denneny in later years. He played hockey for the Ottawa Senators and then he coached Boston. I think he coached Boston the first year they won The Stanley Cup in '27 '28, I think.

JIM: He was with Frank Nighbor, of course. That was quite a line.

EDDIE: What I remember most about Frank Finnigan was he could stick-handle. And he had the smarts. He knew what to do with the puck . . . We can name lots of other Ottawa Senators from the N.H.L. and Quebec Senior days. There was Danny Cox, there was Carl Ross —

JIM: Earl and Des Roache —

EDDIE: Leo Burgo, Ed Milks. And there was Tony Weland. Up until the year that they went out of the league. These guys we mentioned all played with the N.H.L. Ottawa Senators. Why did they go out of the N.H.L.? Money. It was quite obvious. It was a civil service town.

JIM: Everybody in a civil service town budgets their money. You get a factory town, they get paid Friday and they go spend it. They go for three days and they say, "We've only got another day to go till it's pay day." Friday night they get paid again. And Frank Ahearn, of course, things were getting pretty tight as far as money and that was the reason he sold Clancy. He sold Clancy for $35,000 and that kept the operation going eh?

EDDIE: Buck Boucher was one of the best stick-handlers I ever saw. He could control the game pretty well. He'd let Clancy do the chasing up the ice but he'd stay home, but when he wanted to move up . . . And the guy that came from Boston here that stayed here a short time, Cooney Wieland, was a good stick-handler. He later coached for years at Harvard University. He didn't like the corners too much. But he could stick-handle . . .

Oh, I bummed school many times to make hockey sticks with old Herman Proulx, and I remember one night — I'll never forget it — the Old City League they used to do in those days, we used to make these little souvenir hockey sticks about that long. I used to buy the ribbon at Woolworths and we'd put the ribbons on — red, orange, and black was Cornwall and Hull was black and white. And I used to be the agent, eh? You sold them for a quarter and I got five cents, but I used to have the kids sell them for me and I gave them two cents. I didn't do nothing, but I made three cents you see. I just handed them out and they used to check back in to me, eh? Well, one night just before the game started, we were rushing to make as many of these things as we could, eh. And old Herman, the guy that worked with him was his step-son, Elmer Goulet was his name, and doesn't Elmer cut his finger off making these little souvenir hockey sticks. Right here, cut his finger right off. Instead of taking him out the Catherine Street door which was about from here to that door from where their shop was, they bring him down to the front door to take him out which is about 180 feet — the length of the rink. And they're trying to get him out and seven thousand people are trying to get in. In the lobby the place was jammed. To this day, I could never understand why in the name of God did they try to take poor Elmer with his hand and the blood and they put a towel around it, why they'd bring him out the front door. They could have had him out in two minutes, you know, in the back. I met him a couple of years ago, he still has no finger, I can tell you. He was telling me that he still has all that equipment that his step-father, Herman Proulx, made those hockey sticks with. And Elmer was telling me that when the people in the family — when old man Proulx was dead — sold the house, his mother-in-law or grandmother or somebody told him about all the hockey sticks that they had up in the attic. And the people that owned the house wouldn't give them to him. And these hockey sticks — old Herman used to make all the sticks for the Senators and all the N.H.L. teams — were all autographed sticks by all the teams, Stanley Cup champions, all of them. They should have been in the Hall of Fame.

Did the Auditorium have its own Delco or auxiliary lighting system? I wouldn't know about that. But, old Eddie Shore used to turn the lights off. Clancy used to coach the team in the American Hockey League and old Eddie Shore used to have the Springfield team. The Springfield Indians, eh? He had the team there and he also owned the rink there. He owned the team and he run it. And he was the craziest, kookiest, cheapest old bugger there was, eh? Clancy was there one time and they had a practice about three or four o'clock or whatever in the afternoon. So he

Ottawa Senators, 1949–50.
Front row — Legs Fraser, Bobby Copp, George Boucher, Stan Smith, Plumber Craig.

Middle row — Buddy Hellyer, Alex Smart, Jack Irvine, Emile Dagenais, Butch Stahan, Ray Trainor.

Back row — George Greene, Eddie Emberg, Eddie Dartnell, Nils Tremblay, Billie Robinson, Lude Check, Conny Tudin.

said, "Eddie turn the lights on." And Eddie said, "Look if you wait a half an hour the sun will be around and it'll shine in and you won't need the light." So Clancy went down to a hardware store and he bought a lantern, an old coal oil lantern, and just before the game, he lit the lantern and just before the game started he walked across the ice and presented it to Shore. He handed him the thing.

Oh, if you were hurt and you couldn't play Shore used to make you sell programs. Oh, yes. The players. Or he'd make them sell candy bars. He was wild. He'd give you a thousand dollars and then he'd fine you five hundred. For nothin'. He'd call a practice at ten o'clock in the morning and he'd tell you it was at eleven. Then you'd come in late and he say, "Five hundred bucks, you're late." He'd say, "I told you ten. Everybody else was here at ten." If you were sick or didn't feel good, do you know what you got? A spoonful of iodine. He'd make them drink it. The players would say, "Let's get so and so," and they'd say,

"Eddie, Jim doesn't feel too well." He'd say, "What's the matter?"
"Oh something's wrong, he's not well there's something wrong
with his stomach." "Get the iodine. Get the iodine." And he'd
say, "No. No. Eddie, I'm fine. I'm fine. I'm okay I'm not sick."
The guy said it never killed, but it sure did cure me. Tell you who
can tell you about Shore is the guy that coaches the 67s — he
played for him. "Giggy" Kilrea, he played with him. Shore put
hobbles on him. Yes, hobbles like a horse used to wear when they
stood on the streets. The breadman would put them on, and the
milkman . . . in Ottawa. If Kilrea didn't skate the way Shore wanted him to skate, and he wanted him to skate up, so he had this
goddam thing made out of wood and put it on him and he used
to make him practice with this thing on. Like a wood thing.
Kilrea will tell you that. 'Cos Kilrea was the first guy that started
the strike in the hockey, you know. The Springfield team was the
first team that went on strike. And that's when they got rid of
Eddie Shore. Yeah, and when they got rid of Shore the league
people came in and said, "We're sorry Eddie, but it's time to go."
So he gave the team to his son and they say his son was just as
bad as he was. Oh there's lots of stories like that.

They broke training all the time. I mean they smoked, they
drank. We used to leave here, that old Quebec league, and we'd
go down to Union Station and the train was at twelve o'clock,
and we used to get to Bowles Lunch — there used to be Bowles
Lunch down at the old station then — and then they'd get beer.
Dr. Cootes owned Capital Breweries down at the corner of
Preston and Wellington. I don't know if he was a real medical
doctor. He could have been a medical doctor, but he owned the
whole brewery. He bought it from E.P. Taylor or E.P. Taylor
bought it from him one or the other. And we always had a case of
beer after the game. We used to keep it out in the snow at the
back of the rink. And when we went to Quebec City we used to
stop off at a siding in Montreal and lay over overnight. The two
Lemays and a few others all got up and went to mass — cross
over the tracks to church and back. Six in the morning. And
then we'd get to Quebec City and play the game and then the
first thing they did was go for beer. There used to be a little place
right opposite the station called The Hole in the Wall. And
they'd buy six, seven quarts you know and bring them on the
train. And of course in those days they were all the old wicker
seats and they had all this beer, everybody had two or three
quarts, and they walked in and there were twelve nuns sitting —
and they'd been cursing and swearing you know? Twelve nuns.

The Senators were wild, too. I remember Clancy telling me a story. I used to run into Clancy in the Quebec League when the King was refereeing and we used to catch him on the train. He'd get the train in Toronto and that we would catch to go to Montreal and Quebec City, see. Clancy would always be there and he knew everybody. He used to tell us all kinds of stories. What the hell was it? The train broke down in Hawkesbury or somewhere in the dead of winter and they got out and they must have walked about three miles through the snow and went to this restaurant, Chinese restaurant in Hawkesbury. Two o'clock in the morning, and they pounded on the door. They wanted to eat. Buck Boucher, Clancy, maybe Frank and the other guys that were there. And the guy said, "Me closee. Me closee." They said, "We'll break the door down." And they went in and they made him cook bacon and eggs and things till they got the train going. Clancy told me that.

I remember in Montreal they used to take a pail of water . . . you know, in the hotels in those days there was always a transom and they'd put the goddam pail up there and just tip it. They'd phone somebody and say, "Come down to my room, I've got something to show you." And when he'd open the door, down came the water. Things like that. Louis St. Denis, I remember he used to be down in the Windsor Hotel or the Queen's Hotel, and there was a big sumptuous dining-room there and they had the orchestra and the violins, you know. St. Denis be there and he'd have a suit coat on and he'd have this red cravet with white polka dots. Course we knew what he had on underneath. He used to wear a sweatshirt from the Rideau Aquatic Club. Then they'd grab him and take the goddam coat off him and he's sitting there with all these people in evening gowns with Rideau Aquatic Club in front of the thing. Crazy you know.

The best one there was about Alex Connell. Well, Alex Connell he was apparently quite a mimic, impersonator and everything you know. He was down there one time and he got up on the stage and took the violin away from the guy and played some beautiful operas all by himself. And what he'd done, he'd put the guy that played the violin behind the curtains and Alex was just mimicking — he wasn't playing at all. And the people applauded and applauded. And this guy's behind the curtain playing the violin and Connell's out there and he's like this. That was in Montreal too. At the Queens or the Windsor Hotel . . .

Eddie Finnigan, Frank's brother, I knew better than Frank. Eddie played for The Senators after they disbanded professionally and became part of the Quebec Senior Hockey League. They all got paid but they were not supposed to be paid. And Eddie was famous for sleeping, absolutely famous.

Jim McCaffrey, the team owner, used to discover just before game time that Eddie was missing. And he'd yell at me, "Eddie, for Chrissakes, get over there and waken Eddie up!" So I'd have to run over to Arlington Street, a few blocks away from The Auditorium, and waken Eddie up and get him over to the game, still with the sleep in his eyes.

One time I was in the dressing room between periods with the players and Eddie was away over in a corner with a newspaper over his face. And McCaffrey yelled at me, "For Chrissakes, see what Eddie's doing in the corner there," And I went over and lifted up the newspaper and my God! He was asleep under it! Asleep between periods!

Eddie one time badly needed a new pair of skates and Jim McCaffrey wouldn't, or couldn't, buy them for him. So Eddie got an old pair of black boots, walking boots, and put them on with his uniform and went out onto the ice for practice with the working boots on — to shame McCaffrey into getting him new skates. It worked!

One time when the Ottawa Senators were staying at one of the big hotels with a swimming pool — a big thing back in those days — Frank "King" Clancy bet Charlie Conacher fifty dollars that he could high-dive off the tower in his tuxedo. Conacher took the bet and Clancy duly did a clown dive off the board. After Conacher had paid over the fifty dollars, Clancy took off the tuxedo , dripping, shriveled, and handed it to Conacher. "Here, Charlie," he said. "It's not mine. It's yours!"

Connie Brown from Ottawa, he used to play a bit for Detroit, and he went to St. Malachi's school and in those days you had to pay a two-dollar fee to take your entrance examinations (Grade Eight), so the principal of St. Malachi's School — Father Somebody or other — and this was in the Depression, remember — phoned Connie Brown's father and said to him, "Mr. Brown, don't spend your two dollars on Connie. He'll never make it."

One time in some game or other, I can't remember, Connie Brown ended up in a terrible donnybrook on the ice facing Red Kelly. With a twinkle in his eye Brown said to Kelly, "Say, Red, I can't box, you know."

"Neither can I," said Kelly. "Let's wrestle!"

During the 1940s and 1950s Howard Riopelle not only followed the fortunes of amateur hockey in Ottawa but also came to play for The Senators in the Quebec Senior League after a brief career in the N.H.L. with the Montreal Canadiens. In this interview, conducted in April 1992, he recalls the great hockey played in Ottawa during the "lost years" and offers some advice on managing the new Senators N.H.L. team:

Johnny Quilty (left) one of Ottawa's most renowned athletes. Photographed here in hockey action with the Canadiens, he was also an exceptional football player.

Howard Riopelle (right), again one of a renowned Ottawa family of hockey-playing brothers. After a brief sortis into the N.H.L. with the Canadiens, Riopelle joined the Ottawa Senators in the Quebec Senior League.

The Riopelles, being a big family, we had our own hockey team at one time. Some of my brothers played with me in the City League here in Ottawa. There was Montagnards, eh, and of course they had a team in Eastview at that time they called St. Charles, and Lasalle, that's a few of the teams and Hull, of course, they had a team in that league that was very good. They played for the Allan Cup here one year. They were playing against Cornwall.

Most of my family were involved in Junior hockey and Senior hockey. In elementary school I played for St. Malachi's and we won the first Joe Miller Trophy. Joe Miller was a great

great athlete. He donated this trophy for the elementary schools and we won the championship in the old Auditorium. First time we, as children, like that played in the old Auditorium. Big celebrations. That was one of the greatest thrills I had in sports, to tell you the truth. That would be in '36.

The Ottawa Senators of the N.H.L. were gone by then but still The Senators belonged to the Quebec League.

So then after St. Malachi's I went to St. Pat's College and I played for Alex Connell. Great man. He was the goalie for The Senators when they won the last Stanley Cup in 1927, and when he died he gave me his Diamond "O" Ottawa Senator ring. Yes his Stanley Cup ring. And I kept that for many years until I gave it to his grandson. I played for him in Junior hockey for about four years, I guess, and he was just an exceptional man. He formed a lot of great characters. He had great ethics and great morals and he had a real way of life. He had it all together. Great integrity. He was a great man.

I played with Johnny Quilty at St. Pat's. In my opinion he was the greatest all-around athlete that I've ever seen or witnessed. He was an exceptional football player — a quarterback, a great passer, a great kicker. Had he chosen football I'm sure he would have been a star in the Big Four. No question about it. He had the size. Very mature at a young age. Strong, eh? Great boxer. He was never defeated in the assault of arms — that's for high schools in Ontario. He was never defeated. And then of course in '41 he went to the training camp for the Montreal Canadiens — that would be '40, '41 I guess — and of course he won the Calder Trophy as the best rookie of the year in the N.H.L.

When I finished Junior I joined the service automatically, eh, and I went into air crew and of course I had the privilege of playing for a great coach, he proved that, he's won Stanley Cups, Memorial Cups, and Allan Cups — all three. Joe Primeau. Great center ice man. And he was a great storyteller. He was coaching the Toronto Airforce Team. In 1943 we went to the semi-final playoffs for The Allan Cup but the Ottawa Commandoes beat us out that year. They had Kenny Reardon and Joe Cooper and Bingo Kampman. Dick Irvin coached (I played for him later for several years in Montreal). Irvin always said Bingo Kampman was the strongest man he ever seen in hockey. Tremendous shot. Low shot, very hard shot. Terrific. He was a great hockey player.

We had Ernie Dickins who was a real good defenceman — played for Toronto Maple Leafs — and Eddie Bush who played for Detroit and played in that famous series where they'd beaten

Toronto for The Stanley Cup three games in a row and then Toronto won four straight. Murray Wilson and another fellow by the name of Murray Conacher who was a cousin to Lyle — he was a defenceman, played with Boston after. Gee, at that time you see we only dressed ten players, so I'm trying to think of some of the other fellows that played there. Butch Wytcherly, he was a goal player too. And another fellow by the name of Wilson, Don Wilson. He was at the end of his career in the National Hockey League. And I always remember him because he said, "I wish I could play like you with so much enthusiasm. I have no more enthusiasm to play." But anyway we had a great time that year and of course I went on to train as a pilot, eh, and then I came to Ottawa.

The Ottawa Commandoes had the famous line from New York — Mac Colville, Alex Shibicky, and Neil Colville. They were good, a real top line. So good you couldn't get round them.

Here in Ottawa while I was taking my course in flying at Uplands they used to fly me over Arnprior. Allen Shields was coaching at Arnprior. It was an amateur type of league, the different service teams, you know. It wasn't of the caliber of hockey the year I played before in Toronto where they were really all pros coming out or going back into the service.

When I came back from overseas in '45 — the summer of '45 one of the first groups back — I could have gone to Toronto because Joe Primeau wanted me to go there and of course Mr. Gorman who was managing The Canadiens wanted me to go to Montreal. So I chose to go to Montreal. I went there and I went to training camp. I was the last cut — I'd been off skates pretty well nearly two years. So then I played with the Royals. We missed The Allan Cup the first year — which we should have won — but in '46–'47 we won the Cup. Then some of us turned pro the next year. Doug Harvey, a fellow by the name of Bob Campeau, myself, Floyd Curry. Doug Harvey was one of the greatest defenceman I ever saw.

I was with the Canadiens for three years, but in 1950 I was having a lot of trouble with my back, so under Dr. Penfield I spent most of the summer there. They wanted to operate but the club wouldn't go for it because nobody had had a disk removed. So I went back to training camp the next year but I decided — well, I had a business started here in Ottawa so I came back and I played for the Senators, you see, till '55.

Bill Gurney coached us one year and Peanuts O'Flaherty another year. We'd different coaches nearly every year, but they were good fellows, but we never did win The Allan Cup. Then I got engrossed in the business here. Forty-three years ago on the first of May . . .

Johnny Quilty, well, that's sort of a very, very sad story, a very, very sad story. I really pine about him because I really love the fellow. He's a great great humanitarian and a very, very good man. He brought back . . . the fellows were telling me he

Shown here are stars of the Ottawa Senators during the 1950s — Goalie Ray Frederick, Leo Gravelle, Captain Howard Riopelle, Dusty Blair.

brought back to sobriety seventy-five to a hundred men through A.A. did great work in it. He was a great, great fellow. But he really got into the booze and he didn't continue playing. It was a sad thing. He had a great mind. Just a super guy, what an athlete. I would certainly rate him with Lionel Conacher as all-around athlete of the century. He was an exceptional boxer. He also was on the Grey Cup team. The night before they played the Grey Cup — he was playing for the Navy team — the night before he was called out to sea and he missed the final game. But he was a star with them all here. See, he was exceptional playing football, eh, and he was a good boxer and a great ball player . . .

Joe Primeau was a great storyteller. I'll tell you one. You see, Primeau, Jackson, and Conacher — they were the famous names for decades. Still are today. Now you don't always see the same line playing at all time. They mix them all up. It's just like the Kraut Line and the trouble is Joe used to tell us that Conacher and Jackson always wanted the puck. See Joe was the play-maker and a real good player. One of them always wanted the puck and would complain because you passed too much to the other fellow. They would complain to Joe, "You passed too much to Conacher." or "You passed too much to Jackson." So when they were at practice Joe played a trick. "I had a puck split in half one day," he told me, "and I gave them each one half." Joe, oh he

The Kraut Line — Milt Schmidt, Woody Dumart, Bobby Bauer — not only starred with the Boston Bruins but also with the Ottawa R.C.A.F. team which won The Allan Cup in 1941–42.

was really exceptional. What I liked about him was he was a very very quiet man, eh?

A fellow like Dick Irvin, now he as a new breed. Oh man! Would he ever get upset if things weren't right! And if you weren't playing up to your capability, eh, he'd get really upset. Oh, yeah! And at some of the meetings we'd have in Chicago before key games and stuff — Boy! — He'd have the individual guys come in and he'd say, "You'd better get moving because Buffalo is not too far away." Right down to the minors. Joe was completely the opposite. Very very quiet and, in between periods, if you made a mistake or did something stupid, he'd go and sit beside you and talk very very quietly. Like a father to his son. Oh, he had a different approach altogether and look at the success he had. Course, Dick Irvin had great success, too . . .

The Quebec Senior League was a full league but it was The Allan Cup type of thing, not the National Hockey League, but they were really good players and were well-known and people went to see that. They were exciting skaters and carried the puck down. They were dramatic players. Colorful players, that's it.

Ottawa has produced some great players. Look at Steve Yzerman, isn't he some kind of a hockey player? I think right now that Yzerman is one of the purest scorers I've ever seen. He has so many ways of scoring goals. He's a very good hockey player. And Denis Potvin, there's never been a better defenceman than him. A great defenceman. I'd compare him with Doug Harvey and Doug was the greatest. Oh, boy! Denis Potvin, I think he's an underrated superstar like Red Kelly was an underrated superstar. It's a strange thing, you know. Now can you imagine if Denny had been playing with The Canadiens. It's like American baseball players, they don't want to play in Canada 'cos they don't get the coverage they do in the States . . .

The Senators died out in 1934, all gone, the N.H.L. And then Ottawa went on to be — it fielded all kinds of teams like the Commandos and the R.C.A.F. and the Senior Senators. There was the Quebec Senior Hockey League and other Junior leagues and there was this fair amount of hockey that went on at different levels. Well, you see during the war they had the Commandoes and the Ottawa R.C.A.F. with the Kraut Line — Schmidt, Bauer, and Dumart. They were the tops and at that time the National Hockey League didn't have anything compared to them. So fans in Ottawa were watching better hockey actually in the Quebec Senior League than they'd be watching in the N.H.L. during that period. The Commandoes won The Allan Cup in 1943, following the R.C.A.F. victory in 1942. They were really a hot, hot team that could have beaten any of the teams in the N.H.L. which was depleted of players because of the services. There was a period in there where you were really seeing in Ottawa N.H.L. caliber of hockey, eh. Well, then, after the war, of course, all the players went back to their teams; that's why the Quebec League became diluted a bit. Suddenly all these great players were pulled from the Senior and Junior leagues to play in the N.H.L.

Today we have many more players than we ever had before. There's better players today than ever. There's more teams, eh? I was in Moscow in '72. My wife and I went. My own feelings there was that I thought this was the greatest miracle I'd ever seen in sport 'cos I thought the Canadians were outplayed, outplayed completely by the Russians. A different style of play. Dick Irvin used to say, "You know, you fellows think you have to be university professors to play this game. But it's a very simple game. All you do is you take the puck, you pass it, and you skate to get it back." I just thought of him when I saw the Russians in Moscow. I says there's no team I ever saw in my life did what Dick Irvin said. The simple part of the game — it's so simple — head man the puck, skate to get it back. And they play so well together that I found it hard to find an outstanding player.

Perfect unity, you know. Beautiful. That's what I would like to . . . what went through my mind when the new Ottawa Senators were trying to form, eh, that I would hire that Russian who coached the Russians to beat Canada in last winter's Olympic Games. Why wouldn't they bring him over here? Not as a coach, because language would be too much of a problem, but to tell them his principles, his way of playing hockey. Now you'd have to develop a different hockey player. You don't get guys that are seven feet tall and two or three hundred pounds that would drive guys into the boards. But you get guys with talent. You have to have real talent to play that game. It's more difficult to skate with the puck than skating without it. A winger can go up and down all night and do nothing. He'd hardly break a sweat. But when you're skating with the puck and passing it now you see action, but you have to have talent for that kind of a game. Oh, yeah! I love the way the Russians play!

The management of the "new" Ottawa Senators would seem to agree with Howard Riopelle, given the fact that they made Alexei Yashin, a young Russian player, their first choice in the N.H.L. entry draft in June 1992.

Frank Finnigan's life after he retired from the Toronto Maple Leafs in 1937 was as rough and tumble as the post-N.H.L. years of The Senators. The glory years quickly became lost in the ignomy of alcoholism, as did our family. In this reminiscence, my father recounts events during these lost years:

Today there are books being written about when you finish your hockey career. Gordie Howe and his wife have written one about all the trauma and pain of finishing, and they have given the hockey players of today courses in how to adapt themselves to "retirement" so young. In my day you were just thrown out. No, I quit. I wasn't thrown out. I always said I'd quit before they shipped me to the minors. And I did.

Most hockey players retire. They know that they're slowing

up and you realize that. You just can't do what you could back two or three years ago.

We had the Olde Colonial Hotel before I retired. It was on the corner of what is now O'Connor and Queen, right across from the back door of Murphy-Gambles. Right down from the Windsor Hotel. Frank Ahearn fixed it all up for me and we paid rent monthly, my partner and I, Ashe. Tom Ahearn, Frank's

Frank Finnigan returned to Ottawa after retiring from The Leafs, where he took up a second career as a hotel manager. This ad appeared in a program for the Senior Senators.

father, owned the property, but Frank talked his father into giving me the hotel as my "second career." Old Tom was never for it.

Well, then I started working for Brading's Brewery. I was head of the salesmen. And then, after three years I guess, I sold my shares to Ashe. I had controlling shares in the Old Colonial Hotel which I shouldn't have sold. I should have stayed in the hotel, but I was drinking. I sold my shares and then I lost my job at Brading's, so I was in trouble. I went back to Mr. Ahearn, Frank Ahearn. He was Member of Parliament for Ottawa at that time. So he got in touch with somebody and he told me, "Britain will declare war before too long." He said, "Go up to the cottage and have a rest and get straightened out and I'll see if I can't get you into the government." I went into the government and I worked there for about a year or about six months, and then we were making pretty fair money — more that the Grade Twos or Threes, and they were doing the same work as we were. I was in Printing and Stationery. And anyway, they wanted to put us through as a Grade Three. That was only ninety dollars a month and we were making double that. We were temporary, you see. So anyway, I decided that I'd go into the Air Force. So I went into the Air Force which was very good. Then after seven years I got out of the Air Force.

Out of the Air Force I got my gratuities and I decided to buy a hotel. Then I looked at the Portage Hotel. And they were going to put — Russ Boucher was the Member of Parliament for Ottawa and he told me about that — they were going to put a big hydro dam up there. He wasn't a member for Quebec, but he knew what was going on there. And the Portage Hotel was going to boom. So, they were getting ready to build the Chenaux Dam when somebody stepped in and bought it or they decided to keep it themselves — I can't say which.

Now Russ Boucher gave his seat up to George Drew in Ottawa West End — he was MPP for the West End, so George Drew could run as the Premier of Ontario (he was defeated.) Anyway, Russ said to me, "They're building a big hospital in Smiths Falls and there'll be a lot of work up there and Merrickville's not too far from there and they're also building a correctional home or prison at Buritt's Rapids." He said, "Go up and try and buy the Merrickville Hotel." So I took the train and went up to Merrickville and saw the owner and he wanted to sell it, so I bought it. I told him I'd be back in a few days.

Now the license had to be transferred. The problem was, the beer quota at each hotel was rationed before I went to Merrickville. Anyway, I knew some people who had some pull — still. I'm not going to say who. So this party said, "Frank, don't worry. You'll have them up there with lots of beer. You mightn't have the grants you want, but you'll have lots of beer." And I did. And I had a place where I stored some for a bank. There was a secret passageway beneath the Merrickville Hotel and that's where I hid the extra beer.

I got a really good offer for the Merrickville Hotel and I decided that maybe if I was out of the hotel business that maybe I'd "straighten round," you know? Got a good price for it. We doubled our money and we took quite a fair amount out of it. We went back to Ottawa thinking I'd probably get a job in Ottawa but there wasn't much that I could see there where I could make a living. So then we decided that we'd move back up the Pontiac. The Clarendon Inn in Shawville was for sale and we bought it.

Years later in 1950 when I sold the Clarendon the people who bought it had a really tough time getting their liquor licence because, you see, Quebec had changed and if your name wasn't "Bertrand" you were in trouble — it took them six months to get their licence but when I bought the hotel, I got the licence in fifteen minutes! I went to see Ray Johnson. He was the Member for Pontiac at that time. And he said, "I'll have the license down there in fifteen minutes Frank." And I had it.

We lost our liquor licence in Merrickville one time. I had a lot of good friends — maybe old fans — in high places. In Merrickville they had a big festival day every year. Harry McLean would come out in his nightgown and ride around on the donkey and passed out money. Well anyway, there was a big crowd and the bar got packed and everything, and they'd be in the tavern, and, of course, there's not too much room in there, so they'd take their beer and go out and drink it in the backyard — against *the law*. So anyway, the O.P.P. saw this out in the yard and they raised the devil about it. And I said, "There's nothing I can do about it. There's no room in here and I guess they just took it — we didn't sell it out in the back yard — they just took it out there to drink it. There's no room in here for them. I had nothing to do with it. I didn't tell them to go out in the yard and drink it."

So anyway, the O.P.P. phoned or wired or something to the Liquor Control Board in Toronto and the Liquor Control Board called me and told me to turn in my licence. So anyway, I took the licence up to Toronto with me and went up on the train. Took the train and went up. So I got a hold of Connie Smythe at Toronto Maple Leaf Gardens and Mr. Bickle who was the biggest broker in Toronto then and he was vice-president, I guess, or president of the Leafs then. So anyway, Smythe and Bickle called Judge Robb up and I went up to the Liquor Control Board with my licence to Judge Robb. Judge Robb was very nice with me. He was an old lacrosse player and played around St. Catharines and that area years ago. So he said, "What's the trouble Frank?" I said, "There wasn't any trouble. It was a big picnic or fair or whatever you want to call it, and our tavern's not that big and there wasn't too much room in the tavern so when they'd get a beer they'd take it out and drink it out in the yard." And I said, " There wasn't anything I could do about it."

"Well," he said, "that's too bad, Frank, but we'll fix that up." So Judge Robb said, "Let me see your licences." And I said, "Here they are." "Well," he said, "you just take those back with you and there'll be no charge or anything . . . '' So I landed back and put the liquor licences up the next day in the tavern in Merrickville. They wondered where I got all the drag. The O.P.P. officer who sent in the report on me called my brother Eddie in

Ottawa and asked Eddie please to not have him fired. Well, I had no intentions of doing a dirty trick like that. The O.P.P. was only doing his job and thought it might help him.

We had bought the hotel in Shawville — and it was a gold mine — but I was still drinking, making all the promises to quit, and then having another one. Well, anyway, this time I was down in Ottawa, making the rounds of my old haunts there, "touring" as they call it in the Valley, and I'd been to The Alexander, and The Belle Clair, and The Albion, and The Windsor. And I'd met different people at the hotel and had a drink with them. At one of the hotels I'd met my old drinking pal Dick Lamothe — he and I used to chum around together and he liked to drink, too. Birds of a feather, you know, flock together, as your mother used to always say. Anyway somewhere along the line that day we must have parted and I went down to The Windsor. But they wouldn't give me a room there. So I sat down in the big lounge chair and fell asleep. And then they'd wake me up because they didn't want a drunk sawing it off in their nice lobby. So I made my way to the Lord Elgin — I must have abandoned my car — sometimes I had sense enough to do that — or I just plain forgot where it was, but the Lord Elgin wouldn't give me a room either.

I was desperate for sleep, drugged in truth — and I went outside and somehow or other crawled up into the back of a loaded dump truck. I don't ever remember getting up into it. But I fell asleep on top of the load of stone they were carrying. And when I woke up it was morning and I was going bumpity-bumpity down some city street. I guess the driver was going to work at eight o'clock in the morning and I suddenly was sober enough to realize that he was going off to dump his load! And I was going to be dumped with it! I knew I had to get off — or else. So I went to the back of the truck as they came to a stop street and I got down at the back and I went with the truck. I didn't jump off. I went with it. If I'd have jumped off while it was going I would have probably fractured my skull — or killed myself. No, I was smart enough to know I had to "go with the truck." I let myself down over the box, and hung on, and just went with the truck.

I sobered up after that. I remember saying to myself. "Well, this is it. I've hit bottom. Maisie always told me I'd never quit until I hit bottom."

To this day I don't remember my journey back to Shawville. I don't know whether I hitch-hiked or walked. I went upstairs and lay down in a room at the hotel until next morning.

I came down next morning, and when I'd come down in the mornings usually before that I'd always go to the fridge and pour myself a shot of gin and 7-UP or something like, gin and orange juice, and then I'd have a couple of those, and I'd be back on my feet. But that morning I never went near the fridge. Frankie, John, Ross, they were all wondering, "What's wrong with him today?" So the next day the same thing, and the next. And the next. They were all beginning to say to themselves, "What the devil's up with him these days?" So from that day forward I'd get up every morning — never take a drink. Never take a drink all that day, all that night. So I never took another drink after that and I've never taken another drink since . . .

There can be no question that the hockey played in Ottawa during the 1930s, 1940s, and 1950s — even the 1960s and 1970s when the Ottawa 67s of the O.H.A Junior "A" League featured such Ottawa born future N.H.L. stars as Denis Potvin and Bobby Smith, and when the Ottawa Nationals of the W.H.A. boasted stars like Dave Keon — was high caliber and highly entertaining. But the fans still longed for the "show" of N.H.L. hockey, where they might see such Ottawa Valley home-grown talent as Larry Robinson, Guy LaFleur, Steve Yzerman, Doug Wilson, Denis Savard, and Sylvain Turgeon playing for the Ottawa Senators.

6

THE RETURN OF
THE SENATORS

"We won't back down."

— **Bruce Firestone**

"In seven years I expect to have three rings on my fingers — my engineering ring, my wedding band, and my Stanley Cup ring." So Dr. Bruce Firestone declared to me in a 1992 interview given at the Ottawa Senators office suites on Moodie Drive in Nepean.

Firestone said it with the kind of quiet determination and tautly drawn resolve that got him — and his team — the Ottawa N.H.L. expansion franchise in Florida, December 6, 1990. This first landmark was to be followed by financing problems, fund-raising ups and downs, difficulties with the Ontario Municipal Board (O.M.B.) re-zoning of the Palladium site. All conditions were met in November 1991 and Firestone and his seasoned team moved towards the next targets.

"When I got the news of the O.M.B. approval, the first thing I did — after telling my wife — was to phone Frank Finnigan. He had contributed so much to our bringing back The Senators."

Firestone's love of hockey and association with the national game goes back three generations to a time when his grandfather, Sam Torontow, arrived from Russia in 1907, came to Ottawa, and began an immediate love affair with hockey in a town which in that era was a ferment of sporting activity. Sam passed this passion for what Firestone now calls "ballet on ice" on to his daughters, including Bruce Firestone's mother, Isabel.

"We were brought up with a love of the game," Firestone says. And when the old Ottawa Senators folded, the whole clan became rabid fans of Montreal Canadiens. "When I was growing up in Rockcliffe, *Hockey Night in Canada* was an institution in our house. Not only that but I played hockey continually all winter long, pick-up teams, outdoors on Rockcliffe Park rinks and the Ashbury College rink. On Saturdays we played from nine to twelve, had a quick lunch, returned to play until 5:30, grabbed supper, went back and played under the lights until 10:00 p.m."

Bruce Firestone dreamed of returning an Ottawa Senators team to the N.H.L. His dream has come true.

"I knew I didn't have the ingredients, the body build to play advanced hockey. But I have a son coming up who has . . ."

Firestone's resumé reveals a distinguished academic training: Ashbury College in Rockcliffe, Civil Engineering at McGill, a Masters in Engineering at University of New South Wales, PhD in Economics at the Australian National University, and other studies at Harvard, University of Western Ontario, University of Laval.

Why the Masters and PhD in Australia? "The beaches were great there," is Firestone's reply.

Now Chairman and Governor of the Ottawa Senators Hockey Club and Chairman of Terrace Investments Limited, Firestone worked from 1972-78 as a Civil Engineer for the New South Wales Government — and presumably enjoyed the beaches. But, after those six years working within his engineering field, Firestone returned to Canada "not," he said, "because I missed hockey" but "for family reasons."

Back in Ottawa he worked for the Canadian Government Bureau of Supply and Management and organized a real estate

Randy J. Sexton, Chief Executive Officer, Ottawa Senators Hockey Club, was playing pick-up hockey with Bruce Firestone and Cyril Leeder when Firestone announced his dream of a new franchise for Ottawa.

company, Terrace Investments. One evening in March 1988, he was playing pick-up hockey with Randy Sexton and Cyril Leeder at the Westboro arena. In the dressing-room after the game Firestone dropped his bombshell, one he describes as having been nursed for a year and a half and not even communicated to his wife, Dawn.

As Firestone tells the story, "I told them that the N.H.L. is due for another round of expansion franchises and I think Ottawa is ready now. Let's put together a bid."

"Both Randy and Cyril fell off the bench," Firestone added with one of his rare smiles.

But an idea had been sown, a vision was being nurtured, and talks began among movers and shakers.

"I had grown up in Ottawa," Firestone explained, "and I knew Ottawa had changed. It had grown much bigger, it was more diverse, and it was much richer. I simply believed that it was the logical choice in Canada for the upcoming N.H.L. expansion franchise."

The fire had been ignited at that Terrace Investments game of shinny at the Lions Arena in Westboro in March 1988. For the next six months Randy Sexton and Cyril Leeder began to gather information about the N.H.L., its expansion process, financial details concerning the 21 teams, historical data on the original Ottawa Senators. Meanwhile Master Planner Firestone was laying out an overall strategy, the essence of which was:

Buy a Site
Win the Franchise
Build the Building

And somewhere in here the team rallying cry became, "Don't Back Down," from the Tom Petty ballad.

After Firestone had revealed his dream to Randy Sexton and Cyril Leeder and promulgated his three-pronged plan — "buy a site, win the franchise, build the building" — an earnest search began for land for the proposed Senators Palladium. And it was not so easy. There were few suitable sites along the Queensway and some of them were already owned by the National Capital Commission. Then the trio got their first real break; the Central Canada Exhibition Association allowed their options to lapse on land along the Queensway near the Kanata-West Carleton town line, an ideal site. Six months of negotiations with the landowners resulted in a site for the home of the new Ottawa Senators.

On June 12, 1989, a letter was sent to John Ziegler, Jr., President of the National Hockey League, stating the intention of Terrace Investments to seek an expansion franchise on behalf of the citizens of Ottawa. Terrace Investments announced publicly its bid for the new franchise, and on September 6, 1989, held a press conference at the Chateau Laurier in Ottawa to announce its "Bring Back the Senators" campaign.

In my interview with him, Bruce Firestone described one of the special events of this press conference. "We were all ready aware of Frank Finnigan's career in hockey both with the Toronto Maple Leafs and the old Ottawa Senators and we knew that he was an invaluable link with the past history of hockey in Ottawa. It was decided to invite Frank to this conference at the Chateau, and with this intent in mind, I phoned his family. With one of his sons I discussed the possibility of Frank appearing as an honoured guest at the head table. There was some hesitation on the part of Frank's son at this point," Bruce said. "I'll try him," the son finally responded, "He might, and he might not."

At the unveiling ceremonies May 23, 1991, Bruce Firestone and his team presented Frank Finnigan with a replica of his old Ottawa Senator sweater No. 8. The sweater will be retired at the opening game of the 1992–93 season.

"The conference at the Chateau had already begun," Firestone explained to me, "when I sensed a well silence at the entrance to the conference room as Frank Finnigan, the last of the Ottawa Senators, aged eighty-eight, white-haired, straight backed, distinguished and steady came into the room. As I announced his arrival the whole room rose to its feet and gave the old pro a standing ovation. And in that moment I realized the depth of the love affair between Ottawa and the Ottawa Senators."

At that watershed press conference, Finnigan was presented with a new Ottawa Senator word-logo jersey with his old Senator No. 8 on the back.

Firestone continued: "The minute I announced the 'Bring

The architect's dream of the new home of the Ottawa Senators.

Back the Senators' campaign and it was known that we had begun actively seeking a new franchise, I was slapped with three law suits disputing our right to use 'Ottawa Senators,' one from surviving members of the Gorman family (old Tommy Gorman had been an original part-owner with Frank Ahearn of the old Ottawa Senators); one from the Central Junior 'A' League Ottawa Senators, and one other. We fought them all successfully and secured the trade marks for the name The Ottawa Senators."

In September the season ticket reservation drive began; in exchange for a $25 non-refundable pledge, subscribers received a "Bring Back the Senators" sticker and a registration number which reserved a season ticket for the Ottawa Senators first season.

Now began a frenzy of activities and decisions, all of which had to be coordinated in order to meet deadlines as dictated by the conditions of the franchise. Firestone and his original circle began gathering around themselves teams of experts outstanding in their individual fields: in June hiring Rossetti Associates, (architects of the "Palace of Auburn Hills," home of the Detroit Pistons) as architects for the Senators to design the Ottawa Palladium, projected to be a multi-use sports and entertainment facility; in

July Burson-Marsteller Limited and Executive Consultants Limited (of Calgary's bid to stage the 1988 Winter Olympics) to design a Public Relations campaign; David O'Malley of Aerographics in Ottawa to design a campaign logo incorporating Ottawa's Peace Tower and the Canadian flag.

Announcement was made of the names of political figures and business leaders who would comprise the Senators Ad Hoc Advisory Committee. As well, Bruce Firestone continued to gather around himself a team of educated, articulate professionals — lawyers, MBA's, CA's — men and women who were very much in contrast to the old N.H.L. prototypes, self-made "macho" rednecks with short attention spans and faulty grammar but whose homegrown talents and aggressions combined with their love of the game had moved them to the top on all levels of the hockey pyramid, player to coach to manager to executive administrator. Members of The Terrace team began a systematic campaign to visit each N.H.L. city, meet with respective team owners, governors and officials, learn more about the N.H.L. inner workings, and promote the city of Ottawa. In September 1989, the architectural firm Rossetti Associates attended a Terrace press conference and unveiled "the white on white" model for the Ottawa Palladium.

Meanwhile, behind the scenes, work was going on apace on written and visual promotional material. Terrace produced a 26-page color booklet illustrating the beauty and strength of the city of Ottawa for distribution to the N.H.L. Board of Governors. This was simply the forerunner for the 600-page leather-bound official application, a superlative production which was to play a major role in achieving the franchise for Ottawa and said by some to be the factor which tipped the delicate balance in favor of the Capital City.

A few months later Terrace unveiled its plans for a long-term 600-acre development in Kanata surrounding their proposed arena, and including a 408-room luxury hotel, a shopping center, a hi-tech business park, several commercial office towers, two new residential neighborhoods, and a transit station. Just as with the Ahearns fifty years before with the old Ottawa Senators, part of the larger plan was transportation of ticket-holders to the hockey arena.

During a December 1989 meeting at the Breakers Hotel in West Palm Beach, Florida, the N.H.L. Governors announced the expansion plans which would incorporate seven new teams by the year 2000. The entry fee was set at $50 million U.S., a figure that would stagger hopefuls in most fields — except for professional sport in North America. During the official announcement, N.H.L. president John A. Ziegler Jr. said, "North America is our market and we will expand to areas where the game is known, is played and is loved." In hindsight reading between the lines this statement could have been key.

The Terrace people fought the good fight to keep Ottawa

This 600-page, leather-bound, gilt-lettered Official Application was influential in the decision to award a new franchise to the growing Capital of Canada.

and its bid for the franchise consistently in the media with supportive statements from hockey legends like Scotty Bowman, "the winningest coach in N.H.L. history"; Winterlude parties for the Ottawa Senators Original Sponsors, Consultants and Ad Hoc Committee; blessings from Regional Chairman Andy Haydon and an amendment to the Regional Official Plan to permit an N.H.L. arena to be built on the town line; with Terrace Team appearances at all events with N.H.L. overtones or associations like the N.H.L. "All Star" classic in Pittsburgh.

On May 31, 1990, just a few days after Regional Planning Committee unanimously voted to amend the Official Plan to allow Terrace to build in Kanata, Terrace received an official invitation from the N.H.L. to submit an application for an expansion franchise in its "Plan of Sixth Expansion."

On June 14, 1990, Terrace PR people proudly announced that 10,000 season ticket reservations had been received, buoying hopes for winning a franchise. The same day Cyril Leeder, Randy Sexton, and Charles Hamilton of Terrace arrived in Vancouver for the N.H.L.'s 1990 Congress and Entry Draft. It was very much a learning experience for the team.

"We met with lots and lots of people," Randy Sexton said later, "from the governors of the N.H.L. to minor league officials. And we gathered data, valuable date, on expected revenues form board advertising, the market itself, the corporate market, the target audience, and the demographics of the audience."

On August 14, 1990, ten precious 600-page copies of the *Official Expansion Application of the Ottawa Senators Hockey Club* were loaded into a limousine, along with Vice-President Randy Sexton and Jim Steel, Director of Marketing, all headed for the N.H.L. Offices in New York. The following day President Cyril Leeder was quoted in *USA TODAY*: "We believe we have the best hockey market not currently served by an N.H.L. franchise. If the N.H.L. said we could have any market, we'd still take Ottawa." Nine other cities had announced their intention to contest the franchises for two new N.H.L. clubs: Phoenix, Miami, Houston, Seattle, San Diego, Milwaukee, Tampa, St. Petersburg, and Hamilton.

The franchises were to be awarded at the N.H.L. board of Governors meeting in December in West Palm Beach, Florida. As the decision date approached, the Terrace Team was encouraged by N.H.L. executive response to the written application. The team was invited to a question-and-answer meeting with the League's Franchise and Marketing Analysis committee on October 18th in New York, at which Bruce Firestone stated: "We are not looking back. We really believe we are the leading bidder in Canada and in the U.S.A." By mid-November The Senators had 11,000 pledges for season tickets, an achievement which led Randy Sexton to declare, boldly, "We are more confident and optimistic with each day. We will be ready for the Florida meeting and we won't back down." On December 2nd the Terrace Team along with a delegation of 150 enthusiastic supporters and fans traveled to West Palm Beach to make a final presentation at the Board of Governors meeting. To the surprise of Bruce Firestone, The Senators were awarded a franchise on December 6th.

Randy Burgess, in the inaugural issue of Bodycheck, *the official Senators magazine, recounts the experience of that day:*

N.H.L. President John A. Ziegler raises Bruce Firestone's arm in victory.

Firestone, Ziegler, and Phil Esposito of the Tampa Bay franchise join hands in celebration.

"I felt like I did on the night my son was born," said Randy Sexton, Vice-President of Terrace Investments Limited. National Hockey League Governors had awarded a conditional expansion franchise to the City of Ottawa and welcomed Terrace Chairman and Chief Executive Officer, Bruce Firestone, President Cyril Leeder, and Sexton into the "big leagues" of professional sport.

Firestone believed winning a franchise would be much like winning an election and the bid was designed accordingly. "Ottawa has a rich hockey history and that gave our campaign an edge on other cities," Firestone said.

When N.H.L. Governors gathered for their expansion meeting in Florida last December that "edge" was obvious. The slogan "Bring Back the Senators" was visible all over Palm Beach.

Crack open the Champagne! The victory is ours!

Over 150 fans marched in support of The Senators in West Palm Beach. Even more attended the Entry and Expansion Draft in Montreal, marching from the train station to the Forum.

Billboards, bumper stickers, and hats reminded hockey visitors that the Senators were "Winners of Nine Stanley Cups." If the printed message was somehow missed, the spoken (sometimes shouted) word was delivered by an entourage of 150 supporters who traveled south to help win a team.

"We were just starting our presentation to the Governors when the band started up," recalled Sexton. "There was a crash of cymbals and trumpets, trombones and tubas started playing 'Ca-na-da' by Bobby Gimby. It was great!" "Are you the guys with the band?" joked one N.H.L. governor to Sexton. The Ottawa Fire Department Marching Band may have been too much for the conservative clientele at the posh Breakers Hotel, but the band was playing for the governors. The governors listened.

After the formal presentation off the bid, the Ottawa entourage adjourned to The Senators hospitality suite. It featured a mock hockey rink, complete with boards, Senators merchandise and hockey videos. No other expansion candidate provided such a room and the Ottawa suite became a popular spot. It was another "edge" for Ottawa.

Later that evening Senators supporters gathered at a local restaurant, but for Terrace executives the work continued. At a private dinner, they and other bidders had one last chance to lobby the governors.

"One governor actually told us there was no way we would get in and that was devastating," said Cyril Leeder. The governors who supported Ottawa's bid advised Terrace to do nothing else. They said, "Let us handle it, you've done all you can."

The next morning, December 6th, Bruce Firestone was out jogging when the governors summoned his team for a meeting. After a quick change of clothes Firestone prepared for the worst. "A governor's representative took us through a series of back hallways and the kitchen," said Firestone. "I was sure we did not get the franchise." But Jim Durell, then Mayor of Ottawa and now President of the hockey club, told Firestone, "We are going to get it because we deserve it." He was right. The N.H.L. governors decided it was time to bring back the Senators.

"I looked down and saw Ottawa and Tampa written on a piece of paper and I burst into tears," said Firestone. Randy Sexton remembers jumping up and down and hugging Cyril Leeder and Jim Durrell. Durrell called it "the single most important event in Ottawa's history since it was named the capital of Canada." That night, as the Ottawa delegation in Palm Beach celebrated, the N.H.L.'s newest governor, Bruce Firestone, quietly went home. Days earlier his wife Dawn had given birth to a baby girl.

Back in Palm Beach Randy Sexton was also thinking of family. He phoned his father. "My father always told me no matter what you set out to do in life, you have to see it through. You have to bring home the bacon." That night Sexton's father told him, "you took my advice, you brought home the bacon."

"You always gave me good advice," was his son's response.

The Ottawa Citizen *published a special report on the Expansion and Entry Drafts, featuring a two-page story by Roy MacGregor.*

Eighteen months later in June 1992 at the N.H.L. expansion and entry drafts, Randy Sexton would again play a central role in building The Senators team, watched over by his father Al Sexton, seated in the stands at the Montreal Forum while his son "worked the floor" at ice-level, selecting the new Senators for the 1992-93 season. By this time Senator management included not only Sexton, Cyril Leeder, and Bruce Firestone, but also General Manager Mel Bridgman, Director of Player Personnel John Ferguson, Coach Rick Bowness, and Scouts Tim Higgins, Jim Nill, Andre "Moose" Dupont, Paul Castron, Al Patterson, and Glen "Chico" Resch. Ottawa Citizen sports columnist Roy MacGregor chose to tell the story of how the new Senators team was built from the perspective of Al Sexton, a story that proves the art of great sportswriting has returned to Ottawa along with The Senators:

High in the fourth tier of the Montreal Forum, a 62-year-old pensioner whose Gaspé family had been so poor he had never owned a pair of skates, never played a single game of hockey, sat shaking his head in amazement.

Al Sexton's only son, Randy, was moving across the far end of the Forum ice surface, every eye, several television cameras, hundreds of hopes upon him as the chief executive officer of the brand-new Ottawa Senators moved to the microphone with his general manager, Mel Bridgman, and his director of player personnel, John Ferguson.

The last time Al Sexton had sat in this hallowed sports arena and looked for his son he was nowhere to be seen, just another fourth-liner the Cornwall Royals had decided not to dress for the night even though his parents had driven down from Brockville to see him.

Now the son was in the process of naming the most important player in the wild plans that had been mentioned three years earlier in the Sextons' Brockville living room, wild plans that Al Sexton at first took to be nothing but "kidding" but now were about to be broadcast live across the country, splashed across the front pages.

Alexei Yashin, an eighteen-year-old Russian, would become the key building block in a team that was never supposed to happen.

And Al Sexton, sitting with his wife, Pauline, high in the farthest seats away from the action, could only shake his head and speak for all of us.

"Unbelievable"

"Almost unbelievable."

Months before the computer failed, months before the key page went missing, months before Phil Esposito did his unexpected about-face, there had to be a beginning — and Al Sexton was there as well.

The wild plans that he had taken as "kidding" — the idea that Randy Sexton and Bruce Firestone and Cyril Leeder would redesign their Terrace Investments and go after a national Hockey League franchise — had somehow taken root. Through guile, luck, brass and simple determination, the three had managed what no one believed possible: the N.H.L. had awarded one of two new franchises to Ottawa, the other to Esposito and his Tampa partners.

The mayor of Ottawa — then Jim Durrell, now The Senators' president — was throwing a celebration at the Civic Center for the victors. Al Sexton was having a hard time getting to congratulate his son, but when he did, he advised him he'd better start "thinking about what kind of a team you'll have.'

The father figured he already knew. "Big and rugged and —

I wouldn't say 'dirty' — but tough and aggressive." The way Randy had played in Brockville and Cornwall and at St. Lawrence College. And big because, as Al Sexton put it, "another four inches and I honestly think Randy would've had a shot at the N.H.L."

When the younger Sexton and Firestone and Leeder finally sat down and thought about putting their new team together, they had only a few unpolished ideas and a single, overriding philosophy.

They wanted to keep in mind three key franchises: Montreal Canadiens, Edmonton Oilers, Pittsburgh Penguins. The Canadiens because of decades of success; the Oilers because they had demonstrated how to build a modern franchise; Pittsburgh because they were the style of the moment.

The Ottawa Senators, they decided, would have to be a team that could adjust. If the opposition wanted to skate, Ottawa would have to skate. If the game was going to be decided by finesse, Ottawa would have to finesse. If grinding was the style, Ottawa would grind as well. If they were not going to win right away, they would not want to be humiliated.

The emphasis would be on size, on toughness, on leadership and skill. Size no one can control. Skill is somewhat within a team's control But a team can exercise considerable control over "character."

And character would come to count for most on this new club.

In Sexton's mind, he wanted "to control those things we can control." They would establish an environment, "set the culture." If the Montreal Forum had an aura, if pulling on a Boston Bruins' sweater meant something, then being a Senator would have to mean something. The very first game, they decided, they would make a ceremony of hoisting the nine Stanley Cup banners that already belong to the Ottawa Senators of another era.

They set down a five-year plan for the team. To build, slowly, the *core* positions. To build down through center. Strong in goal. A strong defence. Strong centers.

In late August 1991, Terrace hired Mel Bridgman to become the team's first general manager. He had absolutely no experience. But then, neither did they. They hired him on the same basis they intended to measure their team: toughness and character.

Sexton and Bridgman met in Toronto with the N.H.L.'s Central Scouting staff and begged advice, which was freely given. They then put out word that they were looking for scouts and

Bridgman received nearly 100 resumes. Again, experience was rarely offered.

They hired mostly retired players who had played with Bridgman, and again they gave highest points to character. Tim Higgins would handle Ontario; Jim Nill would look after the professional leagues. Andre "Moose" Dupont for Quebec. Paul Castron, a friend of Sexton's and Leeder's from St. Lawrence

Shown here at their inaugural press conference, Mel Bridgman and Rick Bowness have taken on the task of leading The Senators to their tenth Stanley Cup Victory.

Mel Bridgman

Rick Bowness

College days, would handle American college scouting. Al Patterson would handle the west; Chico Resch would look after goalies.

Their one great oversight was Europe — which, ironically, would eventually become the team's first footing for its foundation. Bridgman, who had played briefly in Switzerland at the end of his career, made an arrangement with an old coach, and Castron was somewhat knowledgeable after having played in Scandinavia, but clearly this was not enough experience to keep up with the quantum change in style that is currently sweeping hockey.

The Russian players they laughed at the year The Senators were awarded their franchise are no longer being ridiculed. The four most exciting players in the 1992 Stanley Cup were a Canadian (Mario Lemieux), a Czech (Jaromir Jagr), and two Russians (Pavel Bure and Sergei Federov). Don Cherry suddenly seems hopelessly dated.

To Bridgman's credit, he acted on this shortcoming and in mid-winter placed a call to an out-of-hockey N.H.L. executive who in many ways pioneered the European invasion: John Ferguson. Ferguson was working for a racetrack in Windsor and very unhappy with it; the former general manager of both the

New York Rangers and Winnipeg Jets would indeed be interested in getting back into hockey. And yes, he still had all his contacts in Europe and what had once been the Soviet Union.

A few weeks later, after an emergency N.H.L. Board of Governors meeting in Chicago regarding the possibility of a players' strike, Firestone, Sexton, and Bridgman chartered a light plane home, stopped off in Windsor to pick up Ferguson, brought him on to Ottawa and, during a morning meeting at the Chateau Laurier, like what they heard. Ferguson was shortly named director of player personnel. His immediate responsibility would be the preparation for the upcoming draft.

Meanwhile, the scouts were preparing their lists. As the information came in to The Senators' second-floor offices on Moodie Drive it was dumped onto hard disk and then broken down by computer into a master list, professional list, amateur list, European list. They compiled the expected information on each player's size and age and abilities, but then added two other files, one containing such information as the names and interests of members of the subject's family — the same technique the three had utilized on the 22 N.H.L. governors as they were chasing their franchise — and one containing an evaluation of the all-important *character.*

It was precisely this measure that led The Senators very early to the player around whom they would build their franchise. The early scouting reports on Czechoslovakian teenager Roman Hamrlik were outstanding, but it was only when Bridgman and Sexton traveled to the Four Nations Cup in Vierumaki, Finland, that they understood his character. On a leg he had just fractured blocking a Russian shot from the point, Hamrlik walked on icy street for a mile to meet with the two, refusing a ride and refusing, as well, to admit he was in any pain.

"Mel," Sexton said, "he's our guy."

Hamrlik was instantly tagged as the first player they would draft. If they won the upcoming flip to decide which would select first, Ottawa or Tampa, they would have him for certain. But even if they lost the flip and had to go second, they figured Hamrlik would still be available.

The Tampa Bay Lightning was having a very hard time selling tickets. How would Phil Esposito sell a single seat in aging, conservative Florida with a teenaged kid from a recently communist country who couldn't speak a word of English and, besides, is still a year away from being ready?

Ottawa, with all seats sold out and knowledgeable, patient

fans, would have no such worries. Hamrlik was declared a sure thing. They even began thinking about building a marketing scheme around his first name: a *Roman* to wear the centurion crest for The Senators . . .

In May, during The Memorial Cup tournament in Seattle, Washington, The Senators scouting team was assembled in a hotel meeting room where they debated the prospects. Ferguson

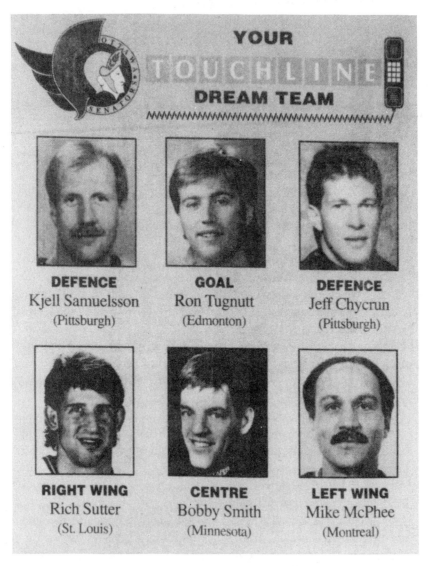

Prior to the Expansion Draft, **The Ottawa Citizen** *compiled a dream team based on a poll of fans. Ottawa-born Bobby Smith was a sentimental favorite of the fans.*

directed the meetings and controlled the talk, whipping them through hundreds of potential players. They then integrated all the North American information, did their final rankings and emerged with a master list they believed, wrongly, would be their most crucial resource.

At the same time, the National Hockey League was going through what may eventually amount to a paradigm shift in attitude. Europeans — more specifically, Russians — were suddenly the talk of the game. The strike over, there was further talk that the game itself would be changing: a new president might be in the works, stricter rules against fighting and stickwork were being discussed, "grinder" hockey was not only passe, it clearly did not work. Toughness mattered, yes, but nothing so much as pure *skill.*

In Seattle the backup choice — in the unlikelihood that one might be needed — was a huge giant from the Medicine Hat Tigers, Mike Rathje. If grinder hockey survived, Rathje was certain to be a superstar.

By this point, "character" had taken on almost religious proportions. One extraordinary Junior prospect was even expunged from The Senators' list on the basis of spelling and grammar mistakes he had made on the hand-written report each junior must fill out for the N.H.L. Central Scouting Office.

Back in Ottawa they continued to meet — Ferguson and Jim Nill handling the rankings for the June 18 expansion draft of fringe N.H.L. players — and Ferguson, Bridgman and others working on the June 20 expansion draft, in which Europeans were daily becoming more of a presence.

"There's no denying it," Sexton said at the time, "we don't have as good a handle on Europe as we should." By the next draft, he promised himself, The Senators would have as much staff concentration on Europe as they have on North America.

Already impressed with a young Russian named Darius Kasparaitis, The Senators made an effort to see another young Russian named Alexei Yashin at the Prague championships, but schooling had kept him at home, so Yashin was not high on any Senators list. And The Senators were beginning to get calls from other teams: Toronto Maple Leafs trying to find out whom Ottawa would pick and whether or not anything might be done to land Ryan Sittler, former Leaf captain Darryl Sittler's son, in a Leaf uniform, Detroit and New Jersey to talk possible deals, Phil Esposito to see if he could find out whom Ottawa was after.

During The Stanley Cup final in Pittsburgh, a coin flip was held and Ottawa lost. They would pick second in the all-important entry draft of amateurs. They would pick first in the almost mean-ingless expansion draft where they would have their choice of play-ers no one else wanted.

They expected Minnesota to offer up Bobby Smith, the for-mer Ottawa Junior star and a sentimental fan favorite, but they had no interest in his contract. If, on the other hand, Edmonton were to offer equally aging Craig MacTavish, The Senators were determined to take him. After that, they would have to see who was available.

The Senators tried to put a brave face on it, claiming they had won "one out of two," but no one was fooled. They took consola-tion in the growing certainty that Esposito would go for the good-looking, highly marketable young Windsor scorer, Todd Warriner.

They were headed for Montreal with confidence. It was all on computer, all available on paper. It would probably happen as predicted.

"I remember one coach saying to me," Al Sexton recalls, "that Randy's moves would never make anybody too dizzy."

They were talking about him on the ice as a player, not as an executive.

Before the Montreal draft was history, the Ottawa Senators would leave a lot of heads spinning, including some of their own, and more than a few heads turning.

On Monday The Senators' brand-new head coach, Rick Bowness, was driven by Bridgman down to Montreal. Bridgman briefed Bowness on the way. Tuesday morning they gathered over a breakfast of fruit in Room 1322 of the Bonaventure Hotel. An Apple computer held all the information for both drafts. A fax machine was taking messages. The JVC ghetto blaster was silent, the stack of CDs offering a choice of irony: Crash Test Dummies, Tears for Fears.

Bridgman was extremely nervous. At noon the N.H.L. was supposed to release the final list of players the other teams would make available. At that moment — in theory — the guesswork would be over, the strategy could begin.

But already the strategy was taking on a life of its own. The Senators had a chance to sign a free-agent goaltender no one else seemed much aware of, Lake Superior State's Darrin Madeley, who'd just been named college player of the year by *The Hockey News*. Signing him would immediately shift the plane to go for two quality goaltenders in the expansion draft. They could now afford to take the one they most wanted, Peter Sidorkeiwicz, and perhaps do something with the other choice.

So far Bridgman had refused to indicate whether Ottawa would select the first and fourth goaltender or the second and third. The thinking had been second and third — but Madeley changed all that.

Bridgman and some of the others were also rattled by a rumor that Tampa had signed a free agent, but no one knew whom. And they still didn't have the N.H.L. list.

Bridgman sat on the couch, Higgins to his left, then Ferguson, Bowness, Castron, and Nill. Chico Resch arrived late, stood around for a while, and eventually pulled up a chair between Higgins and Ferguson. They passed the time going over their own computer lists and bringing Bowness up to scratch.

Finally, too edgy to concentrate in the hotel suite, they moved operations over to the Sun Life Building where the N.H.L. set them up in the ninth-floor boardroom where they waited under the stares of the only four presidents the league has so far had — Frank Calder, Red Dutton, Clarence Campbell, and John Ziegler. On the wall were paintings of the way it's supposed to be: Montreal and Boston facing off, a goaltender making a remarkable save, a player firing the puck so hard it leaves a blurred tracer as it moves across the canvas, the packed and excited crowd rising in anticipation.

But on the huge boardroom table the game slowed to a snail's pace. Some lists arrived and The Senators congratulated themselves on how accurate their forecasts had been. There were few surprises. They had expected the Montreal Canadiens to leave forward Mike McPhee unprotected, but then, so did everyone else.

Bowness talked about what it is like in the Forum when the top picks have gone and the entry draft has dwindled down to the last few rounds, and how team managers have to sit there and stare up into the stands where kids and parents are beginning to stare so desperately down, some of them openly weeping, and he talked about how he once saw a kid picked at the very end come down and seek out the general manager who had chosen him and who was just packing away his notes. No sweater or cap for this kid, but all he wanted was a handshake, and when he reached out to meet his new boss the manager would only growl, "Who the hell are you?"

None of them wanted that to happen to anyone they picked.

At one point no new list arrived for some 40 minutes. Chico Resch was bouncing around, very nervous. Ferguson and Nill were calm. Bridgman, anxious for something "constructive" to do, had them work on assembling a new master list, but there was really nothing constructive to do but wait.

Clearly the N.H.L. had run into a glitch. A mistake had been made in the first list sent in by the Edmonton Oilers. New lists were being drawn up. New lists would continually be added as the first draft grew closer — an annoyance, but no one in The Senators group realized it would soon also be their greatest embarrassment.

Finally, the N.H.L. delivered its master list to The Senators on Wednesday morning. The list was photocopied and entered into the books each scout and executive carried. At 2:00 in the afternoon the list was handed out to the media.

The morning list contained the name "C.J. Young" of the Calgary Flames, a player The Senators had tagged as one they would like if he were made available. The afternoon list had no such name.

Bridgman met in the evening with the press, but there was nothing to say and virtually nothing to ask.

At one point he jumped up and used his sleeve to wipe clean a scheduling chart that was taped to the wall, fretting that someone had seen details of tomorrow's meetings.

"I'm not really nervous," he said. "Anxious."

Thursday morning they met and reviewed the situation and the strategy. They had decided that Ottawa would select first but refused to tell Esposito just to make sure they didn't "give Phil an edge."

A potential deal might also be possible with New York. Now that The Senators weren't so worried about their second goal-tender, they might do the Rangers a favor by taking young Mark LaForest, whom the Rangers hadn't been able to protect, and then perhaps return LaForest to New York for another prospect.

The Senators felt they might even get two players down the road for such a favor.

New Jersey also might lead to a future deal. Word was out that several teams, including Detroit, were after veteran defenceman Viacheslav Fetisov, whom New Jersey wished to keep. The other teams had been after Ottawa to do them a favor — but Ottawa was forbidden by league rules to enter into any formal agreement until the draft was over. Ottawa, however, would do New Jersey the favor by taking defenceman Brad Shaw, whom they wanted anyway, and thereby ensure that New Jersey, under the draft rules, could not lose two defencemen.

In return for this favor, New Jersey might give Ottawa hockey's

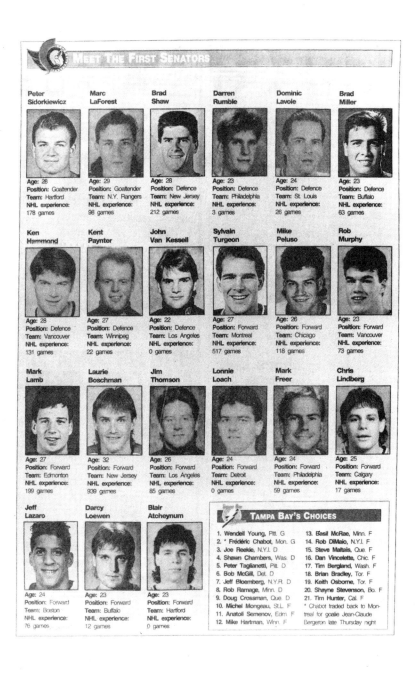

MEET THE FIRST SENATORS

Peter Sidorkiewicz
Age: 28
Position: Goaltender
Team: Hartford
NHL experience: 178 games

Marc LaForest
Age: 29
Position: Goaltender
Team: N.Y. Rangers
NHL experience: 98 games

Brad Shaw
Age: 28
Position: Defence
Team: New Jersey
NHL experience: 212 games

Darren Rumble
Age: 23
Position: Defence
Team: Philadelphia
NHL experience: 3 games

Dominic Lavoie
Age: 24
Position: Defence
Team: St. Louis
NHL experience: 26 games

Brad Miller
Age: 23
Position: Defence
Team: Buffalo
NHL experience: 63 games

Ken Hammond
Age: 28
Position: Defence
Team: Vancouver
NHL experience: 131 games

Kent Paynter
Age: 27
Position: Defence
Team: Winnipeg
NHL experience: 22 games

John Van Kessell
Age: 22
Position: Defence
Team: Los Angeles
NHL experience: 0 games

Sylvain Turgeon
Age: 27
Position: Forward
Team: Montreal
NHL experience: 517 games

Mike Peluso
Age: 26
Position: Forward
Team: Chicago
NHL experience: 118 games

Rob Murphy
Age: 23
Position: Forward
Team: Vancouver
NHL experience: 73 games

Mark Lamb
Age: 27
Position: Forward
Team: Edmonton
NHL experience: 199 games

Laurie Boschman
Age: 32
Position: Forward
Team: New Jersey
NHL experience: 939 games

Jim Thomson
Age: 26
Position: Forward
Team: Los Angeles
NHL experience: 85 games

Lonnie Loach
Age: 24
Position: Forward
Team: Detroit
NHL experience: 0 games

Mark Freer
Age: 24
Position: Forward
Team: Philadelphia
NHL experience: 59 games

Chris Lindberg
Age: 25
Position: Forward
Team: Calgary
NHL experience: 17 games

Jeff Lazaro
Age: 24
Position: Forward
Team: Boston
NHL experience: 76 games

Darcy Loewen
Age: 23
Position: Forward
Team: Buffalo
NHL experience: 12 games

Blair Atcheynum
Age: 23
Position: Forward
Team: Hartford
NHL experience: 0 games

TAMPA BAY'S CHOICES

1. Wendell Young, Pitt. G
2. * Frédéric Chabot, Mon. G
3. Joe Reekie, N.Y.I. D
4. Shawn Chambers, Was. D
5. Peter Taglianetti, Pitt. D
6. Bob McGill, Det. D
7. Jeff Bloemberg, N.Y.R. D
8. Rob Ramage, Minn. D
9. Doug Crossman, Que. D
10. Michel Mongeau, St.L. F
11. Anatoli Semenov, Edm. F
12. Mike Hartman, Winn. F
13. Basil McRae, Minn. F
14. Rob DiMaio, N.Y.I. F
15. Steve Maltais, Que. F
16. Dan Vincelette, Chic. F
17. Tim Bergland, Wash. F
18. Brian Bradley, Tor. F
19. Keith Osborne, Tor. F
20. Shayne Stevenson, Bo. F
21. Tim Hunter, Cal. F
* Chabot traded back to Montreal for goalie Jean-Claude Bergeron late Thursday night

The Ottawa Citizen presented the new Senators in a special report on the Expansion Draft.

euphemistic "future considerations" — yet another young player.

With the expansion draft scheduled to begin at 6 p.m. The Senators organized early. They would have their lists in their binders and they would bring in a laptop computer to access their files. The computer program would cross index players. Data entered would allow the team to track the progress of the draft. The computer would help them make decisions, keep them from making mistakes.

At 5:45 p.m. John Ferguson was handed an envelope by a young N.H.L. "runner" as he entered the draft room. Inside was yet another up-to-date list. No indication was given that there were changes. Ferguson stacked it with his other papers.

The laptop computer was brought out and plugged in and turned on, but nothing happened. Frantically, they checked the power line: no electricity. They checked the battery: no power.

They were now without the computer. They had to rely completely on their printed lists. And the list in their notebooks was already out of date.

"We are approaching the witching hour," announced N.H.L. Vice-President Brian O'Neill.

He had no idea how right he was.

Ottawa selected first, taking Sidorkiewicz, and after Esposito took two goaltenders, The Senators stalled, slowing the televised proceedings to an embarrassing crawl. Yet while most observers thought it was indecision holding them back, it was actually the complicated deal worked out with New York.

With Jim Nill hurrying between The Rangers' personnel and The Senators' center table, the television audience was forced to wait. New York was willing to talk about future considerations, but was also looking for a late-round selection. Nill returned to his seat and a message came down from the N.H.L. officials at the podium: no fiddling with the process. The Senators gambled on a future deal and took LaForest anyway.

For a while the draft went smoothly. Esposito appeared to be aiming for older players, for rougher players, and Ottawa was pleasantly surprised to be getting more or less the players they had targeted.

As planned, they selected Brad Shaw from New Jersey. They got three of the six defencemen they were hoping for, and six of what they had determined to be the top nine forwards, including potential star Sylvain Turgeon.

They lost Michel Mongeau to Esposito, and Brian Bradley, and they were considering Esposito's final forward pick, Calgary's belligerent Tim Hunter, who appealed to the Senators on the basis of *character*.

It was when The Senators began pursuing their own "tough guy" that the lack of computer caught up to them. They selected Montreal's Todd Ewan, only to be told Montreal could lose no more players. Someone at the table hadn't been counting. They selected a Toronto Maple Leaf immediately after two Leafs had been taken in a row by Esposito, meaning a third could not be selected. And finally, they tried to take C.J. Young, whose name wasn't even on the list.

Furious, Sexton, Ferguson, and Bridgman all approached the podium to argue the point. They carried with them the master list with Young's name. The N.H.L. pointed out that the working master list held no such name. No one else in the room had Young's name on a list.

Esposito, turning toward the Tampa area media, rolled his eyes back in his head.

It was, all agreed, "unbelievably embarrassing."

And unfortunate, for if the results had not been clouded with the long delay and three *faux pas* it might have been reported that The Senators did a far superior job on the expansion draft than had Tampa Bay.

Jim Nill had done his job. The expansion picks weren't much, but they were certainly worth more than Esposito was taking back to Florida.

By Friday, however, the hotel corridors were filling with rumors that Esposito was beginning to move toward taking Hamrlik in the all-important entry draft. His own scouts were rating Hamrlik highest and the other scouts moving about the Bonaventure and Intercontinental and Radisson hotels were raving about the big youngster with the "killer instinct" and the astonishing skills.

Ottawa was beginning to worry. It was clear, as well, that the Europeans were having an impact. As John Ferguson was saying, "You gotta have them." And coming into Montreal, Ottawa had been thinking about a 6'5" kid from Medicine Hat if Hamrlik wasn't available.

In a matter of hours they completely changed strategy. Thanks to a large contingent of Russian prospects, they were able to do some fast interviewing, including Alexei Yashin, whose name was being heard more and more often.

They met Yashin and were most impressed with his intelligence, his demeanor, and his intent. While Hamrlik was walking around telling reporters he would soon be buying a Porsche, Yashin told The Senators his goal was "to play in the National Hockey League and move his parents and brother to a cleaner environment."

Character.

The Senators used the interviews to ask all the young Russians two key questions: first, who was a possible leader, and

Ottawa Senator executives welcome their first draft choice to the team — and to Canada. Left to right— Randy Sexton, Mel Bridgman, Alexei Yashin, Bruce Firestone, Cyril Leeder, Jim Durrell.

second, who had the greatest skill level among them. All named Yashin as the leader. When it came to skill, many names were mentioned, including the highly-rated Darius Kasparaitis but just as much they talked about Yashin.

Friday evening Rick Bowness and Sexton took the young Russian out to dinner and were very impressed. Sexton came to the conclusion that Yashin should have been the chosen one all along.

But there was still one slim chance to get Hamrlik. Esposito had offered a deal. The Senators could get the player they wished if they would give him a draft pick. The Senators refused. They would go with Yashin.

"Even if in the end Phil had gone with Warriner we would have taken Yashin," says Sexton.

Esposito went with Hamrlik.

Ottawa took Yashin.

Rathje went to San Jose.

And Warriner, who was expected to go first, ended up with Quebec.

The laptop computer worked fine.

Ottawa made no more mistakes.

On the computer and in the yellow folders each Senator carried at the table, Chad Penney of North Bay and Patrick Traverse of Shawinigan were both listed to go in the first round. They picked up Penney in the second, Traverse in the third.

The reason was the very charge Ottawa and Tampa launched when first one then the other went for a "European." From that point on, Sexton says, it became "trendy."

When it was over, Ottawa had five players from the top 25 they had tagged in their folders.

And as a bonus, they had one final pick courtesy of The Rangers for future considerations.

And they used it to take another European: a nineteen-year-old Swedish goaltender none of them has even seen but who has, according to scout Kent Nilson, great potential *character*.

"They're all futures," John Ferguson said as he packed up to leave.

"We don't have to rush any of them. That's what this is all about — building your stockpile for the future."

As for Al and Pauline Sexton, they were coming down out of the stands after a long, long day, anxious to head back to Brockville and home, two hockey parents who finally got to see their son play in the Montreal Forum.

"Unbelievable," Al Sexton concluded.

"Almost unbelievable."

How well this team will perform in the N.H.L. cannot be predicted with certainty. We do know that the new Senators will be inspired by the achievements of the old Senators. This team has some old scores to settle with N.H.L. rivals like the Toronto Maple Leafs, the Montreal Canadiens, the Boston Bruins, the New York Rangers, the Detroit Red Wings, the Chicago Blackhawks — even with teams from Quebec, Pittsburgh, Vancouver, Edmonton, and perhaps especially St. Louis. The team also has several new goals, but none greater than winning The Stanley Cup for the tenth time in history of The Senators. The Montreal Canadiens may be well-advised not to boast of any Stanley Cup record victories. The Senators would like nothing better than to trump their rivals from down river.

Recently while doing research in Ottawa I stayed at Mary and Andy Haydon's Bed and Breakfast, Haydon House, on the

Driveway near Lisgar Collegiate. It was shortly after my father had died and Andy and I engaged one morning in conversation and condolences:

I knew Frank slightly. I sat beside him at a couple of dinners — I can't remember what ones — maybe Hockey Hall of Fame

The Ottawa Sun *also published a special souvenir report on the making of The Senators.*

— or something like that. I was a fan of his and I followed his appearances and publicity in regard to the Ottawa Senators getting the N.H.L. expansion franchise. I think he was one of the greatest contributing factors to their success. I mean, I don't think they could have done it without him — he was just such a presence, so effective, such a guy . . . . When he died, everyone said, "Oh, how sad! He didn't make it to face-off the puck for the first new Ottawa Senators game." But I don't feel that way at all. I feel his work was finished and he just signed off. Ended the game.

Somehow I know that the new Senators will honor the legend of The Shawville Express and bring home The Stanley Cup to Ottawa, the sporting town, resting in the Ottawa Valley, the cradle of Canadian hockey.

ACKNOWLEDGEMENTS

I wish to acknowledge my indebtedness to the following people for memories, stories, data, photos, and cartoons contributed to this book: Mrs. Leta Horner; Mrs. Sam Farrell; Mr. and Mrs. Bob Beatty; Keith Milne; Mr. and Mrs. Johnny Finnigan, North Bay; Edward Zeally, Toronto; Barbara Audie of the Champlain Trail Museum; Gary Howard, Pembroke; Ross Finnigan; Mr. and Mrs. F. Finnigan, Shawville; Bill Galloway; Roy MacGregor; Bob Wake; Ken Roberts; John Dunfield; Eddie Albert; Frank Cosentino; Eugene Cornacchia; the John Kirby family; Howard Riopelle; Jake Dunlap; Bill O'Farrell; Bob Hursti; Lilias Ahearn; Bruce Firestone and staff. As ever Joan Litke of Burnstown, Ontario, did her faithful transcribing of the tapes. This book was written around and through the deaths of my father on December 25, 1991, and then six months later my mother on July 11, 1992. I will be eternally grateful to Bob Hilderley, publisher and editor, for his understanding, patience, and forbearance during the difficult times.

Photo Credits

Photographs and memorabilia reproduced in this book come from the private collection of Joan Finnigan, except for the following: Bill Galloway — 113, 158, 171, 174, 178, 182; Howard Riopelle — 178, 181; Hockey Hall of Fame — 41, 44, 46, 54, 66, 74, 87, 94, 100, 101, 104, 107, 114, 134, 137, 140, 141, 145; Ottawa Senators — 192, 193, 195, 196, 198, 200, 201, 206.